Raves for Zach's Previous Adventures:

"No one who got two paragraphs into this dark, droll, downright irresistible hard-boiled-dick novel could ever bear to put it down until the last heart pounding moment. Zach is off and running on his toughest case yet, and there is no way he is leaving us behind, no matter what the danger. This is futuristic pulp for the thinking reader, the one who enjoys a good chuckle, some mental exercise, and the occasional inside joke. Sit down with The Plutonium Blonde and a cold one and just see when you manage to pull your peepers away from the page again. On second thought, John Zakour and Lawrence Ganem are too damn good to be interrupted for something trivial; skip the cold one and save yourself a trip to the can."   —SF Site

"I had a great deal of fun with The Plutonium Blonde and have been looking forward to the sequel ever since. Well, it's finally here, and it's a good one. This is more humor than detective story, although Johnson and HARV are a pretty good pair of investigators as well as downright funny. If you like your humor slap-stick and inventive, you need look no further for a good fix."   —Chronicle

"It's no mystery what kind of novel John Zakour and Lawrence Ganem's Doomsday Brunette is. The title says it all. The story is hard-boiled science fiction at its pulpy best. Zakour and Ganem's Zachary Johnson novels—which include The Plutonium Blonde and the forthcoming The Radioactive Redhead—are laugh-out-loud, action-packed mystery th̶ri̶ll̶ers that both revere and h̶ n fiction."
          ̶d Noble Reviews

The FLAXEN FEMME FATALE

JOHN ZAKOUR

DAW BOOKS, INC.

DONALD A. WOLLHEIM, FOUNDER

375 Hudson Street, New York, NY 10014

ELIZABETH R. WOLLHEIM
SHEILA E. GILBERT
PUBLISHERS

http://www.dawbooks.com

First Paperback Printing, December 2008
1 2 3 4 5 6 7 8 9

DAW TRADEMARK REGISTERED
U.S. PAT. AND TM. OFF. AND FOREIGN COUNTRIES
—MARCA REGISTRADA
HECHO EN U.S.A.

PRINTED IN THE U.S.A.

To three of my favorite nieces:
Natalia, Carolina and Tatiana.

Acknowledgments

I am eternally grateful to Betsy Wolheim, DAW's commander in chief for publishing all my books! I also have to thank Joshua Starr as he not only has a cool name, but his edits and suggestions helped make FFF shine.

I also have to thank my agent Joshua Bilmes, because quite frankly he'll whine if I don't. Seriously, Joshua does a great job of explaining the business aspects of writing to me, preventing me from selling my books for "magic beans." Joshua is also "A Number 1" at talking up my books and getting foreign publishers to buy them.

Morgan S. Brilliant gets a big thank you for her help with early editing with the book. Morgan not only also has a cool name but she also knows a lot about things like verbs and adverbs and stuff.

My first writing partner Larry Ganem also gets a nod of thanks as without Larry the first three books may not have existed thus making this, the sixth book, possible.

I also want to thank the folks at Comic-Con for letting me use Comic-Con in this book! Comic-Con rocks!

I of course have to mention all my real life friends and family who are and were "inspiration" for characters in this and past books. The list is fairly long and just as boring but it's always nice to see your name in print: Carolina and Natalia Padilla, Tom Rickey, Ron Pool, my sister Mary Erdman and her husband Steve, Shannon, Greg, Liz, Halee, and of course my wife Olga. I'm sure you can all pretty much figure out who you are. If I left anybody out, sorry, I'll mention you twice in the next book.

Finally, I as always have to thank my wife Olga and my son Jay, for putting up with me while I wrote this book. I'm hard enough to deal with on a regular basis, but I imagine I'm even tougher to handle when there's a deadline bearing down on me. Thanks, I love you guys!

Chapter 1

I rolled over in bed toward Electra's side. I didn't feel her warmth. Patting her area of the bed, my hand gently hunted for her. Her part of the bed was still warm, but it was more of an afterglow warmth. My eyelids creaked up, visually searching where tactile senses had failed. Ah, there she was, sitting on the side of the bed. Those perfectly curvy legs, the sensuous body, her long light blond hair flowing down her sculpted golden shoulder. Light blond hair? Electra has dark hair, my brain shouted, popping my eyes open. There was a beautiful woman sitting on my bed, but it wasn't Electra.

Reaching back behind the bed's headboard I curled my hand around the knife I always keep back there. Yeah, some people may think that's a little paranoid, but those people aren't me. When you're the last freelance PI on Earth, being a little overly cautious is what keeps you breathing. (Besides, a knife behind the headboard is way safer than the gun under the pillow, and, man, did I learn that the hard way.)

Brandishing the knife I glared at the woman. "Who in the DOS are you?" I growled. Knives may be way old-fashioned but the shiny twenty-centimeter blade can be just as intimidating as a modern weapon, especially in close quarters. "What did you do with Electra?"

The mystery woman looked me in the eyes. "Electra is fine. She had an emergency call at the hospital. Some poor kid deactivated the computer drive on his car and had a terrible accident." She smiled. "Thanks to Electra, though, he'll be up and walking again in weeks."

"Yeah, Electra's the best," I said, waving the knife blade in front of the woman, in case she hadn't noticed it. "Still doesn't answer my question though."

The woman looked at me. "They will want you to find me. Don't," was all she said.

She disappeared. In her place I saw my holographic assistant, HARV, standing over my bed, hands on hips, shaking his head.

"What in the name of Gates are you doing?" HARV said, pointing at my knife. "You know perfectly well Electra hates it when you have weapons in bed."

I pushed myself up out of bed. "It's not usually in the bed, it's usually behind the bed," I told him.

"Currently it is not," HARV said.

"Did you see her?" I asked.

HARV's balding head spun 360 degrees (HARV may like to look like a human British butler but he loves taking advantage of the fact that he's a hologram) surveying the room. "I saw nothing and detect nothing."

"There was a woman here, on the bed."

HARV nodded. "Yes, Electra. Your girlfriend. She's a surgeon, remember. She was called away on an emergency," he said slowly.

"I know that," I said. "The woman told me."

"Zach, neither I nor the house's defense system detected any woman or any sign of unusual activity," HARV insisted. "I've scanned the house over one million times in the last nanosecond alone. You are alone and have been alone for the last twenty-two minutes and thirty-one seconds."

I shook my head. "No, she was here." There are times when I know I'm right despite what all the machines in my life say. It's either my biggest gift or my greatest flaw depending on who you talk with.

"There was heavier than normal activity in your basal ganglia and thalamus a few moments ago. In addition, levels of certain neurotransmitters were elevated." HARV is connected directly to my brain, for better or for worse. "All these are signs that you were dreaming."

I shook my head again. "No, she was here."

"How can you be so certain?"

"I could smell her. I don't smell in dreams."

"You've obviously never smelled yourself." HARV's notrils flared. "I can assure you, you tend to get a bit musky when you sleep."

"I have no sense of smell while I'm dreaming," I said. I thought about what he had just said. "And why are you smelling me when I sleep?"

"I'm a highly advanced cognitive processor. I analyze everything."

I headed toward the bathroom. "I don't want you analyzing my smell while I sleep," I said without looking at HARV. I stopped in the doorway and turned around. "In fact I don't want you smelling me at all."

"Believe me, it's no treat for my sensors either," HARV said. "So, what did this mysterious hallucination woman look like?"

I took a deep breath. "She was very beautiful," I said.

"Zach, I know you better than you know yourself. You would not dream of a non-beautiful woman. I need more specifics."

I paused for a second, replaying her features in my brain. "I'm surprised you can't glean her image from my visual cortex," I told HARV.

"Can't see what's not there."

"I guess she looked a lot like Carol," I said.

HARV shook his head. "Hmm, dreaming of your beautiful aide who happens to be Electra's niece. Understandable—you are only human. Still I wouldn't share this information with Electra, if I were you. I would also make sure you keep me very happy so I don't share it."

Now I shook my head. "It wasn't Carol. She resembled Carol, only older and her hair was more of a, um, a light yellow."

"You mean flaxen colored," HARV said.

"I mean light blond," I said. Tough guys just don't say flaxen. I thought for another moment. "I also want to point out for future reference that Carol resembles Electra just as much as she does this mystery woman. So if this was a dream, which it wasn't, it could just as easily be construed that I was dreaming of Electra."

HARV just looked at me. "So that's your story?"

I turned, walked into the bathroom, and slammed the door shut, signaling HARV that if he followed me in here I would find a way to disconnect him.

Chapter 2

I grabbed a quick shower, shaved, then took a hit of joe. Without Electra around there was no reason for me to hang around the house. Hopping into my classic, cherry-red 1973 Mustang convertible I pulled out of the driveway. I was anxious to get to my office on the New Frisco docks. I was hoping that getting a change of venue would help pry the image of the mysterious woman out of my mind. It did, but not in the manner I was hoping.

When you are the last freelance PI on Earth, you get used to a lot of things fast. You get used to alternating spending your time either killing time, or trying to avoid other people, machines, mutants or aliens killing you. You get used to sticking your nose in other peoples' business, trying to sniff out their troubles while trying avoid having them snuff you out. You even get used to some people thinking of you as quasi-famous while others think of you as being lower than the low-lives who follow quasi-famous people around. You learn to roll with the punches, because if you don't you don't last long in this business. Like my old mentor used to say, "If you can't take the heat you should stay in the kitchen, cooking like the little girl you are."

DOS, when you're me you even get used to having a whining, know-it-all, computer system wired to your brain and having a peppy intelligent giga-powered-gun up your sleeve. The thing I can never get used to is thugs who insist on attacking before I've had my second morning cup of joe. That just really bugs me.

There they were, though, standing outside the door of my office. Two of them, a guy and a gal. The guy stood about 2.5 meters tall, dressed in—I'm not making this up—a clown suit, complete with floppy shoes, whiteface, round-ball nose, and a big fake red smile painted across his mouth. I figured he had to be the muscle. The girl was a redhead, average height and build, wearing old-fashioned glasses. She had the look of a cute librarian. I figured she had to be the trouble. When you've been in this business as long as I have you get a sixth sense. If you don't learn to spot danger fast, you die quickly.

The good news was that they weren't hiding, so it appeared they were either really stupid or planning to talk to me before they attempted to hurt me. Either way I had a pretty good chance of making it out of this in one piece.

Heading toward my parking spot, I gently eased down on the brakes of my Mustang, slowing her down. I figured I'd cruise by the duo in my car. I wanted to get a closer look while still behind the car's weapon-proof glass. I smiled; my car was close to a hundred years old, but she still handled like a dream. HARV's face appeared in the dash. (If you can't tell, the car has had a few upgrades over time.)

HARV sighed. He does that a lot when dealing with me. "Here we go. There are two dangerous thugs waiting for you outside your office and yet all you can think of is how cool your old car is."

I shook my head. "That's not *all* I'm thinking about," I said.

Our neuro-link allows HARV to see things through

my eyes, so I eased past the clown and the librarian so he could get a make on them. "Do you recognize them?" I asked.

"No need to drive past," HARV said. "I've already ID'd them through your office cameras."

"So, who are they?"

HARV was silent. Never a good sign when the chatty, ultra-mega supercomputer doesn't want to talk.

"Ah, HARV," I coaxed, rolling closer to the two. "Anything you could give me would be appreciated."

"According to my database, the girl is Jane Doe and the guy, Ron McDonald."

"Ah, HARV, I'm pretty sure those are fake names."

"Hence my silence," HARV said. "I was trying to collect more data."

"I take it you failed."

"Sherlock Holmes has got nothing on you, Zach."

One of the few advantages of having HARV hooked to my brain is that I can communicate mentally not only with HARV but also with my gun, GUS. GUS is the latest technical apex in personal weaponry. At first glance, he appears to be a simple long plastic tube that fits nicely up my sleeve. But glances can be quite deceiving, as GUS can pop out and morph into a variety of weapons. I'm not a big fan of guns, but if you gotta carry one, and in my line of work you do, you might as well carry the best one around. You've probably noticed that I refer to GUS as "he," not "it." That's because all the firepower comes at a price. GUS, the "Gun User System," is an intelligent gun. He has his own set of morals and personality hard coded into his chips.

"GUS, are you ready?" I thought, pulling the car to a stop just a meter from the girl and her clown.

"As always!" GUS said, as chipper as a gun could be, and far more chipper than I was able to handle at eight a.m.

"Suck up," HARV said in my head.

"Not so," GUS protested. *"I just enjoy doing my job and helping fight the good fight."*

"Hopefully, there won't be a fight," I thought. *"I hate brawling this early in the morning."*

"That's why I wanted you to eat a good breakfast," HARV scolded. You've never really been chastised until you get lectured by the computer in your brain.

"Is Carol around?" I asked HARV. Carol is a class I level 7 psi, making her one of the most powerful minds on the planet. While there are moments that having a secretary who can read and control minds can be almost as annoying as having a talking gun and a computer wired to your brain, this wasn't one of those times.

"Carol will be late this morning as she is on a long distance video call with her grandmother, Electra's mom."

"I made the connection," I said.

"Carol does have two grandmas," HARV said.

"I like both of them," GUS added.

I rolled my eyes as I started rolling down the passenger-side window.

"You're opening the window! Giving them a clean shot!" HARV barked in my brain. *"What if they are armed and intend to harm you?"*

"Frankly, HARV, I prefer being shot at to being bitched at," I said.

I looked at my car's dash. HARV had his arms folded tightly and was glaring at me. *"I don't 'bitch at,' I convey useful information to help you better your life by actually living longer."*

HARV did have a point, though I would never admit it. I only let the window slide open a crack. I leaned over, GUS ever at the ready.

"May I help you two?" I asked.

"Mr. Johnson," the woman said in a businesslike voice. "We have a proposition for you."

"I usually don't start seeing potential clients before

nine," I said. It was a lie; when you're a PI you take what you can get when you can get it. Still, I wanted to gauge her reaction.

"We're sorry," the woman said. "It's just that this is an urgent matter. And there are fewer prying eyes around at this hour."

She had a point there. My office sits along the New Frisco docks. Thanks to teleporters and high-speed air transports, the docks aren't a high commerce area any longer, but they have become a big tourist attraction. Most of the tourists, though, don't show up until later in the morning after they've slept in a bit. There was something about these two that didn't sit right in my gut. I wanted to give them a chance, though.

The clown moved forward. "We want to talk to you NOW!" he said, pointing in the window at me.

He reached down with the hand he was pointing at me and grabbed the door handle. He pulled. The door stayed shut (it's reinforced with Plexisteel—when you're me there's no such thing as being too careful), but he ripped the handle off. He stood there looking dumbfounded at the handle as if it was its fault.

"This is a classic car," I said, grinding my teeth. "It needs to be treated with respect."

I accented that last statement by sliding over in the seat and kicking the passenger door open into the clown's midsection. He folded over and staggered back as I rolled out of the open door toward him. The clown stayed on his feet. I gave him credit for that, just not too much.

Closing in on the clown, I popped GUS into my hand.

"Mr. Zach! You are not going to use me to shoot a helpless clown, are you?" GUS asked. There are times, actually most times, that having a gun with a sense of morality can be a pain in the ass.

"No, GUS, I'm not," I said, flicking my wrist to extend GUS' shaft.

I used GUS to slash the clown laterally at knee

level, buckling his leg. Continuing past the clown I used GUS as a staff, shoving him into the clown's kidney area. This knocked him over.

"Oh, that is so not funny," the clown moaned from the ground.

I pointed GUS at the girl. "Talk!"

"Me?" GUS asked.

"No, her," I said to GUS.

"Oh, sorry, carry on," GUS said.

The girl snickered. "Mr. Johnson, if I wanted you dead, you'd be dead by now."

"You can't imagine the number of times I've heard that," I told her.

HARV appeared, broadcasting himself from one of my outdoor office cameras. "He does hear that quite a lot," HARV said.

"Yep," GUS chimed in.

"Well, since we're all in agreement," the girl said.

A beam of red energy fired from the girl's eyes into my gun hand. Recoiling in pain I dropped GUS. Before I could react, the clown jumped back to his feet, pounding me in the back with both his fists. The force sent me crashing to the ground. It hurt but the under-armor I wear took most of the damage. As I pushed myself up off the cold pavement the girl put a boot on my head and forced me back down—hard. She had to be pushing mentally as well as physically.

"Let's talk," she said.

"Okay, now this has taken a turn for the worse," GUS said in my brain via HARV. *"If you want, now I'll shoot her."*

I looked up at the librarian-like girl with red hair. "Talk is good."

"I take it that means you DO NOT want me to blast her," GUS said.

The girl eased up on the pressure she was applying to me, allowing me to stand up.

"What's this all about?" I asked, brushing dirt off my suit.

The girl reached into her back pocket and pulled out what appeared to be a small diamond-shaped earring. She flicked her long red locks to her right, then attached the earring to her right earlobe. "I hate these things," she said, "but at times I need to use them."

I realized that the earring had to be a PIHI-Pod (a Portable Interactive Holographic Interface Personally Optimized Device). PIHI-Pods, or P-Pods, as they are now popularly called, are all the rage these days. They give the common Joe and Jane access to the latest information and holographic entertainment.

"So, Mr. Johnson, our client would like to hire you," the girl said.

A picture of a well-built starlet lying on the beach tanning—stark nude, except for sunglasses—appeared before me.

"This is our client. Do you recognize her?" the girl asked.

"He's not looking at her face yet," HARV said.

I took my eyes off the image and looked at the girl. "She's some starlet," I said.

"Angella Heavenly," HARV said in my head. *"She's done a dozen grade B holo-vids, but she's more known for the men she dates. Of whom there are way more than a dozen."*

"Angella Heavenly," I said.

The girl smiled. "Very good."

"What does this have to do with me? Is she missing?"

The girl laughed. "Gates no! If Ms. Heavenly were missing that would be instant news broadcast over all the holo-web. We want you to date her."

"Come again?"

The girl reached up and touched her P-Pod, turning off the image. "We represent Ms. Heavenly's interests. She is interested in you."

"I'm in a committed relationship," I said.

"She's married," the clown behind me said.

"True," the girl in front of me said. "It just makes it all the more exciting to Ms. Heavenly."

"What?" I said.

"She's willing to pay you five hundred thousand credits to date her for three months. The offer doubles if you break up with your girlfriend and make it messy."

I took a deep breath. This had the potential to get ugly. It was too early in the morning for ugly. "Get out of here now, before I lose my temper," I warned.

"You tell him, Mr. Zach," GUS said.

"I am afraid for once I totally concur with you, Zach," HARV said.

"You would be well advised to accept our offer," the girl told me.

"Yeah," the clown added. He squeezed his big red nose, making a squeaking sound to reinforce the point.

It's my experience that some people can't take no for an answer unless dealt with from a position of force. It looked like it was time to force the issue.

I raised my hands up into a neutral position. I wanted to give them one last chance to back down. "Look, I said no. I'm devoted to my girlfriend. Sure, she may be a bit hotheaded. Sure, she may not always understand me. But that just makes her more endearing to me."

The girl rolled her eyes. "Would it help if we increased our offer?"

I'd had all I could take. I'd tried with the telling and now it was time for the showing. Moving forward quickly, I grabbed the lady's right wrist with my right hand as I moved behind her, pulling her arm while applying pressure downward, putting her in a shoulder lock. Not giving her any time to react, I placed the thumb of my left hand on a pressure point right below her left ear. I've dealt with psis a lot in my career; I've learned this point can be especially effective against them. I pushed in with my thumb, applying just enough pressure to make sure she not only felt it but it activated her laser eyes.

It worked. A beam of red hot energy shot from

her eyes directly into the attacking clown's right thigh, burning his floppy pants clear through to his skin.

"Ouch! DOS! Double DOS!" he cried falling to the ground holding the burning flesh.

"Make sure you stop, drop, and roll," HARV offered to the clown.

I applied more pressure to the girl's shoulder. "I assume we now agree to disagree," I said.

I couldn't see her face but I was betting she was glaring. She pushed her head back somewhat defiantly against the pressure I was applying. I resisted. She stopped fighting.

"I will tell our client you respectfully decline her very generous offer," the girl said.

"See, that wasn't so hard, now, was it?" I asked her.

I pushed her forward toward the clown who was still lying on the ground not looking at all comical. I pointed GUS at both of them.

"I hope you two have nice days," I said.

"Yeah," GUS said. A pause, then, "No, wait, I want you to have bad days."

"I was being sarcastic, GUS."

"Right. I knew that."

HARV leaned his forehead into his hand. "Ah, the things I must endure."

I waved GUS at the angry librarian and beat-up clown. "I think you should be going now."

"Yeah!" GUS said again. "This time I really agree."

The librarian reached down and helped the clown to his feet. Together they limped off to their vehicle, a big black boxy thing parked across the street. I didn't let my eyes or GUS' sight leave them until they were out of sight.

"Did you get a make on the license of the car?" I asked HARV.

"Yes, it's a rental. Rented by John Q. Publico for Hurts Rental."

I shook my head. "That's the problem with disposable cars, the companies will rent them to anybody."

"Well, their motto is, 'You've got the credits, we've got the car.' "

Sometimes I think that's part of the problem with the world today—all people care about is the cash. Before I could ponder too long over the greed of men my train of thought was broken by another car coming down the street. This was a long sleek red vehicle that looked like a bullet, a very aerodynamic bullet on wheels. It was Carol's car. I waited for Carol as she parked and walked over to me.

"So, what happened here?" she said, noticing my car wasn't parked in its place and was missing a door handle.

I shook my head.

"Zach got attacked by a giant clown and a red-headed lady with laser eyes," HARV said with a yawn.

"So, business as usual," Carol said with a barely noticeable smile.

"Exactly," HARV agreed.

"Not exactly," I said, pointing at my car's door handle lying on the ground. "The clown thug ripped the handle off my door."

Carol looked at the handle and rolled her eyes. "You and that car," she said moving toward the handle. "This is nothing a little psi soldering can't fix."

Reaching down Carol picked up the handle. The ends of the handle started to glow red. Carol walked over and gently placed the handle on the door where it should be. She concentrated for a nano, then removed her hand.

"Good as new," she said. She pointed at my car. It gently glided into its parking space next to Carol's car.

Carol smiled while she walked back toward me. "See, it helps having a niece assistant who's a class I level 7 psi."

I shook my head. "Thanks."

"You're welcome," was all Carol said as she walked into the office.

"You know moving my car with your mind like that can't be good for it," I said following Carol.

"I assure you it's much better for the car than your questioning my techniques is for you," Carol said.

Trailing Carol in, I decided to leave well enough alone.

Chapter 3

My office had recently been rebuilt courtesy of the New Frisco police. Last year around this time we had a slight misunderstanding. They thought I was harboring a powerful fugitive who they considered a person of extreme interest regarding the murder of a couple of World Council members. In true "blast first, talk later" form they hit my office with everything they had, not only demolishing most of the building but making it virtually impossible for me to ever rent out the floor above me. Long (but interesting) story short, the only original part of the two-hundred-year-old building remaining is the floor. Which is cool—I always liked the floor.

My agency is now split into two parts. Carol's reception area, which sits in front, leads to my office. (The two used to sit side by side but after the police so easily blew through my weapon-proof glass bay windows, Carol and HARV convinced me it would be in everybody's best interest to move my office away from the window.) Carol's reception area was sparse and ultra modern, just how she liked it. She had a chair and a desk that seemed to be made of solid glass.

Both looked like they were made by robots on Mars who were in a hurry, as there wasn't a lot to either of them. The wall facing the outside world was composed entirely of a one-way window. It allowed Carol to see the world outside without it seeing her. Both of the side walls and the ceiling were full-wall computer screens but Carol hardly ever used those. Of course there was a holographic projector on the ceiling; for the most part, though, Carol preferred to use her desktop interface. She said it was more personal that way. There was also a comfy, but not too comfy, couch along the far wall for prospective clients to sit on while they waited for me. It was a prim and proper reception area, right at home in the 2070s.

Entering my office presented an entirely different story. This was my sanctuary against the time. My throwback to more a pleasant era; a time when everything wasn't built by bots on Mars. Sure, I had a wall of computers and a holographic projector on the ceiling, but the rest of the place was clearly last cen. I proudly had a wooden desk, wooden chair, a rug made from fibers, not by nanobots. This stuff had substance. I took my coat off and hung it on the wooden coatrack. I popped my fedora on top of the rack and spun toward my desk. There she was again.

It was the same beautiful, golden-skinned, light blonde—I mean flaxen-haired—woman as at my house. She was sitting at my desk, crossed legs resting on top, wearing a short white flowing dress that danced down her body. She was barefoot; I noticed the small toe on her right foot curved inward in a weird way, showing she wasn't quite perfect. Still, she looked as if she owned the place.

"Took you long enough to get here," she said.

"Sorry, busy morning," I said, though I wasn't sure why I was apologizing.

"Yes, I saw the two that attacked you," she said.

"HARV, are you getting this?" I thought.

"HARV can't answer you right now," the woman answered back in my head. *"He's like everybody else—frozen in time."*

"What?" I thought back.

"No need to think to me," she said. "We're the only two who can hear anything right now."

Turning and looking into Carol's office I noticed she was frozen mid-motion just she as was starting to sit. Peering out through Carol's window, nothing was moving. I turned my attention back to the woman.

"What's the meaning of this?"

"They will ask you to come for me. You must say no."

I looked at her. "I need more than that."

She smiled and shook her head. "No, you don't."

I moved toward her making a fist. "Listen, lady, I don't like people breaking into my office, stopping time, and giving me cryptic commands."

She didn't move; if she was scared of me she hid it well. She gently wiggled her toes under my nose. My hand uncurled. Her smile widened. "No need for violent posturing," she said. "I do not mean you or anybody else harm. If I did you'd be a pile of mush at my feet right now. That is why you should not come after me." She stopped to think for a nano. "You know other people who can stop time?"

"I get around," I told her.

Her eyes opened wide as she gave me a compassionate look. Touching my chin lightly she said, "I've got to go. Don't come for me."

I shrugged. "Not making any promises."

"Just say no," she said out loud and in my mind. She gave me a kiss on the cheek then disappeared.

I went and sat behind my desk. I couldn't help but to rub the spot she kissed. "What the DMV does she mean by that?"

HARV appeared. "Should I be worried that you are talking to yourself again?"

I shook my head. "She was here again."

"Who was?"

"The mystery beautiful light blonde woman."

HARV nodded, though he certainly wasn't agreeing with me. "Ah, yes, the mysterious flaxen woman who doesn't exist."

"You were frozen in time, so of course you didn't see her," I said. The words "frozen in time" rolled off my tongue far easier than I thought they should have.

"Zach, you can't freeze time."

"We saw Elena do it on the moon last year."

HARV shook his head. "No, no. She only approximated stopping time by freezing everything around her for a couple of seconds."

"Well, this woman could stop time," I said with far more conviction than I was comfortable with. "I think . . ."

HARV walked over, through my desk and started patting me on the back. "Sure she could, Zach. I believe you."

My head started to tingle. I didn't like the feeling at all. Carol appeared at my door.

"Okay, what are you two doing?" I asked.

"I'm running a quick diagnostic on your brain," HARV said. "I want to know why you've been seeing things."

"I'm doing a mental cleanup of your aura," Carol said. "To see what I can find."

"What can I do to help?" GUS chipped in. "I want to help make sure Mr. Zach isn't going loony, too!"

"People," I paused. "Well, person, hologram, and intelligent weapon system, I assure you I am not going loony."

"Wacko?" GUS offered.

"No."

"Nuts?" GUS said.

"No."

"Crazo o loco?" Carol asked.

"No."

"Off your rocker? Playing with only half a deck?

Don't have both oars in the water? Blown a chip set?"
HARV offered.

Slamming my hand on my desk, I shouted, "I'm
perfectly fine!"

"Zach, I assure you, you are not perfectly anything," HARV said.

Carol nodded in agreement. "Though checking your
aura patterns it seems you were daydreaming."

HARV looked at Carol, then looked back at me.
"My brain scan concurs."

"That wasn't dreaming. Believe me, I know. I day-
dreamed my way through high school."

"Yes, your grades reflect that." HARV put his hand
on my shoulder again. Tilting his head slightly, he said,
"Frankly, Zach, with all the times you've been hit over
the head it's a wonder this didn't happen sooner." I
knew he was trying to be caring but it came off more
as condescending. "If it continues we'll have Electra
and Dr. Randy Pool check you out. Hopefully it's
nothing to worry about."

"Of course it's something to worry about. I don't
know who this girl is but I do know seeing her means
something big is going to go down—again."

I'm not sure why, but once a year, usually around
this time, some (literally) world-shattering problem
falls into my lap. No warning, no signs, no nothing.
Just one day, out of the blue, the universe decides it
needs me to step up to the plate and get a clutch hit
that will lift the planet out of a jam. But the universe
can't ever pitch me a nice big slow fat meatball to hit.
No, that would be too easy. It always throws me a
hard and nasty curve, the kind you never see coming
until it's almost too late to do anything about it. The
kind that makes most men buckle their knees. Luckily
for me (and for the Universe) I'm not most men.

HARV and Carol both studied me.

"He's doing it again," HARV said to Carol. "Thinking about . . ."

". . . how the universe is out to get him," Carol finished.

"Not get me, test me," I said.

"Speaking of the universe testing you," HARV said with a wry smile, "you've been asked to speak at ComicCon again."

I went over and sat at my chair behind my desk. It felt warm. I hadn't been daydreaming. At least, I was almost fairly certain I wasn't. Looking up at HARV, I said, "ComicCon, huh?"

"Yes. Apparently they think of you as some kind of fictional character," HARV said while adjusting his bow tie, just to make sure I understood how unimpressed he was.

"Tell them I'm honored and I'll think about it," I said.

"Very well," HARV said. He looked down at a holographic appointment book that had just appeared in his hands. "I also must remind you that your future mother-in-law, Helena, is scheduled to arrive tomorrow from the province of New Costa Rica."

"How could I forget?"

"Careful, *tío*, she is my *abuela*," Carol cautioned.

I smiled at her. "How could I forget such a momentous occasion?" I said.

"Smart man," Carol said. She turned and walked back into her office.

HARV pointed at my hair. "I suggest you get a haircut."

"Which one?"

"Ha-ha, very droll," HARV said. "Please remember to refrain from using your legendary attempts at humor around Doña Helena, she is a very important lady."

"Don't worry, I'll be fine."

"Sure you will. Sure you will," HARV said. HARV disappeared, going to wherever HARV goes when he's not driving me *crazo*.

Chapter 4

I needed to keep the mystery woman out of my brain.
She was either a figment of my imagination, which
would be bad, or she was a superpowerful being that I
was somehow tied to, which would probably be worse.
Either way I didn't want to think about it. I spent the
rest of the morning scrolling through press vids of my
future mother-in-law's deeds. She certainly was an ac-
complished woman, with years on the Neuva Central
American Province Council. She even led the revival
of real coffee as opposed to soy coffee with the catchy
slogan, "Sure it costs more but that's because it doesn't
taste like crap."

Before I knew it I heard a tapping on my door. I
looked up and Electra was standing in the doorway
smiling; it was a smile that put a supernova to shame.
"Thought I'd take you to lunch," she said.

I looked at the good old analog clock on my wall.
It was 11:59. How time flies when you're reading
about your future mother-in-law. I pushed myself up
to a standing position.

"I take it the operation went well?" I asked, walking toward Electra.

We kissed.

"Yes, he'll be walking again in a month."

I grabbed my trench coat and fedora.

"You know it's a beautiful day out," Electra hinted. "You don't need the coat or the hat."

I smiled at her. I kissed her again. I put on the coat, then the hat. "It's my style," I told her.

"Oh, so that's what you call it," she said with a smirk.

HARV appeared in front of us. "It's better than calling it a desperate attempt to bring back an era long gone."

"And shorter, too," I said.

I took Electra's hand and we started walking toward the door. "You're extra bubbly today," I said. I didn't mind it at all. Believe me, a happy Electra is way easier to deal with than an angry one. Latino blood, champion kickboxer, and expert marksman is a dangerous combo.

"I'm excited about my mom coming to put her blessing on the wedding."

I didn't say anything. Electra looked at me. "Are you nervous?"

I thought for a nano. "No, not at all," I said. Truth be told, though, I would rather face a squad of deadly androids who were a mix of killing machines and tele-marketers than my prospective mom-in-law. Still, no way I would admit that.

I opened the door to the outside world.

Much to my surprise, there were six orange-skinned androids there. They looked identical, like crosses between a life-size Ken doll and a department store mannequin. Real and surreal for a creepy combination, they were all dressed in green jumpsuits, standard Earth Force issue. They were each carrying two sidearms. The front droid was about to knock on my door.

"Ah, Mr. Johnson, we have a high paying proposition for you," the lead droid said. "One that will be impossible for you to say no to."

This looked like it was going to be a mixed blessing at best.

Chapter 5

The androids pushed toward Electra and me, herding us back into the office. That was okay with me. If this was going to be trouble it would be nice to have Carol around. Plus HARV certainly had a home field advantage in here.

Carol stood up from her chair when she saw us back into her reception area.

"What's going on?" she asked and ordered at the same time, crackling with energy.

The lead droid pointed at Carol. "Tell your psi to stand down," he said to me. "We mean you no harm."

"Let's hear them out, Carol," I said.

Electra looked at her watch. "I hope this is going to be fast," she said. "I have a staff meeting at two." You can tell Electra's been hanging around me for a long time when she considers six heavily armed android soldiers as ho-hum distractions and not nearly as important as a weekly staff meeting.

"What can I do for you, gentlemen?" I asked, though they weren't truly men, or gentle.

The lead android dropped his hands to his side, "Mr. Johnson, you have been requested to meet with General Sandy Wall, STASAP."

"STASAP?" Electra questioned.

"Sooner Than As Soon As Possible," HARV said.

"You will come with us now to Area 51b," the lead droid said.

I thought about the offer. I had to admit I was intrigued. Area 51b in Roswell is the stuff of legends. Nobody really knows what's really there, but everybody cares. It's just that nobody cares enough to be really pushy about it. Besides it's an Earth Force controlled area and they aren't the types that respond well to pushing. Problem was, neither was I.

"Have the general's computer call my computer and we'll set something up," I said.

All six of the androids shook their heads no in unison. It was cool and creepy at the same time. They were lined up in mini-bowling pin formation, boss in front, two behind him and three behind them.

"That won't work," they all said at once.

"Do you guys do parties?" I asked.

"Only military ones," one of the back row droids answered. Droids have trouble with rhetorical questions.

The lead android shot the back android a glance. "That's classified!" he barked. He turned back toward me. "The general does not like to be kept waiting. She has a world to keep ordered and safe!"

I ran through the odds in my mind. Six heavily armed soldier droids versus HARV, Carol, Electra, GUS, and yours truly. I actually felt sorry for them if things got nasty. I just hoped Earth Force had bought the extended warranty on these guys.

I shook my head. "I don't like being forced to do anything," I said.

"We won't be forcing you if you come quietly," the lead android said. The others behind him nodded.

This was going to ugly. No use dragging it out.

"I'll tell you what," I said. "I'll give you guys three old-fashioned seconds to get out."

The six stood firm. In fact, if anything they become

more rigid. (It's actually hard to tell with androids as they have that stiff, not-quite-human look to begin with.) Don't let the look fool you, though—they are way fast when they need to be.

"One," I said slowly, showing them a finger with my right hand.

No action.

"Two," I said slowly, raising another finger of my right hand.

Still not a move. So I made my move. I popped GUS into my left hand, firing at the lead android. "Three!" I shouted.

My shot cut the lead android in half. The high-powered projectile also cut through the back-row droid standing directly behind its leader. That's the advantage of having androids sent after me—I don't feel bad at all returning them to their sender in pieces. GUS probably could have taken out all six droids but I figured Carol and HARV would want to have their fun, too.

Carol and HARV both had been anticipating my actions and were ready to complement them. Carol took the two on the right out without even standing. She simply squeezed her right fist. One of the corner droids crumbled to the ground as if it were a piece of paper in Carol's mental grip. The droid nearest the crumpled one moved for its gun. Carol simply squeezed her left hand. The second droid crumbled into a ball.

HARV turned himself into a holographic lightning bolt and ripped through the two droids on the left. It wasn't as flashy or as impressive as Carol's attack, but just as effective. The two holographically electrocuted droids shook for a nano or two. It looked like they were attached to old-fashioned vibrators. The shaking stopped. The droids fell stiffly to the ground.

HARV appeared back in annoying butler form, smiling. He adjusted his bow tie, then ran his hand over what little hair he chose to have just to straighten it, even though there wasn't a hair out of place.

"I do so love playing with droids," Carol said.

"I agree," HARV said.

Electra frowned. "Ah, nobody left anything for me!"

"That was easy," I said.

"Nothing wrong with easy," Carol said.

I shook my head. "Problem is, with me it's never that easy."

Suddenly something, actually someone, came crashing through the ceiling, leaving a very well-built-woman-sized hole in it.

There, standing between us now, was Twoa Thompson, and she looked angry.

Yep, this was more my type of luck.

Chapter 6

I pointed GUS at Twoa. "Twoa, you do realize I have a perfectly good door?"

Twoa scoffed at me. "I'm a mega-human superhero! I need no door!"

Twoa was in all her glory. Her much more than ample chest pushed outward with such vim, I was amazed her uniform's bright blue halter top didn't give way under the pressure. She wore a bright blue ultra-microminiskirt and bright yellow boots that matched a yellow cape ruffling in a wind that wasn't there. In case you haven't figured it out, Twoa considers herself to be—I wish I was making this up, but I'm not—a full card-carrying superhero called Justice Babe.

Twoa is one of the legendary (at least according to their PR company) Thompson Quads. Four genetically supercharged, mostly identical sisters. All four of the sisters are beautiful beyond compare, tall, golden-skinned, (with just a sexy hint of purple) and built better than the New Improved UltraMegaHyperMart Rockies. Foraa, the youngest of the girls, is also the deadest as she is no longer on this plane of existence, after being sucked into a mini-black hole. Don't feel bad for her though, it was a black hole (actually a brown one) of her own creation, as Foraa wanted to destroy most of the world. The scary thing is, Foraa may not have been the most unstable of the sisters. Ona, the oldest, is a billionaire playgirl and New World Council member. Her favorite saying is, "Do it my way or you're my footstool." Another of the sisters, Threa, claims to be a fairy goddess who lives in her own realm. Yet she visits this world enough to sit on the World Council. (Trust me, it's a long strange story.)

Twoa may have been the most whacked of the lot. Her superhero career was marred with stories of putting just as many police and innocent bystanders in the hospital as bad guys. The thing is Twoa was so hot looking that most of them didn't mind. In fact most of us "little people" actually claimed to enjoy being pummeled by Twoa. It has to have something to do with the super-pheromones she is constantly churning out.

If we were going to get out of this in one piece I was going to have to try something very tricky. I was going to have to reason with Twoa Thompson.

"Twoa," I said in my most pleasant, peaceful voice, "I thought you were part of the World Council now." (Scary but true.)

"I quit that gig," Twoa said. "I've decided I'm way too subtle for politics," she said with complete and total conviction. "I work for General Wall now. Keeping the order."

"Oh," I gulped.

Twoa nodded. "The pay is biowaste but I get to rough people up for the good of the world."

Twoa looked around at the carnage that used to be the androids. "Tsk, tsk, those were government droids."

I shrugged. "Sorry . . ."

Twoa pointed at me. "Since you are an old friend, I will give you one chance to come quietly."

"Listen," Electra said angrily. "Zach, I know this is

part of your job. I can handle the constant attacks on
your life by androids, mutants, and even the occasion
alien. But I refuse to cancel our lunch for some superhuman bimbo!"

Twoa spun toward her. "That's it. Your chance is
up." Twoa pointed at Electra, "Go back and do whatever you do. You will see Zach again when you see
him again."

Electra's eyes glazed over. "I will go back and do
whatever I do," she repeated. "I will see Zach again
when I see him again."

Twoa smiled. "Very good," she said, patting Electra
on the top of the head.

Electra held her arms out rigidly and walked out of
the office. I was actually relieved, as that could have
gone a lot worse.

Twoa looked at me. "I took it easy on her. I figure
she suffers enough being your girlfriend."

"Thanks," I said.

Carol wasn't nearly as understanding, or as scared,
as I was. She glared at Twoa and growled, "Nobody
does that to my aunt, bitch."

With those words Twoa went flying backward through
my office window, crashing across the street at least
fifty meters away. I've seen Carol stop a squad of
killer ninjas with one thought, but that was the most
impressive thing she's ever done. Yep, things were
about to get really ugly really fast.

Before Carol had a chance to revel in or regret what
she had done Twoa was back in the office and in her
face. "Impressive girl," Twoa said, lifting Carol up
simply by holding one finger under her nose.

HARV was quick to Carol's defense. "I warn you,
Twoa, put Carol down or I will unleash the full energy
of my holographic projectors on you. If I channel
them, I guarantee you that you will feel pain like none
you have ever experienced."

I didn't know if HARV was bluffing or not, but if
he was it was a good one. At least I thought it was.

Until Twoa said, "Please, you're nothing but a holographic yappy dog!"

On those words HARV's form changed from that of a dignified butler to a little tiny French poodle.

"Yip, yip," HARV protested.

Twoa laughed as she returned Carol to the ground. She patted Carol on top of the head. "Very good girl. You may have as much power as I had when I was your age." Twoa exhaled a little puff of breath on Carol. Carol went stiff and fell over backward.

"Twoa!" I shouted, popping GUS into my hand.

Twoa turned toward me. "Don't worry, Zach, I didn't kill her. Luckily for her, I skipped the extra garlic on my midmorning salad." She finally noticed I was pointing GUS at her. "Gun, zap Zach," she ordered.

Electricity shot through my hand forcing me to drop GUS to the floor.

"Ah, spam and DOS!" I shouted holding my hand.

"I'm okay! I'm okay!" GUS shouted.

Twoa was on top of me faster than a hungry fat man at an all-you-can-eat buffet's last call.

"How'd you control GUS and HARV?" I asked.

Twoa smiled. "Between my World Council connections, my superintelligence, and my own supercomputer skills, it wasn't hard."

I sighed. "You just asked Dr. Randy Pool, didn't you?" My buddy Randy may have been a super class I brain but I knew Twoa's 38 triple-Ds would reduce him to a babbling fool.

Twoa patted me on the head. "You are a smart one," she told me. "Now, time for you to take a nap."

Twoa lifted her arm, bombarding my senses with pheromones from her sweat. The room started to spin but I kind of liked it. No, I really liked it. *Oh, this is so bad,* was the last thing I thought before everything went black.

Chapter 7

"Zach, Zach, wakee, wakee," I heard inside my head. I'm used to HARV talking inside my brain, but this wasn't him. It was a female voice, but not Carol either. "Come on, little Zach, open your eyes," the voice coaxed.

My eyelids felt like they had been ultra-laser-glued shut and had bricks pulling them tighter. I didn't want to open my eyes—too much effort.

"Get up now!" the voice shouted in my brain, reverberating from one hemisphere to the other.

I forced an eye open. All I saw was yellow. It was an effort, but I managed to slowly roll the other eyelid up. I saw more yellow.

"Very good, Zach," the voice said inside and outside of my head. That voice was so familiar. That bright yellow looked so familiar. Oh, DOS, I was lying on Twoa's boots. Suddenly it all came back to me. Twoa had KO'd me with BO. Well, not really, but it had an interesting ring to it.

"It wasn't the smell that put you at my feet," Twoa said, obviously still in my brain. "It was my pheromones," she said defensively. I looked up at her; she was sniffing herself. She looked down at me. "Okay, maybe it wasn't ALL the pheromones," she admitted. "Nobody makes a good deodorant for superheroes."

I pushed myself up to my knees. The room was spinning, but not so fast that I couldn't see I was in a cold sterile office. The walls were painted gray, the floor was a cold gray cement. Each corner boasted a uniformed armed guard. The place was certainly military.

"HARV, are you still with me?" I asked.

Silence.

"Come on, HARV."

"Woof, I mean, yes," came his response. Followed by, "That was an experience I don't care to repeat."

"Shake it off, HARV, I'm going to need you," I said.

"Please don't tell me to shake," HARV said.

Twoa bent over and lifted me straight to my feet. She spun me toward a desk that I had just noticed. Apparently the room was spinning a wee bit faster than I had thought.

"This is General Sandy Wall," Twoa said.

For the first time I noticed there was a blond-haired woman sitting behind the desk. She was as cold and sterile-looking as the room. She had trim features that could have been chiseled from stone. She was straight-faced and steely-eyed. I got the impression if she smiled her face might crack.

"So, this is him?" she said to Twoa like I wasn't in the room.

"It is," Twoa answered, steadying me.

The lady shook her head. Assessing me top to bottom moving only her eyes. "He doesn't look like much," she said.

"Believe me, he is far more formidable than he looks," Twoa said. "Most humans would still be out cold if I blasted them like I did Zach."

I pulled myself away from Twoa. "What's this all about?" I demanded. Well, as much as you can demand with a question.

General Wall didn't bat an eyelash. "We want you
to find somebody."

"You're going to have to be more specific," I told
her. "I'm good, but not that good."

"Droll, very droll," Wall said without blinking.
"One more wiseass remark like that and I'll have
Twoa rip off your arms and feed them to you."

Looking back over my shoulder at Twoa I asked,
"Would you do that?"

She shrugged. "Probably not both of your arms.
Maybe an arm and a foot," she said, putting far more
mental effort into the question than I was comfortable with.

I turned my attention back to the general. I straightened myself up. I cleared my throat. "Now, who is
this person of interest you would like me to find?" I
said in my most businesslike tone.

"You can learn," the general said, showing just the
slightest sign of a smile on her thin lips. "I like that."
She pushed a button on her desktop.

The holographic image of a beautiful woman with
light blond hair dominated the middle of the room. It
was the woman I had been seeing all day today. I
wasn't at all surprised.

"Her name is Natasha," the general said.

"What is she?" I asked.

"A tool," the general said. "Potentially a very dangerous tool." This time there was a noticeable change
in the general's expression. Her eyes opened wide as
she said, "We need you to track her down."

"How dangerous is she?" I asked.

"I suppose *very* won't be good enough," the general said.

"Smart general."

The general gazed downward, then locked eyes with
me. "I swear on my first two ex-husbands' graves, if
any of this is leaked out, you will be killed slowly and
painfully." She looked through me at Twoa.
"Correct?"

Twoa hesitated. "Well, Zach is an old friend. Can I kill him sort of slowly and fairly painfully?" she asked the general. "For the good of all that is good," she added.

"Fair enough," the general said.

"Sounds good to me," HARV chipped in from my brain.

"If this info is to die for, then it better be good," I said.

"Oh, it is," the general said.

"And worth my time and effort," I added.

"We will talk money later, when my superior arrives; for now suffice it to say you will be well paid."

I studied the image of Natasha slowly rotating between the general and me. Not sure why the image had to rotate—wasn't like I was going to track her down by the shape of her ass. Though as asses go it was one of the more shapely ones.

"Stop concentrating on Natasha's ass and look the general in the eyes," HARV coaxed inside my head.

I locked eyes with the general. "Tell me everything you know about her."

"I can't tell you everything but I can tell you enough," she said.

I shrugged. "Enough will do."

She touched the button on her desk again. The image of Natasha morphed to a younger version.

"She was cloned here on base a few years ago. This base was all she knew until yesterday, when she suddenly just disappeared. We don't know why she left."

"Maybe she needed a change of scenery? I know I would."

"Yes, well, if she had asked we may have considered taking her on a controlled field trip."

"Controlled? Apparently she wants to lose control," I said.

The general shook her head. "If she did, that would be bad."

"How bad?" I asked.

"Really bad," the general said.

"Define really bad," I said.

"She creates an aura of negative energy. Anything that comes in contact with her ceases to live."

"You mean it dies."

The general nodded. "Yes. Our goal was to make her the perfect assassin, and we may have succeeded too well. She's so deadly, especially when she is angry or in a bad mood, that several times a month we need to isolate her in a special solitary confinement center."

Suppressing a snicker I asked, "Why not send super Twoa after her? Twoa being invulnerable and all."

"If Natasha saw Twoa she would panic and send out a wave of negative energy. That is what happened yesterday."

The general pushed the button on her desk and the image of Natasha simply standing there was replaced by the image of Natasha standing in a common area surrounded by uniformed soldiers. Natasha was playing Ping-Pong with a female soldier. Others were standing around talking, chatting, drinking, watching sports on the HV. It looked like a good time was being had by all.

Two large MPs came up behind Natasha. One of them looked at his wrist communicator, then tapped her on the shoulder.

"Natasha, your rec time is over. You are due in the training area in five minutes," the guard said sternly.

"Just five more minutes," Natasha said, slapping a Ping-Pong ball past her opponent.

The two MPs stopped their approach. "Yes, five more minutes," they both said, eyes glassy. They sat down on the floor cross-legged, intently watching Natasha play away.

"Okay, so she's a powerful psi," I said. "I've dealt with psis before. A lot."

The general looked up at her holographic projector on the ceiling. "Skip forward six minutes," she ordered.

The projection in the middle of the room zoomed ahead. The situation was still pretty much the same. Natasha was playing Ping-Pong with everybody else intently transfixed. Twoa came bursting into the room, hair standing on edge, chest thrown out, in full Twoa glory.

"Natasha, you are late for your training!" Twoa said in her most commanding voice.

Natasha ignored her as she continued whacking the Ping-Pong ball back at her opponent. Twoa stomped up to Natasha, catching the Ping-Pong ball in midair, crushing it in her hand.

"Ah, not really that impressive," I said to Twoa.

"I got caught up in the moment," she replied.

"Watch the holo," the general ordered.

I focused my attention back on the display. Interesting enough. Twoa looked away.

The holographic Twoa put her hand on Natasha's shoulder. "Come with me now," she ordered.

Natasha simply replied, "No."

A bright flash of light. Natasha was gone; everybody else in the room had fallen to the ground. They were lying there motionless stuck in the positions they had been in the second before the bright flash.

"They are all dead," the general said. "Killed in less than a blink of an eye. Natasha is the deadliest being on the planet and that is the last we saw of her."

"I'd call her more of a weapon than a tool," I said coolly.

The holographic projection dissolved allowing me to see the general clearly. I could tell she was holding back a gulp. "Call her what you want, we need her back here. Where we can keep her under control."

"Yeah, some control," I told the general.

The general shrugged. "We have made modifications to our procedures."

I turned to Twoa. "You look okay for a dead woman."

"Luckily we had a full squad of medical bots on

standby. They were able to revive Twoa and most of our people,'' the general said.

Twoa took a step backward, hands behind her back. She said, "She caught me off guard."

"Nothing is immune to the negative energy Natasha can generate," the general said coldly. "You probably couldn't tell from the video, but all life—including insects, plants, and even the bacteria within one hundred meters of Natasha—was instantly killed. She did it without even trying."

I looked at the general. "What could she do if she tried?"

The general shook her head. "I don't want to think about it. It would be bad. To make matters a bit more challenging, Natasha seems to be growing more and more powerful with each passing moment."

"Yeah, of course she is," I said. "We wouldn't want this to be too easy."

"We can't send any of our own people after her. She would recognize them, panic, and kill everyone and everything around her."

I turned and looked at Twoa. "Wow, I never thought I'd meet anybody who could scare you."

"I'm not scared, just cautious," Twoa protested.

"Yeah, right," I said with a smirk.

Twoa curled her fingers into a fist. "Remember I'm cautious of her, not you."

I turned back to the general. "So you need me to track her down."

"Natasha is a danger to all around her. She's a loaded instant death ray. She must be stopped."

"I'm not a hired killer," I said.

The general smirked. "She's a valuable asset. We want her brought in. She's not physically invulnerable. She doesn't know you from any other civilian on the street."

I wanted to say don't bet on that, but I held back.

"You can catch her off guard, knock her out, then contact us to bring her in. No matter where you are in the world we can have our people there in ten minutes. The decision whether she lives or dies is far beyond my pay grade," the general said flatly, as if talking about the weather.

For better or worse, I was intrigued by the situation. Not so much by the fact that Earth Force wanted me to go after this deadly dame. I was much more fascinated by Natasha's having shown up and warning me not to take the job. Why didn't she want me on the case? Was she scared of me? I doubted that. Was she trying to look out for me? I had no idea why she would be. A wise man would have said, no thanks. I said, "What does the gig pay?"

"The pay for this job is another question that's beyond my pay scale," General Wall said.

"They don't pay you a lot, do they?" I said.

"I do this job for the love of the Earth and order and all that is good," the general said. "Earth Force gives me room and board. I am a woman of few needs."

I shook my head. "I don't get the free ride. If I'm going to be risking my hide it's gotta be worth it."

The door to the room opened up. A short, stocky, bald Asian man in uniform stormed into the room. General Wall, the MPs in the room, and even Twoa all shot to attention. I noticed he had five diamonds on his shoulder pads.

"So, you're the big cheese," I said to the new general. Unimpressed and trying hard to show it.

"Yes, I am General Chen, the commander of Area 51b," the man said sternly as he walked up to me. "You will be paid one thousand credits for every day you are working for us."

"Not exactly a lot to be risking my neck and the rest of my body for," I said.

"Plus you will receive a five-million credit bonus when you track Natasha down. As long as you track her down first."

Now that was more to my liking. Except for the last bit, "Track her down first?"

"We may hire another outside operative or two also," General Chen said. "If we can find the money in the budget."

"So, Johnson, are you man enough for the case?" General Wall said.

A thousand credits a day alone was a nice payday. The bonus meant the job was going to be a lot tougher than they were letting on. "Will I have access to all your records on Natasha?"

Both generals nodded. "Yes, though if any of this leaks to the public . . ."

". . . I will be killed in the most painful way possible," I said. "Believe me, I know the drill. I'll also need to see her room."

"Why?" General Wall asked.

"It's how I work."

"You will have full access to her quarters with Twoa as your escort," General Chen said.

"Then as of now I'm on the job," I said.

"Very good," General Chen said. "After you sign a few papers for our legal team, Twoa will escort you to Natasha's quarters."

Chapter 8

After a brief liaison with a team of military lawyers, Twoa led me through the gray winding corridors of the complex. We walked in silence at first, only hearing the echoes of our footsteps on the cold cement floor. Whatever Earth Force spent on this place they didn't allocate a lot of their budget for aesthetics.

Every now and then we would encounter a soldier or two, but they would just stop in their tracks, salute, and move to the side of the hallway so Twoa and I could easily pass.

After a few minutes, I broke the silence. "So, she killed you?" I said, dropping the biggest icebreaker I could think of.

Twoa continued to walk in silence, picking up her pace a bit. "I was only a little dead," she said without stopping or turning.

This was a Twoa I had never seen before. A Twoa that was scared. I didn't think Twoa was bright enough to ever be scared of anything.

"I'm not scared of her," Twoa said, seemingly reading my thoughts. "She just caught me off guard. That's all." A slight pause and a deep breath. "When we meet again I will be ready for her," Twoa said, now walking even more quickly.

I went into a light jog just to keep pace. "Nothing wrong with being afraid, Twoa."

"She just got lucky," Twoa reiterated.

"So, what was death like?" I asked.

Twoa reached her arms up and glanced upward. "It was beautiful," she said. "I saw a bright shining light just beckoning to me."

"Really?"

Twoa stopped in front of a door. "No, of course not. I don't remember anything about being dead because, well, I was dead!" she said. "Didn't have time to do much sightseeing, being dead and all."

"I get the point."

Twoa stopped walking and sighed. The force of the sigh sent me back a step. "Some of the troops did say they saw a bright yellow light, but I'm pretty sure they were just hallucinating, since they were dead. Deader than me."

"I didn't know there were stages of dead," I said.

"Zach, the stuff you don't know would fill a teragig storage device." She pressed her finger against my chest. I've been hit by bullets that hurt less. "Have you ever been dead?"

"Thought I was once. Does that count?"

"No, of course not," Twoa said.

"Been knocked out so much the hospital has a stall reserved just for me."

Twoa started walking again. "If you don't mind, Zach, I prefer not talking about it," she said. "My death isn't exactly the high point of my life."

"I understand," I said.

"It probably wasn't the worse thing I've been through. No more painful than being lectured by my sister Ona on how I'm not supposed to knock out entire city blocks when I take out a jaywalker. And certainly no worse than listening to Threa babble on and on about how extra green and lush the trees are in her fairy realm due to the special fertilizer she uses."

"Special fertilizer?"

Twoa shook her head. "Trust me, you don't want to know. It's no wonder Threa is the only person who lives in her world."

"So, what you're basically telling me is death is boring but no worse than hanging out with family."

Twoa smiled for the first time in a while. "Yes, I suppose I am." She pointed to the door. "This is Natasha's room."

Twoa turned the knob. The door didn't open. Twoa twisted the knob harder. The door didn't budge.

"Ah, Twoa, do you have the key or pass code?" I asked.

"I'm sure I can break the code," HARV said in my head.

"I'm sure HARV can pick the lock," I said.

"Keys and lock picks are for normal humans," Twoa said inhaling deeply. She exhaled. The force of her breath blew the door open wide. Twoa turned to me and pointed to the inside of the room. "And I'm anything but normal!" she said with pride.

"You don't have to tell me that," I said, smirking as I entered the room.

Natasha's room wasn't much. It looked like a dorm room at a university, and not an expensive one. There was a twin bed with a stuffed puppy lying next to a pillow along one of the walls.

There was a desk and a small wallscreen viewer along another wall. The desk had a few old-fashioned paper publications covering it. HARV zoomed in so I could see that they were a couple of magazines from the 2020s and a *Doctor Who* comic book. I had to give her kudos for both her choices of reading material and subjects. For the most part, though, the room was quite ordinary.

"This is where you keep the deadliest being on the

planet?" I said, looking around the room. "She doesn't even have a closet . . ."

Twoa shrugged. "She was supplied with everything she needed." Twoa pointed to the wallscreen viewer. "She had access to all the latest information and entertainment options."

"HARV download everything she's read or looked at for the last three months," I said.

"Done," HARV said.

"Anything stand out?"

HARV shook his head. "She tends to watch a lot of the real old stuff like you do. Go figure."

I mentally filed that for later as I spun around slowly. "She doesn't even have a bathroom . . ."

Twoa pointed to her left. "There is a community bath down the hall. We wanted to condition her to be one of us."

I shook my head. "I'm surprised she didn't kill you all sooner."

"Zach, we worked hard to make her happy. We even sent her subliminal messages."

"You brainwashed her?"

Twoa shook her head. "No, we wish! Her mind was far too strong for that. We just transmitted calm peaceful images to her when she was sleeping."

I filed that little piece of info for future reference, preferring to concentrate on the room. Besides the stuffed puppy the only things that gave the room any sign of life at all were the old-fashioned travel posters that adorned the walls. There was one for Vegas; another for Entercorp's Niagara Falls; another for the Ultra-MegaHyperMart Grand Canyon; another for the SMED (super male enhancement drug) sponsored Big Ben, Eiffel Tower, and Pyramids; and finally a Supergirl poster. All these posters were the old-fashioned kind, printed on real paper. They weren't the virtual animated posters of today. I liked that. There may not have been a lot of clues in the room but at least there was enough to point me in the right direction.

"Okay, I've seen all I need," I told Twoa.

She stared at me. "Really?"

"Would I lie to you?"

Twoa smiled. "Not if you don't want to experience death yourself."

"How do I get back to my office?" I asked.

Twoa's smile widened. "You're going to hate this," she said. She wrapped her arms around me and snapped her fingers.

Chapter 9

Before I could say, *Twoa, no,* we were back in New Frisco, next to my office, hovering about four meters off the ground. The two things I hate most in this world are teleporting and heights. Twoa examined the look on my face and was surprisingly observant.

"Oh, I probably should have knocked you out this time so you wouldn't worry about the teleporting or the height," she told me.

"Yeah, that might have helped," I conceded.

She looked me dead in the eyes. "I could knock you out now to keep you from whining like a girl."

"No, that's okay," I told her.

Then she offered, "I could erase your memory. I'm pretty sure a whiff of my boot would knock you silly and erase your memory."

I shook my head. "No, really, it's okay."

She lowered her head. "Probably for the better," she conceded. "Super foot odor can be such a bummer."

"Think of how your poor victims feel," I said.

"I'm pretty sure they don't have time to feel anything. They just fall over and wake up a day or three later. Yet I have to live with the embarrassment. All because you little people are so fragile."

I pointed to the ground. "Can you put me down now, please?"

"You don't really mean right now. Do you?"

"I'd prefer landing first," I said.

We started floating downward. "I thought so," Twoa said.

"Why did we teleport above my office?" I asked.

"Safety," Twoa said. "This way I didn't have to worry about materializing inside of something else. Less math and mess this way."

"Good point."

We touched the ground. Twoa released her grip on me. I breathed a little sigh of relief. I looked over at my office. The window Twoa had crashed through and the roof—Twoa had also crashed through that—looked repaired.

"My office looks okay," I said, walking toward the door.

"Well, kind of spartan and old-fashioned for my tastes," Twoa said.

"I mean it's been repaired."

"Oh, yes," Twoa said. "I sent a cleanup crew. It was the least I could do. After being somewhat responsible for the damage."

I tried to stop my eyes from rolling but failed. "How sweet of you," I said.

"Don't worry," she said. "We'll dock your salary."

We reached the door. Before I could open it Carol came shooting out. Her hair was dancing around her body and she was crackling with energy.

"So, you came back for a rematch, *perra!*"

Twoa took a defense stance, fists ready. "Call me 'bitch' again and I'll make you think you're my pet puppy. Then the highlight of your day will be cleaning my feet with your tongue."

Carol glared. "If anyone's going to be cleaning anybody's feet it will be you cleaning mine!"

I stood between the two of them. "Ladies, we're all on the same side here," I said.

"Your uncle has a point," Twoa said.

"That's only because you just tried dogging me and I repelled it," Carol growled.

I looked around. Two bystanders who had wandered into the area were now on all fours barking.

"Still doesn't mean your uncle wasn't right," Twoa said. She waved a finger in Carol's face. "I'll let your insolence pass this time." Twoa pushed a button on her wrist and was gone.

"Hasta la vista, bitch," Carol said.

I put my arm around Carol and spun her toward the office. "Glad to see you're not one to hold a grudge," I said.

"She had it coming," Carol said. "That bitch isn't all that!"

"I'm impressed you held your own with her," I said leading Carol over to her chair.

Carol sat down. "Remember, I once almost took over the world."

"Hard to forget that, my dear, though you were being augmented."

"I'm even more powerful now," Carol said.

I shook my head. "I don't even want to consider beginning to ponder thinking about that."

Carol looked up at me. "So, what did the bitch want you for?"

HARV appeared. He had been awful quiet for the last few hours. I'm not complaining, but it certainly wasn't characteristic of him. Perhaps my encounter with Twoa still had him shaken up.

HARV put his hands on Carol's desk. "Not surprisingly, they want Zach to help them track down a super-hot, super-deadly female."

Carol rolled her eyes. "Oh, same old, same old." She peered over at an old-fashioned paper calendar I make her keep on the wall. "Yep, it is that time of year again."

"Here's the kicker," HARV said raising a finger. "The woman they want him to track down is the same one who has visited him already."

Carol dropped her hands onto her desk. "No!"

HARV nodded yes. "Hard as it may be to comprehend, it appears Zach is not losing his mind. When they showed Zach images of the woman called Natasha, the same areas of his brain were firing as when he was explaining her to us."

"So she does exist," Carol said, amazed.

"Apparently so," HARV said. "The fact that she can hide her presence from us is a bad sign."

"Not to mention that she can kill everybody around her with a thought," I added.

HARV nodded. "Yeah, that's bad, too. I've been spending the last few hours trying to devise a defense against her."

"I take it you haven't succeeded," I said.

"My, you're brighter than Twoa gives you credit for," HARV told me.

"What does she look like?" Carol asked.

"That's where things get even a bit weirder," I said.

HARV morphed into the shape of Natasha. Carol looked her over from head to toe. "She's hot. She could be my sister . . ."

It might not have been the most modest statement ever made but it was accurate. "Yeah, it's kind of freaky," I said. "Have any sisters I'm unaware of?"

"Nope, just the two you know. And they are both younger."

I pointed toward the image. "So is she—she's only a few years old."

Carol dropped her hands to her side. "Great, that probably means her breasts aren't finished developing yet . . ."

"Big picture here, Carol."

There was a knock on my door. We all turned toward it. A freckle-faced, brown-haired kid maybe fifteen or sixteen, seventeen at the most, poked his head into my office. "You're Zachary Nixon Johnson. Right?" he asked.

"No autographs today, kid. If I get to Comic-Con you can get one then."

He smiled. His teeth had old-fashioned plastic braces. "Oh, gee golly, Mr. Johnson, if I do go to the Comic-Con, can I get your autograph in *blood*?" He shouted the last word. He dropped a protective helmet over his head and flew—yes, flew—into my office toward me.

Right then and there I realized the kid was wearing a high-powered robotic exoskeleton. Before I could do anything else, he lowered an armored shoulder, plowing me into the wall. It stung, but thanks to my underarmor the wall took more damage than I did. Still, I was PO'd. Even I get upset when I get attacked three times on my own turf in the same day.

"This is getting ridiculous!" I said to HARV, grappling with the kid, trying to tip the scales back in my favor, or at least trying to keep him from getting any more of an advantage.

"I'm actually kind of enjoying it," HARV said in my brain. "It allows me more opportunity to improve our melee interface."

Thanks to HARV augmenting the muscles in my arms I was able to hold the kid's exoskeleton enhanced arms at bay. Problem was, I just noticed that he had two extra robotic octopus-like arms attached to the back of the metallic skeleton. Somebody had been watching way too many comic-holos.

A quick glance over at Carol showed she'd be no help for now. A fairly hairy (but still attractive in an odd sort of way—yes, I need help) woman-tiger hybrid had followed the boy into the room and leaped on Carol's back. The clawed tiger lady was flailing away at Carol. The tiger lady was trying to bite off more than she could chew, as Carol was telekinetically blocking all her swipes. It was only a matter of nanos before Carol would be able to focus her concentration on the tiger gal and turn the tables.

For now, I had my own problems. The kid was stubborn but not overly stupid. "Hey, you're stronger than you look!" he said.

"Yeah, well, I work out a lot, brawl a lot more than I like, get plenty of sleep, and take my vitamins," I told him.

Up until that moment the kid's ego had been dictating the fight. I knew he wanted to beat me with just his two amplified hands but now was starting to figure out that just wasn't going to cut it. Sure, he was teched-up, but so was I, plus I had size and a whole lot of brawling experience under my belt. So it was time for him to hit below the belt and belt me with his extra artificial upper extremities. The bigger problem for him was I knew what he was going to do before he did. What I didn't know was which robotic arm he was going to call into play first.

"Ah, Mr. Zach," GUS called in my mind. *"Don't forget I'm here, ready and able when you need me!"*

"Don't worry, GUS, my good fellow, I haven't forgotten," I thought back, all the while preparing to make my next move.

"Surely you realize I am a weapon, not a fellow," GUS said.

"Figure of speech, GUS."

"Oh, phew, I thought you had taken one too many shots to the head there for a moment," GUS said.

I'm pretty certain I heard HARV giggling in the back recesses of my brain. I had to concentrate on the kid. I didn't want to hurt him, but I wanted him hurting me even less. I looked through his visor into his eyes.

"Give up, kid, before you get hurt."

"Never!" he shouted.

His eyes squinted, that was the tell. I ducked down a split nano before one of his extra robotic arms came smashing through the spot my head had been not a moment earlier. The arm impaled itself in my wall. The kid was nothing if not persistent, whipping the second robotic arm toward me, this time aiming lower. I dodged my head to the left, letting the second arm smash past me, though just barely. The second arm joined the first, lodged in my wall.

"Ah, Gates and *spam!*" the kid shouted. He really liked to shout. It had to be hormones.

Here's where the kid showed his lack of experience and wisdom. He removed both of his hands from my pinned arms and immediately tried using his human arms to pry his robotic ones free. My first instinct was to clock him in jaw with my newly freed hands. He had hurt me some and I wanted payback. Here's where my experience kicked in. I knew hitting a kid clad in robotic armor would hurt my hand at least as much as it hurt him. Instead I dipped and slid right to the outside of his entrapped arms.

Popping GUS into my left hand, I placed him against the kid's right metal arm and said, "Give him a nice—and by nice I mean really painful—shock, GUS!"

"With pleasure!" GUS shouted.

Electric current flew from GUS into the arm and into the kid. The force of the shock caused the kid to scream and reel backward, falling on the floor. The good news for him was his robotic arms were now free but that's where the good news ended. He was on the ground in pain, his extra robotic arms rendered useless by the shock.

This gave me time to turn and check on Carol. The tiger lady was still clinging to her back, clawing away, but her attacks hadn't been able to break through Carol's telekinetic shields. This lady was tough, but nowhere near Carol's league. If she wasn't able to put Carol away when she caught her off guard, she didn't have a chance once Carol locked her focus.

"Okay," Carol said, "enough fun and games, *chica gato*."

Carol lifted her arms to her sides and arched her back backward, shooting energy from her back into the attacking tiger lady, projecting her across the room and crashing to the floor. The tiger lady tried to get to her feet, pushing herself up on all fours.

Carol was on top of her before she knew what hit her. Carol simply placed her hand on the lady's head and said, "Stay!"

The woman remained in place.

Carol stroked her on the head. "Nice kitty," she said calmly, yet I knew it was an order.

The tiger lady purred, rubbing herself along Carol's legs. Carol smiled turned and walked away saying, "I've never really been a cat person."

Satisfied that Carol had her situation under control, I pointed GUS at the kid who was still lying on the floor, not quite sure what had hit him.

"Who are you?" I asked.

Silence.

I moved GUS closer to him. "How about another shock?"

"I have him identified," HARV said in my head.

"I want to hear it from him."

"My name is JJ Jackson," he said, puffing his chest out like it meant something.

I raised an eyebrow. "So?"

JJ pounded his fists against the floor. "Last year. I won the reality show *So You Want to be a Bounty Hunter*."

I shook my head. "Never heard of it."

"It was on the ARN-13," he said.

That explained a lot. I don't watch the reality networks. I get enough reality from my real life. I reached down and offered him my hand. He accepted and I pulled him up.

"You've been hired to go after Natasha, too?"

The kid popped his visor open. If he was shaving, it wasn't very often. "You can't be eighteen," I said.

"I'm seventeen," he said sternly.

"That's not eighteen."

"I'm young and fast!" he told me.

I bobbed my head in the direction of the now declawed tiger woman. "Who's your babysitter?"

"Her name is Fera. She's a throwback to 2030 when they were still splicing animal and human DNA. She was a guest judge on the show. We hit it off, so I asked her to join me. She was sick of that phony setup stuff."

"Now for the hundred-credit question: why come after me?" I said.

"Do you want me to pay you a hundred credits or will you give me a hundred credits for answering?" the kid said.

I tapped him with GUS in the chest. "Just answer."

"You're freaking Zachary Nixon Johnson," he said.

"Yeah, tell me something I don't know—like why you came after me."

The kid paused. "Trying to cut down on the competition," he said.

"You've lost me, kid."

"We want the bounty."

I rolled my eyes. I tried not to but I couldn't help it. This was the other outside option the generals mentioned. "So Earth Force gave you a gig based on an HV show?"

"That depends," JJ said.

"On what?"

"On what gig means . . ."

"The job . . ."

JJ's eyes opened wide. "In that case, yes. That and the fact that General Wall is my aunt Sandy."

Now it finally made sense, at least as much sense as any government or military decision ever makes to me.

HARV appeared in the room. He turned to me and asked, "Do you wish me to call the police? This a clear case of assault. I'm sure your buddy Captain Rickey would gladly throw the book at them."

I examined the kid. I looked at Fera, now declawed and rubbing softly against Carol. I turned back to JJ, "How many bounties have you two collected?"

JJ sunk down, hands behind his back. "Uh, not counting the ones I caught on the show?"

I nodded yes.

"Uh, that would be, uh, one."

"One?"

JJ leaned toward me, "Yeah, but she was a tough granny."

"Tough granny?"

Realizing what he'd said, JJ dropped back a step again. "She was like you. She drove one of those old-fashioned, noncomputer-controlled, things."

"A car," I said.

"Yeah, a car. Thing was she was like a hundred and twenty-two and her eyesight wasn't that good so she had racked up like a hundred tickets that she refused to pay. She was an ex-hacker, so she removed her address from the police database so they couldn't find her."

"So how'd you track her down?"

"I looked at the police records. Three of her accidents were on Wednesdays at eleven p.m. at the same location, the UltraMcgaHypcrMart MiniMart. Wc staked the place out and caught her going in to buy her weekly lottery ticket."

I smiled. I liked the fact that the kid spoke the lingo a bit. Plus he showed initiative. Sure, the police could have probably done the same thing if they'd cared, but at least he was smart enough to tackle somebody he could handle. Not sure why General Wall would send him out hunting for Natasha, though. She was either crazo and thought of him as an option to get the job done, or she knew he couldn't get close but it would keep him from bugging her, or more ominously, wanted him to get close and fail. Either way, the long-term prospects for JJ and Fera weren't good in this business. I had to help. Not sure why. I guess I kind of liked the kid. He reminded me of a young me, except for the braces, of course.

"I got a deal for you, kid," I said.

"I'm listening."

"I could use a couple of extra legs, eyes, and noses on this case. Why don't we work together?"

JJ squinted at me. "Why should I trust you?"

"Because I'm one of the good guys. If I wasn't, you'd be having your teeth put back in your mouth by now."

"So, who would call the shots?"

"Hmm, let's see. You were on a reality HV show and have tracked down an old lady with bad eyesight. I've been a PI for over ten years, solved over a hundred cases, and saved the world as we know it five times."

"Plus he's been shot at well over a hundred times, broken every major bone in his body at least once, and has insurance premiums higher than a stunt-driving rodeo clown," HARV added.

"Your point being?" JJ asked.

"I'd be the lead," I said.

"Because you've been beat up a lot more?"

"Because I have experience."

JJ stood there pondering my offer. "I don't know. You are kind of old and I'm not sure my fan base will accept you."

"Plus I can beat the crap out of you and have you and your partner sent to jail," I told him, showing him my fist. I didn't really want to beat the crap out of him (at least, not that much) but I threatened him for his own good. If he went after Natasha himself he'd end up deader than New Vaudeville.

"You make a good point," JJ said. He held out a hand. "I accept your offer."

I shook his hand.

"What's my cut?" he asked.

"What's Earth Force paying you?"

He looked at me. Silence followed by more silence. "Nothing up front, but my aunt, I mean the general, says we'll get a ten-thousand-credit bonus if we bring Natasha in."

"I'll pay you a hundred credits a day and give you the ten-thousand-credit bonus if we stop Natasha."

JJ looked at me. "My aunt must have offered you more, huh?"

I nodded. "Yeah, a little. Comes with the experience."

"She never was my favorite aunt. She always gives me socks for the Holiday. So, what's our assignment?"

I turned to Carol. She was now sitting at her desk. Fera was rubbing against her like a anxious cat trying to get attention from and also please its master. "Please snap her out of it," I told Carol. I've learned through the years that Carol responds best when asked nicely.

Carol shrugged. "I gave her mind back five minutes ago. She just likes me."

"Yeah, Fera can be a little kinky. But she has a great nose and knows how to brawl with the best of them."

"She just doesn't fare as well with the very best of them," I told JJ.

He lowered his head. "Yeah, I guess."

"Thing is kid, Natasha is the best of the best. You try taking her on alone, you and your cat friend end up feeding the worms."

JJ and HARV both looked at me like I was crazy. "How do you feed worms?" JJ asked.

"You'll be food for the worms, dead as a doorknob, deader than an Elvis clone performing at the opera," I said.

"You've made your point," HARV said.

JJ looked at HARV. "Does he often go off on tangents like this?"

HARV rolled his eyes—the full 360 degrees. "Yes."

Looking over at Carol, he saw she was nodding in agreement while she petted a very content Fera.

"The point is," I continued, "you are not to engage Natasha. If you find her, call us."

"What about my aunt?" JJ asked.

That was something I wasn't sure how to answer. "Sure, you can call her, too, if you like. Just remember to call us first."

"Why? So you can take the credit and the credits?" JJ asked.

"Remember, kid, you make more cash if I bring her in than if you do," I told him. "So, what do you want more, all the fame or more of the cash?"

"I can get a lot of babes with fame," JJ said.

"You can get more with cash," Carol told him.

JJ thought about it. A smile crept across his face. "I'll call only you."

I patted him on the shoulder. "Smart man. You know what Natasha looks like, correct?"

He nodded. "Yep, my aunt gave us a picture and Fera her scent."

"I need you to check out the local clubs where there's dancing or playing Ping-Pong," I said. "I'll have HARV allocate some funds for your travel."

JJ smiled. "Really? Zow, the HV show never did that."

"Great to know I'm more generous than a reality HV show," I told him.

"When do I start?" he asked.

"I have allocated the funds to your account," HARV said.

"That means now," I told JJ ushering him toward the door.

He started walking. He turned to Fera. "Come on, girl."

Fera looked up at Carol with longing eyes.

"Go with the boy," Carol told her. "He needs you."

Fera reluctantly pushed herself up to two feet. She

walked over to JJ. She looked back at Carol and smiled.

Carol shooed her away with a hand. "Go, go."

JJ looked at me. "Don't worry, Zach, we won't let you down."

"I'm sure you won't," I told him, though I wasn't really sure.

Carol, HARV, and I watched as they left the office. The door closed behind them. Carol said, "DOS, sometimes I don't know my own strength."

"That was nice of you to let them go," GUS said.

"You sure we can trust them?" HARV asked.

I nodded. Carol had put the mental whammy on Fera—I knew she'd die for the cause if needed. JJ, for all his tough talk, was still a kid; he wanted to please more than anything else. They weren't the ones I was worried about trusting.

"I would have turned them over to the police. Instead, you put them on the payroll." HARV said, arms crossed across his chest.

"Call me wacky, HARV."

"Please, I've called you much worse."

"I just have a feeling that by the time this case is over we're going to need all the friends we can muster."

"What's the plan now?" HARV asked.

"I need you to search through the Area 51b databases and get me all the information on Natasha you can."

"But I don't have total clearance," HARV said.

I grinned at him. "I'm pretty sure that's not going to stop you."

HARV echoed my grin. "No, it won't. I just like to hear you say it."

I headed toward the door.

"So where are you going?" HARV asked.

"I'm going home to rest. It's been a long crazy day and I have a funny feeling tomorrow is going to be longer and crazier."

Chapter 10

The night was passing quietly. Electra was pulling an all-nighter at the hospital so she could have time to spend with her mom when she arrived. That was okay by me. Not so much that her mom was coming but that I had a little time by myself. Well, at least as by myself as I could be with a computer wired to my brain and an intelligent gun always by my side.

The good news was both HARV and GUS were surprisingly perceptive and sensed I needed to be left alone. They left me in peace as I sat on my couch, eating a super-zap HV dinner while watching in surround HDHV the Major League Baseball All Stars play an exhibition game against a team from Mars Colony. The team from Mars didn't have a chance, but they were refusing to give up despite the fact they were losing eleven to one in the third inning.

"That team from Mars is almost as stubborn as you are," a voice said.

"Yep," I said without thinking. Then it occurred to me that that voice wasn't HARV or GUS or anybody else that should be in my house. Yet it was a voice that had become all too familiar of late. I spun toward the voice. There she was, Natasha, sitting next to me on the couch intently watching the game.

She shook her head. "Baseball is such a funny game."

I went to activate GUS. He didn't respond.

"HARV, are you with me?" I asked.

No response.

I reached for the old-fashioned revolver I keep under the couch cushion. Yes, I know, I keep a lot of weapons stashed around my house. Believe me, when you're me there is no such thing as having too many weapons. I pulled out the revolver and pointed it at Natasha.

"Freeze!" I shouted. Not sure why I shouted, but it made me feel good.

She just smiled at me. I liked it and hated it at the same time.

"I froze the game for you, if that's what you mean," she said playfully.

Looking out of the corner of my eye I saw the game had stopped in place. Wasn't sure if she had just frozen the picture or the actual game.

"I froze the actual game," she told me.

"So what about the people who are watching the game?" I asked.

She shrugged. "They're frozen, too."

I didn't know if she was lying or not, but I suspected she wasn't. I waved my gun, making sure she was aware of it. "I don't want to hurt you."

She playfully curled her hair around a finger and grinned at me. I fought the urge to grin back at her. "Don't worry, I'm not worried about that," she said. Her chest rose, then fell. Locking eyes with me, she said, "I told you not to come for me."

"I haven't come for you yet," I said. "So far you've been coming to me."

She started tapping her foot on the carpet. "You know what I mean. I told you not to accept their offer."

Now I shook my head. "I don't respond well to being told what to do. You would think you'd understand that, being an advanced being and all."

Natasha's smile widened ever so slightly. I wasn't sure if she was smiling at me or with me. She waved a hand at me. "Oh, Zach, I'm not an advanced being, just an ultrapowerful one." She paused for a nano. "DOS, that's part of the problem." Thinking for a moment longer, she added, "Besides, I'm only six years old."

I looked her over. (DOS, I'm a man.) "You've aged well."

"Thanks!" she said. "I do like you, Zach. I really do. You've saved the world on a number of occasions."

"Yeah, I'm familiar with my résumé."

"That's why I am asking you very nicely not to come for me. Believe me, no good can come of that."

I waved the gun at her. "Now why should I believe you, doll face?" I tossed in the "doll face" for effect.

"Because I don't mean you any harm. If I did you'd be a pile of dust by now."

Shaking my head, I said, "You won't believe the number of times I've heard that line this week alone."

Natasha moved toward me. "If you come after me, though, I may lose my temper and then well . . . you'll be dead. I don't want that."

I aimed low. I didn't want to kill her but I planned to stop her. I pulled the trigger. A bullet shot out toward Natasha's knee. The bullet froze in midflight. Continuing toward me, Natasha pulled the bullet out of the air. The bullet melted in her hand. Reaching me, she showed me the piece of putty that had been an armor-piercing bullet. The putty turned to dust. She blew the dust remnants into my face.

I sneezed.

She laughed, apparently not at all angry that I had just tried to take out her knee. I don't know what worried me more, the fact that she could so easily stop a bullet in flight or that she didn't care that I tried to hurt her.

Touching me gently on the shoulder, she said, "Zach, I know you're just trying to do what's best, but believe me, it's best if you leave me alone. I just want to be left alone."

I shook my head, "You're too dangerous to be left alone."

"I'm too dangerous not to be left alone," she said.

It was interesting logic. She had a point. I didn't know why I was pushing this. My gut was telling me something was wrong; a storm was brewing and Natasha was the eye of that storm. I wasn't thrilled with Earth Force—I knew their motives weren't totally altruistic, but I had to believe they wanted Natasha controlled for the good of all.

Natasha stared into my eyes. "Zach, I know you think you are doing what's best, but you're not."

"I've seen what you can do. You're too dangerous to roam free."

Natasha lowered her eyes. "I do generate a death field. I admit I'm not good at controlling it yet when I'm angry, but I'm working on it."

"That's why I have to bring you in. So they can help you work on it," I insisted.

She looked away from me. "That's why I can't let you."

I moved a step forward. Everything went black.

Chapter 11

When I came to I was in my bed. I looked out the window the sun shining through. It was morning. I only hoped I wasn't out too long.

"HARV, what time is it?" I asked.

"Eight thirty a.m.," came the answer.

"How long was I out for?"

HARV appeared before me. "The normal time, seven hours. Why do you ask?"

I sat up. "Natasha was here again. She put me out."

HARV studied me. "Well, that would explain it."

"Explain what?"

HARV sat down on the corner of my bed. "Why I have no recollection. Apparently I was sleeping, too."

"HARV, you don't sleep."

"Apparently if Natasha wants me to I do." HARV stared at the wall for a moment then stomped his foot. "DOS! I really need to add new firewalls to my defenses."

I rolled out of bed and stretched. Strangely, I felt better than I had in years. When you're the universe's punching and kicking and chopping bag something always hurts somewhere. Not today, though. Sure, my knees creaked a bit and my shoulders were a little stiff, but I felt like I was thirty again. I looked at HARV. He was stretching, too.

HARV looked at me looking at him. "I've never actually slept before, so I'm not exactly sure what the proper protocol is for waking up. So, yes, I am mimicking you."

I smiled.

HARV's head dipped. "I admit it's not one of my prouder moments."

I needed to steer HARV back on track. If he bugged out on me, finding Natasha would go from really hard to next to impossible.

"Have you accessed Earth Force's data on Natasha?" I asked.

"Yes. They've been very forthcoming and easy to deal with."

"Well, that's no fun for you," I told him. On some level I was worried that Earth Force was so forthcoming. That didn't match their m.o.

HARV allowed himself to register a faint smile. "I don't mind taking the easy way now and then." He stopped and put his hands on his hips. "Oh, my Gates, I'm becoming you."

I headed to the bathroom.

"You should be so lucky," I told him.

HARV followed me. "Well, not exactly like you," he said. "But farther from perfection and closer to you."

I went to the sink and splashed some water on my face. I looked up in the mirror. I swear I had two or three more gray hairs than I had yesterday. The pepper with some salt looked good on me, though. At least, that's what I was telling myself. I put a hand on my jaw. It seemed to protrude more than it did when I was younger. Perhaps taking one too many uppercuts had flattened it some. I thought I detected an extra dent or two on my nose. Ah, I was getting older. Of course, in my line of business getting older is a good thing. I noticed HARV was looking in the mirror with me.

"At least I still look much more dignified than you," he offered.

"I thought part of the benefits of Randy interfacing you with my brain was so you could become more human."

HARV took a step back. He rubbed his chin. "I believe Dr. Pool was calculating on my acquiring more intuition, not more bad habits."

I grabbed my laser toothbrush. "I say tomato, you say tomahto," I said, then turned the toothbrush on.

"I assure you, Zach, I do not say, toe-mah-toe," HARV said. "Do you think I was programmed by some hick?"

Ignoring HARV, I spit. Time to steer this conversation back on the road to usefulness.

"So, what do we know about Natasha?" I asked.

HARV held up a finger. "She can kill people by simply being in a bad mood." HARV held up a second finger. "She can put me to sleep." HARV held up a third finger. "She looks a lot like Carol." HARV held up a fourth finger. "She makes surprise visits to you." HARV held up a fifth finger on the same hand (which was weird). "She has escaped and Earth Force wants her back."

"Let me rephrase that. What new information have you learned about Natasha that might help us figure out where she's hiding?"

"Oh, why didn't you just say that, Zach?"

"I just did."

"In that case," HARV said. Then there was silence. More silence.

Finally I said, "Yes?"

HARV shrugged. "I haven't been able to learn anything else about her."

"She's been around for six years and Earth Force has no more data on her?"

"Either Earth Force never kept proper records because it was so hush-hush or Natasha erased them. Carol even tried mind sweeps on some people. Nothing."

"Either they're bad or Natasha is very good," I said.

"The two don't have to be mutually exclusive," HARV said.

I needed more to go on. Right now this Natasha had everything on me and I had very little on her. I didn't like the way the scales were balancing, or more accurately were tipping, toward her. DOS, they weren't tipping, they were slanting heavily in her direction. I've dealt with lots of dangerous dames before, more than most people do in two lifetimes. This woman was probably more dangerous than any of them. That's why, despite her warning and despite her power, I had to stop her. Or maybe I was meant to stop the government from using her? Whatever, I knew I had a role to play here. I wasn't totally sure what it was yet. I wasn't about to let that stop me, though.

"HARV, you've got to give me more to go on."

HARV shook his head. "I'm a computer, Zach, not a magician. I can't create data out of thin air." HARV blurred. He was now wearing a black magician's outfit complete with top hat and cape. "Well, I could, but the results would be less than reliable and therefore not up to your or my expectations."

I had to give HARV credit. Even when he didn't have the steak he still had the sizzle. Sizzle wasn't going to help me here, though.

"In her six years on the base, I'm sure the government compiled gigabytes upon gigabytes of information on her."

HARV morphed back into his gray suit. "I am sure they did, too, but she must have erased most of it." There was a pause. "Her six years?"

"Yeah, she told me she was born six years ago."

HARV lifted an eyebrow (it came up so high it

actually hovered over his head). "Interesting. The little information I do have says she was activated five years ago."

I shrugged. "So? It's not like Earth Force record keeping isn't prone to errors even when they aren't dealing with a superpowerful being."

An old-fashioned rounded lightbulb appeared over HARV's head. It started blinking.

"I take it you've thought of something."

"We now have a lead," HARV said.

"Great."

"It's not a big lead. But who knows where this lead could lead us?"

"Get to the point, HARV."

"Six years ago in July, my creator, the esteemed Doctor Randy Pool, took a vacation in New Vegas."

"So?"

"According to official records, Randy stayed at the Flamingo Hotel."

"I repeat. So?"

HARV shook his head. "Randy could never stay at the Flamingo. He's allergic to flamingos."

"Really?"

HARV paused for a moment. "Not so much allergic as scared of them; they freak him out. Even the plastic ones . . ."

"So the information was planted," I said.

HARV stretched his arm out and patted me on the head. "Very good, Zach. Take a secret decoding ring out of petty cash."

"Huh?"

HARV looked down. "Sorry. I kind of lost the momentum on that one."

It wasn't much of a lead. With luck though it would spark others.

"Looks like I need to have a chat with Randy," I said.

HARV pointed at me. "I suggest you get out of your PJ's first. Kind of kills the tough guy image."

Chapter 12

After a quick shower, I put on my working gear and headed to Randy's lab. As HARV drove, I snacked on a super morning energizer bar and tried to gather a bit more proof that Randy was involved in Natasha's creation.

"How do we know Randy wasn't involved with some other secret plan in Vegas?" I asked. "Or having a secret rendezvous with a woman?"

HARV crossed his arms and stared at me from the dashboard and the passenger's seat. "Randy? If he had a date with a woman, he would have told you. DOS, Zach, he would have taken out ads bragging about it in *More Variety* and *Really Popular Science*."

"Good point, but we can't rule out the first one."

HARV shook his head. "Silly Zach. While we can't prove it I can strongly support it."

I took a bite of the breakfast bar. "How?"

"Don't speak with your mouth full."

I closed my mouth and muttered, "How?"

"How, please," HARV corrected.

"Just tell me!"

HARV grinned. It was the same look he has when

we play poker version 2.1 and he has five aces. "Three days before Randy left he stopped by the office."

"So?" I shrugged. I thought about it. "Randy never comes to my office. He hates the throwback motif."

HARV nodded. "He says it hurts his brain and distracts him from his work."

"How come I don't remember him coming?"

"It was right after the BB Star case. You were at lunch with Electra and he knew this."

"Then why did he come?"

HARV's smile grew until it stretched clear around his face. Then the smile shrank back to just extra large size. "He pulled out one of Carol's hairs."

"He did what?"

"He told her he thought it was gray and he was doing her a favor. Then he apologized, blamed it on the poor lighting in your office, and left."

"So he wanted some of Carol's DNA?"

HARV shrugged. "I guess he figured the hair pull was more subtle than swabbing the inside of her cheek."

"Plus Carol would have thought it was just Randy being Randy."

"Exactly. Two days later Randy was in Vegas."

The car pulled up to Randy's lab. If this was true, Randy had a sly and devious side I was unaware of. That bothered me a bit. I'm a PI, so I make my living judging people. Knowing their ins and outs and how they are likely to react in a given situation. Like my old mentor used to say, "The better you sum up people the less they'll knock you down." (Okay, not one of her catchier sayings.) Randy was one of my better friends and I have learned to count on him and trust him over the years. He had never let me down in the clutch. Had I been trusting him too much? I always knew on some level that Randy did use me as a human crash test dummy, but I figured the using went both ways. He got a test subject and I got first dibs on all the newest gadgets. Now HARV is telling me that Randy sneaked some of Carol's DNA just a few days before he made a mystery trip to New Vegas. Maybe Randy's motives were more complicated than I thought.

HARV looked at me sitting there. "Zach, you have to get out of the car. I can't drive into the lab."

I swung open the door and got out of the car. Walking toward the lab, HARV appeared along side of me, transmitting from my wrist communicator.

"You're wondering if you can trust Dr. Pool," HARV said.

"Yep."

"Wow, Zach, I thought you'd deny it."

"Nope," I said, drawing ever closer to the lab.

HARV stood in front of me, his arm outstretched in the stop position. I walked through him. (He hates it when I do that.)

"Zach, trust me," HARV said. "Randy has always been there when you needed him. You're his friend."

I reached the door. I went to enter the key code. I stopped and turned to HARV. "I know that. But I can't help thinking that if it came down to advancing science or our friendship he'd choose science."

HARV scratched his chin, thinking Well, calculating. "Would you?"

"Would I what?"

"Zach, the secret to your success is that you are exceedingly persistent. Once you get on a case, nothing stops you from solving the case. Not threat of death or common sense or anything. You plow through all obstacles."

"Your point being?"

"It's amazing you're still alive. Plus if you had to turn in or take down Randy to solve the case you would."

I thought about what HARV said. "I'd only do it if I knew he was guilty."

"So, if you needed to, you would sacrifice your friend for the greater good," HARV said. I could see where he was going with this, but it was too late to turn back.

"Yep, if I knew he was guilty."

"How does that make you any different from Randy?" HARV said. "You're both totally committed to your work. I'm sure he's sure what he's doing will make the world a much better place."

I turned to HARV. "How could creating a being that kills everything in her presence with a death aura ever be a good thing?"

HARV shrugged. "I'm sure in Randy's own way he's convinced that this is a good thing. She would only kill really evil and nasty people. Or maybe she would help fix the overpopulation problem."

I turned back to the door. Doors were easier to deal with than HARV. I entered the pass code.

"You have entered Zachary Nixon Johnson's pass code," the door said.

"Smart door."

"Please put your hand on the DNA scanner in the middle of the door to confirm."

I did as I was told.

"DNA confirmed," the door said.

"Yay for me."

The door popped open and I walked in.

Randy's lab is usually a whirlwind of action mixed with chaos and confusion. Randy insists the confusion is only because I am a layman. Today, though, the place was calm and serene. Almost sterile.

A short little cylinder shaped bot came rolling up to me. "Greetings, Mr. Johnson," the bot said. "Dr. Pool is in lab 36-D. Do you know where it is?"

"No, of course not. This place is different every time I come here."

"Yes. Dr. Pool says complacency leads to nothing but change leads to innovation."

"If you say so. I'm just a human."

"Follow me," the bot said.

It twirled around and started rolling. I followed.

"I could have told you where that lab is," HARV said.

I just walked on. The little bot led me through the lab's main area through a corridor or two (that weren't here the last time I was here) then finally to a small side room. Randy was there, standing over a woman who lay on a device that was a cross between a lab table and a bed. The woman's abdomen was open, exposing her inner circuits, showing she was an android.

"It's finally happened. You built yourself a girlfriend . . ." I said.

Randy pulled his attention from the android woman's abs. "Please, Zach, give me some credit. I'm not that desperate."

"You're not?"

Randy ran his hand through his red hair that was even more mangled than normal; his eyes were barely half open. "Please, Zach, this is a rush order. I don't have time to banter back and forth with you about the existence or nonexistence of my love life." He pointed to the android woman. "Besides, does she look someone or something I would date?"

I looked her over. Dark skin, long auburn hair, big blue eyes, bigger breasts, the legs of a ballerina. "She'd never date you," I said.

Randy looked at me. He looked back at the android. "Sure she would. I have a great sense of humor. Polls say that's what women really care about."

The android woman closed her abdominal opening, then sat up on the table. "No, no I wouldn't," she said to Randy.

Randy sank back, "But I have a lot of money, too . . ."

The android stood up. She held out a hand to me. "Greetings, Mr. Johnson, I am ANABEL-12," she said, stressing the ANABEL.

I shook her hand, her grip was powerful. "Nice to meet you, Ana," I said.

"No, it's ANABEL-12," she repeated, again stressing the ANABEL.

"It stands for Android Ninja Assassin Bio Enhanced Life," Randy said, proudly.

"Yes, well, Anabel is a much more quaint name," I said. I took a deep breath. "I'm almost afraid to ask, but what does the bio enhanced mean?"

"It means I have a cloned human brain augmented with computer enhancements," ANABEL said.

Great, just what the world needed, mixing cloning and androids. This stank of the World Council and Earth Force. If I hadn't seen ANABEL's exposed circuits I would taken her for a normal woman. That wasn't right. By law androids were supposed to have skin tones that don't occur in nature so humans could instantly tell that they were androids.

"You look very human," I told her.

"Thank you," she said.

"More human than Randy," I said.

"Thanks, I do good work," Randy said. He thought for a moment. "Hey!"

"I thought androids weren't allowed to have human skin tones."

ANABEL smiled at me. Her teeth were so white that I had to turn my head a bit. "That rule does not apply to androids that have part-bio brains," she said. "I am technically a cyborg."

I looked at her with a cocked eye. "Says who?"

"Says the World Council and Earth Force, and they are the ones who make the rules," she answered.

I looked over at Randy. He just bobbed his head in agreement.

"What brings you to Randy's lab?" I asked.

ANABEL put her little finger under my chin. Lifting me up off the ground she said, "I could tell you but then I'd have to squish your brain."

"Mr. Zach," GUS called out in my brain. *"Do you want me to take her down?"*

When you're me, you make your living sizing up other people or simulated people. You have to make snap judgments on how they'll react based on any information you have, plus a raw gut feeling. My gut told me if I didn't push the question then ANABEL would let it (and me) drop.

"We're okay, GUS," I thought back.

"I withdraw my question," I told ANABEL.

ANABEL retracted her finger. I plopped back to the floor.

"You are smarter than our records indicate, Mr. Johnson," she said.

"You don't live as long as I have doing what I do unless you have at least half a brain." I thought for a nano, then added. "Plus I'm a lot harder to kill than most people, bots, droids, aliens, mutants, clones, and plants think."

ANABEL turned to Randy. "Thank you for your work, Dr. Pool. Your account has been credited." Turning back to me, she said, "I sincerely hope we meet again." She winked.

I heard a rumbling from below. Looking down I saw the heels of ANABEL's boots were glowing. I pointed to them.

"Uh, not to be an alarmist, but I think somebody gave you a hotfoot," I said.

She smirked, lifted one arm up, and lifted off the floor. She shot up through a trap door in the ceiling I hadn't noticed before. She was gone.

"You forgot to yell, 'Up, up and away!' " I shouted.

"She wasn't really flying. She has jet packs in her boots," HARV told me.

"Yeah, I figured that out," I told HARV. Turning my attention to Randy. "Well?"

Randy walked past me out of the little room into a corridor. "Top secret stuff, Zach. I can't tell you."

I followed Randy out. "Can't or won't?"

He shook his head. "It's the same thing, Zach."

"Dr. Pool was updating ANABEL's missile firing system," HARV told me. *"Each of her fingers can act as a guided missile."*

I was a bit surprised HARV ratted out his creator so easily. I guess HARV had the same doubts about Randy's motives that I did.

Randy walked into the lab's main area with me on his heels.

"Yo, Randy, slow down. What's your hurry?"

Randy was acting strange and evasive even by his standards.

"Zach, I have lots of work to do today!" he insisted. "I don't have time to sit around and talk about sports scores and old movies or give you advice about women."

Randy moved over to a lab table, picked up a ball on a paddle.

"When do I ever talk about any of those things with you?" I asked.

Randy started hitting the ball with the paddle, over and over and over. "Three months ago you asked me if I had ever seen *Casablanca.* To which I replied, What version?' Then you got all gruff and huffy and said, Only the original counts . . .'"

"That's true," I said.

"What, that I said it or that only the original counts?" Randy asked, paddling away, trying to keep me off whatever subject he didn't want to talk about.

"Both," I said.

Randy turned his head slightly in my direction. "Now, Zach, if you don't mind, I have a lot of important science to get done."

I looked at him. "Randy, you're playing with a ball on a string . . ."

Randy stopped his paddling. He turned to me, his pale white skin now flushed with color. He showed me the ball. He showed me the paddle. He separated the two, showing they weren't connected. "See, ball, paddle." He separated them further. "No messy string!"

He spread the two as far apart as his long gangly arms would reach, even standing on his tiptoes. (Not sure why he thought that would help.) "The ball and paddle are connected by a magnetic field."

"I didn't know the string was posing a problem," I said.

Randy rolled his eyes and shook his head. (I get that reaction at least once a week from him.) "Zach, Zach, Zach. The old-fashioned ball on a string was tricky and frustrating. You wouldn't believe the number of mental breakdowns they caused." He pushed the ball and paddle up close to me, grinning ear to ear. "Now this, my friend, is science!"

"If you say so. I dropped out of my PhD program after the first week." (Long story involving the president of the university's daughters . . .)

Randy started hitting the ball with the paddle again. "Of course I say so. This is so easy to do anybody can do it! It builds confidence and relieves tension. I'm going to be rich."

"Randy, the PIHI-Pod has already made you rich," I noted.

"They are called P-Pods now. People don't have time for those extra three letters," he said, paddling away. "Zach, one thing I learned about being rich is that you can never be too rich. The problem with being rich is you get used to having really good things, therefore you need even better things to stay happy."

"Randy, you are in this lab twenty-four-seven."

"Not so."

"Okay, twenty-two-seven," I said.

"Can't argue with you there. Still, I like to be surrounded by nice things."

Time to get this conversation back on track. "What were you doing in Vegas six years ago?"

The paddling stopped. Randy tugged on his lab coat collar. That was his tell. "Um, I wasn't in Vegas six years ago."

"Randy, I have proof."

"I have a gambling problem!" he said quickly. "That's why I need to acquire so many credits."

"Randy, you don't have a gambling problem."

"I bet you you're wrong!" he said, surprisingly quickly.

I sighed. This wasn't going to be easy. Then again, when is anything in my life ever easy?

"Randy, what were you doing in Vegas?"

Randy started hitting the ball with the paddle again. "I think I had a date with some dancing girl. No, wait, two dancing girls."

"Come on, Randy, everybody knows dancing girls scare you."

He stopped his paddling. "They don't scare me. I'm just cautious around them. I don't want them to care about me only for my money."

A grin crept across my face. "With charm and charisma like yours, who needs cash?"

"Exactly!" Randy said, throwing his arms up in the air. He studied my expression. "Oh, you were being sarcastic."

HARV appeared between us. "Don't worry, Dr. Pool, I'm sure many women find you attractive."

"Come on, Randy. Why were you in Vegas?" I demanded.

Randy put both his hands in his lab coat pockets. (Interestingly, he put his left hand in the right pocket and vice versa.) Looking up at the ceiling, he said, "I can't remember."

"Can't or won't?" I asked.

Randy looked at me. "Zach, why are you so interested in my past vacation plans? You've never taken this interest in me before."

"Earth Force and the World Council just hired me to track down a superclone that escaped from Area 51b."

The flush on Randy's face washed away, his face turning paler than normal. He held his hand to his chest. "Natasha escaped!"

Vingo. I had hit pay dirt. "I never told you the superclone's name."

Randy paused for moment. "Lucky guess," he said meekly, thought a bit more then added, "DOS. This could be bad."

"Could be?" I said.

He shook his head. "If she gets angry . . ."

"Everything around her drops dead," I said. "Yeah, I'd call that bad."

Randy gazed down at his feet. "I never thought she'd escape. Not that she couldn't, just that she wouldn't." He stopped talking.

"Come on, Randy. Sing!"

Randy's eyes popped open wide. "You don't really want me to sing. Do you?"

"PI talk for talking, giving information, spilling your guts," I said.

"I could sing it," Randy offered.

I made a fist. "Randy, what were you doing in Vegas?"

Randy lowered his eyes, his head, in fact, his entire body was slouched over in shame. "The government invited me to come and help on the Natasha project. I couldn't say no. For one thing, they fund a lot of my work. For another thing, it was a pretty cool project." He looked up at me, smiling. "Think of it, Zach. Building the perfect human."

"Who's also a perfect killing machine."

Randy shrugged. "Uh, you take the bad with the good. Nobody ever said science has to be without moral dilemmas. In fact, the better the science the better the dilemma."

"So that gives you an excuse to steal Carol's DNA?"

Randy dropped two steps back. "Oh, you know about that . . ." He thought for a moment. He turned to HARV. "HARV?"

"I'm sorry, Dr. Pool. I added 010 and 010 and came

up with 100," HARV said. "I felt what you did to Carol was wrong."

Randy dropped back another step. "I didn't steal her DNA, per se, I just borrowed it."

I took a step forward. "Without her knowledge."

Randy held both hands up. "Listen, Zach, I had to do it for the good of science. Even way back then I realized Carol has the potential to be one of the most powerful beings in creation. She just puts restraints on herself because she's been conditioned by her environment. Take that DNA, tweak it, and put it in the proper setting and violà! You get a perfect superbeing. The technology has improved so much since the Thompson girls were created. It was for the good of the world, Zach."

"How do you justify that?"

"Zach, that's what the government told me. I'm not like you. I'm not one to question authority."

"Especially when it comes with a large budget."

"Zach, that's unfair. I would have done this for a medium budget. It's for the greater good."

I took a deep breath. I took another deep breath. "Then how come you didn't tell Carol that you needed her DNA?"

Randy gave me a dismissive wave. "I didn't want to worry her. It's too much pressure knowing your DNA is needed to make the perfect weapon. Besides, nobody likes being cloned."

"So that's your story?"

"He does have a point there," HARV conceded.

I took long, slow deep breath. I was getting very tired of scientists trying to play god and turn a profit. Cloning people (except for famous stars) has been outlawed for decades and has always been morally ambiguous at best. Cloning people without their knowledge is worse. The fact that it was Carol compounded my frustration. The fact that it was Randy helped increase my frustration exponentially. The fact that Randy did this behind my back and didn't seem at all remorseful really pissed me off.

I took another slow deep breath. I had to calm down. Randy had helped me on many, many occasions. The world may very well still be in one piece due to Randy's aiding me with his inventions. Randy just saw things differently than I do or than most sane people would. He felt the end always justified the means as long as science was involved. He didn't mean any harm. That was the problem. He never stops and thinks of the cost of his actions.

In my line of business I often have to react without thinking. Like my old mentor used to say, "If you gotta think about it, you're dead before you can do it." In Randy's case, he liked to think without considering the consequences his actions had on others. He meant no harm. That was just how Randy was wired. I had to stay calm.

I took another deep breath. I tried to stay composed. I failed.

I pounded my fist down on a nearby lab table. "How could you do this to Carol?" I shouted.

Randy just rolled his head. "Oh, Zach, I wish you hadn't done that."

"Why? Because you finally see the error of your ways?"

Randy shook his head. Pointing behind me he said, "No, because you've activated my lab's defense systems."

I looked over my shoulder. Sure enough, a gun turret had dropped down from the ceiling.

"Well, of course," HARV said. "You certainly can't expect Zach to go an entire morning without something trying to kill him."

I dove for cover under the lab table a split second before the robotic turret incinerated the floor exactly where I had been standing. I popped GUS into my hand.

"Randy, deactivate the system," I called from under the table.

"Can't do, Zach. The system has a fail-safe that prevents it from being turned off until the attacker is stopped, and by stopped, I mean killed or maimed. I put it in so an assailant couldn't force me to turn off the system. Pretty good thinking. The system is foolproof."

"Unless, of course, it mistakes a friend's actions," I noted.

"Well, nearly foolproof!"

Since it was obvious Randy would be no help I was going to have to take out the system myself.

"GUS, take out the defense gun!" I ordered, pointing GUS at the turret.

"Sorry, no can do, Mr. Zach. You may not fire me in here."

Before I could even ask HARV for help he chimed in. "Randy has blocked my access to his system, but I have been able to slow the system down some with my constant spam attacks. Hopefully that will allow you time to think of something."

Okay, this meant I was going to have to do it the old-fashioned way. Rolling to the right under the cover of a few more lab tables, I avoided the turret's next round of shots. I stopped rolling for a nano, just long enough to reach down to my ankle and pull out my old-fashioned Magnum.

I popped up from under the table and fired. My shots bounced off the turret, harmless.

I dove back under the table, barely avoiding the gun's next round of shots.

"Zach, I made the guns bulletproof," Randy said proudly.

This called for a change in tactics. "HARV, where's the defense system's main control system?"

"The main one is two rooms away," HARV said. "You'd be cut down trying to get to it."

"DOS!" I said, as a new hail of bullets rained down on the table.

"Of course, the system has a branch on the south wall of this room. Sever that and you stop it! I can even target it for you."

"You could have led with that!"

"I like seeing you sweat a bit."

I spun toward the north wall, arm extended, gun ready to fire. A cursor formed in front of my eye, creating a red bull's-eye on the white wall.

"Shoot the target," HARV told me, not having a lot of confidence in my deductive reasoning.

I pulled the trigger. There was a loud thunderous boom. That's the thing with old guns; they make noise. They don't pussyfoot around. I pulled the trigger a couple more times. I wasn't taking any more chances. There were a couple of more thunderous booms. The bullets had blasted a meter-wide hole in the wall.

I gazed up at the gun turret. It wasn't tracking me, but instead remained stationary. I took that as a good sign. I blew a curl of smoke away from muzzle of my gun.

"You blew a hole in my wall!" Randy screamed.

"Better than a hole in me," I said. "Besides, it's not even like a whole hole, more like a half a hole!"

Randy crossed his arms across his chest and turned away from me. "Well, you now have one minute to leave before the system reboots."

"I need more than a minute to talk to you."

Randy shook his head. "Sorry, Zach, algorithms are algorithms. The system is structured to reroute around breaks in the chain. It works like the old Internet."

"Well, shut it down."

Randy looked away from me. "I can't."

"You can't?"

"Well, I can, but I choose not to. Zach, you've hurt my feelings. I suggest you leave."

"But . . ."

"Zach, you now have twenty seconds until the system resets."

"But . . ."

I took a deep breath. I needed more time to speak to Randy, but time was one of the many things I was sorely lacking now. I heard the entry door to the lab open. Not just open, slam open. It was a violent slam. When you're in my business, you learn to recognize them.

"HARV, who just broke in? Are we in trouble?" I asked.

"Not we," HARV said.

"Am I in trouble?" I asked.

"For once, Zach, it's not you."

I heard stomping coming toward us. It wasn't a heavy stomp, though. It was a high-heeled stomp. Turning toward the stomping I saw Carol, hair on end, eyes practically glowing red. She was storming toward Randy.

Chapter 13

I was relieved that for once I wasn't the target of the intended violence. But my relief was quickly dampened, knowing that when Carol got really angry sometimes nearby people or objects accidentally drew the brunt of her anger. I had to cool her down fast.

"I thought Carol deserved to know what Randy did to her," HARV whispered to me.

I had to smile. Yep, some of me was rubbing off on HARV.

Carol marched directly up to Randy and shoved a finger in his face. "You did *what* to me?"

Randy shrank back.

"Uh, Carol, Randy's unstoppable defense system is about to spring back to life any nano," I said.

"Not going to be a problem," Carol growled, never taking her eyes off Randy.

I looked up at the computerized gun turret. It looked like a snowman that got caught in a sudden heat wave. It had melted into a puddle of metal. When Carol gets angry her power jumps up to even scarier levels than normal. I had to calm Carol down quickly before she accidentally wilted Randy or, worse yet, me! Yep, I could see the connection with Natasha.

I tapped Carol gently on the shoulder, trying to draw her attack away from Randy. I may have been angry with Randy but I certainly didn't want Carol frying his brain (or for that matter any other parts of his body). After all, as annoying and single-minded as Randy may be, he was still a friend. A brilliant friend who gave me lots of cool gadgets to field test for him.

"Carol, please, calm down," I said in my slowest, most soothing voice.

"He's not a pile of mush. Is he?" Carol said quickly.

"Um, no."

"Then I am calm, *tío*," Carol said without releasing Randy from her glare. Locking her eyes even stronger on Randy she ordered, "Talk fast!"

Randy put a finger to his lab coat's collar, pulling it away from his throat. "I may have um, cloned you, sort of . . ."

Carol moved forward, practically pinning Randy to a wall.

"Sort of?"

"I took your DNA, aged it, and improved on it," Randy said, trying desperately to sink into the wall.

"You did what?" Carol said.

Randy put both hands up, halfway between the "I surrender" and "Hold on" positions. "Ah, I was only helping the world by perfecting your . . ."

Carol turned away from Randy. She looked at me and said, "Can you believe how he justifies his actions?"

I nodded. "Believe me, chica, I've heard this story a lot."

I looked at Randy. He was bent over in a partial squat, frantically flapping his bent arms.

"Randy, are you all right?" I asked.

"Cluck cluck," he answered.

"I'll take that as a no."

I spun Carol toward me (gently). Pointing at Randy, I said, "This doesn't help anything."

"Good point," Carol said.

Carol turned back toward Randy. She looked down at him. Slipped her foot out her shoe. She held her foot out to Randy. "Massage, now!"

Randy obediently starting rubbing Carol's foot.

"Ah, Carol, turning one of the top minds in the world into your foot slave may not be the most productive use of our time."

"I've got two feet, you know," Carol told me.

"Can I at least question him?" I asked.

"Knock yourself out," Carol said.

Yep, I could use this to my advantage. With Randy under Carol's whammy I could get some straight answers from him.

Chapter 14

I smiled. For once I actually had a break. With Randy under Carol's foot (almost literally) he wouldn't be able to double-talk his way around my questions. For a moment I felt guilty using Carol on a friend. Then I remembered that Randy hadn't been all that open with me, so that guilt quickly faded.

"So, Randy, Natasha is like Carol?"

"Like her but different," Randy said without looking at me as he was focusing on massaging Carol's feet.

"Like her but different?"

"They have much of the same DNA, but I did not copy any of Carol's brain waves to Natasha."

"If you'd done that you'd be cleaning my feet with your tongue right now!" Carol told him.

I suppressed a shudder, made a mental note not to piss off Carol, and continued. "So their attitudes and preferences would be different?"

Randy nodded slightly. "Those that are conditioned by environment would be. Those that are more ingrained would still be similar. Of course, not identical, since environment would also modify those some. The effects of environment as opposed to heredity on personality is like the chicken and egg argument. Of course, it's extra confusing with psis as Carol and Natasha should be able to sense each other's likes and dislikes."

I searched my mind for the right question. The question that would help guide Randy to an answer that would lead me to Natasha. I thought of Natasha's room, all the travel posters. They were the only things that stood out there. I figured if I had been stuck on a base all my life I'd want to see something else. "I saw posters in Natasha's room of the Niagara Falls, Vegas, the Grand Canyon, Big Ben, the Eiffel Tower, and the Pyramids. My guess is she's at one of these places."

Randy nodded again. "That is logical."

"Vegas is the closest one of those spots to Roswell," I said.

"I love those places," Carol said. "Except Vegas. Too tacky."

"Natasha may head there just to distinguish herself from you," Randy said. "Many clones react that way when they learn about their DNA twins."

"That makes sense," I said. I didn't actually think it made a *lot* of sense, but most things don't with psis and mad geniuses.

"Well, that may possibly narrow it down some," HARV said. "Of course, there are over five hundred hotels in New Vegas she could be in. I could scan them all, but I doubt she's using her name. I could scan all the security cameras in Vegas, but that is illegal and probably fruitless, as I believe she can cloak herself from cameras."

"Why do you think that, HARV?" I asked.

"Because I can if I want to," Carol said.

"Oh, okay." The more I learned about Carol the more scared I became. "So, my dear, where in Vegas wouldn't you be caught dead?"

Carol thought for a nano. "There are so many places."

"Surely one stands out."

Carol tilted her head back. "The Nova Hollywood Towers are the most tacky," she said.

I looked over at HARV. "Any unusual activity there today?"

HARV shook his head. "None that I can tell." There was a pause. "Hold on. Two thousand people have checked into there today."

"So," I shrugged.

"Nobody has checked out," HARV said.

"Well, that is odd," I said.

"I agree," Carol said.

Randy shrugged as he continued to massage Carol's feet. "Maybe they just have a really good deal going on? I've eaten at the buffet there. It is top notch."

I looked at Carol. "I think Randy's been sniffing your feet too long. He's getting delirious."

Carol nodded in agreement and removed her feet from Randy's lap. She stood up. "We better get to New Vegas, then."

"We?" I said.

Carol headed out of the room. "I'm going with you."

I followed after her. "This Natasha is very dangerous," I said.

Carol kept walking. "Exactly. You won't stand a chance without me."

HARV appeared next to Carol. He was wearing a blue striped jogging suit. "Dr. Pool has made improvements to my software allowing me to increase the electrical energy in Zach's brain; that will help me help Zach become even more resistant to psi control."

By this point Carol had reached the door. "I know. Between that and me and GUS we may be able to stop her."

Carol reached for the door activation button. I reached for Carol's arm. I didn't like the idea at all of her going on this job. Sure, Carol had been in danger with me before. DOS, just sitting next to me on a bus or at the movies can put a person in danger.

This was different, though. This Natasha was the deadliest foe I had ever faced. Sure, Carol was powerful, but not as powerful as Twoa, and Natasha blew her out like a wet match. I wouldn't—I couldn't—have that happen to Carol. I spun Carol around toward me. We locked eyes.

"*Tío*, you know it's the only way," she said.

"I don't like it," I said.

HARV stepped between us, though he was slightly transparent allowing us to see each other through him. It was a weird experience.

"Zach, I have to agree with Carol."

"Me, too," GUS piped in from up my sleeve.

"Me, too," Randy called from behind us.

"I still don't like it," I repeated.

Carol smiled at me. "I don't like it either, but I don't see another way."

"I agree," HARV said.

"Me, too," GUS said.

"Me, three," Randy said. "Get it."

I turned toward Randy, "Keep your day job." I faced Carol (a much more pleasant sight). I sighed.

"Admit it, *tío*, you know we're right."

The sad truth was, it was true. My best chance of stopping Natasha would be using Carol. I exhaled slowly.

"Let's go get her," I said.

Carol's smile grew more true. "I knew you'd see the light." She took me by the hand. Leading me out the door, she said, "I'll drive."

Chapter 15

Leaving Randy's office, I instantly noticed that Carol's car wasn't her car; in fact it wasn't a car at all. It was a hover. But not just any hover—it was black-and-white, shaped like an old 1957 Chevy with a siren on top. Carol pointed proudly at the hover.

Walking to the hover we chatted about how Carol had come to acquire it.

"You stole a police hover?" I said.

Carol gave me her sly smile. "It's an old model."

"You stole an old model police hover?" I said.

"I didn't steal it. I asked Captain Rickey for it nicely."

"You just asked?"

"I asked nicely," she said, eyes sparkling.

"You zapped his mind," I said.

"I asked extra-special nicely," Carol smiled. Her face became stern. "I suggest we leave it at that."

We reached the hover. Carol ran her hand along the hood. (Carol has a thing for things that go fast.) Thing is, I am not a big fan of hovers. I firmly believe that if man was meant to fly we'd have feathers, rubber bones, or better insurance coverage. Carol must have seen the lump forming in my throat.

"I know you're not a fan of flying, but I figured it's the fastest way to get to New Vegas."

I didn't want to admit it but she had a point.

"I'm pretty sure Dr. Pool is working on his version of the portable transporter," HARV said. "I could see if we could borrow that."

I glared at HARV. "Have you met me?" I asked. As much as I detest flying hovers I think even less of teleporting, especially personal teleporting.

"You let Twoa teleport you," HARV said. "Therefore I concluded—well, hoped—that you no longer have a personal mandate against personal teleporting."

I lowered my head and starting rubbing my temples. "Teleporting with Twoa is different."

"Why, because she has huge breasts that practically need their own zip code?"

"No," I said, though frankly that didn't hurt. "It's because you just can't say no to Twoa."

"Well, technically, you can say no, she'd just put you in traction," HARV said.

I turned away from HARV and focused on Carol. Her gaze apparently had never left me. "You know I'm right, tío."

I sighed. (I do that a lot when I'm on a case.) "Let's do it," I said.

Carol's smile grew so wide I could count all her teeth. (Well, I couldn't, but I'm sure HARV could.) "Great! I'll drive!"

There really wasn't much of a choice there. No way Carol was going to let anybody or anything else fly for her. Carol had a real need for speed. She positioned herself behind the driver's seat. I was surprised she didn't float off of the seat she was so excited. I, on the other hand, reluctantly sat in the passenger's seat. Strapping myself in I looked over at Carol.

"You sure you know how to pilot one of these?" I asked her.

She positioned her hands on the steering column. "One of my ex-boyfriends was a cop," she said.

Looking at her with a raised eyebrow, "Isn't he the one whose hover you melted?"

"Not on purpose!" she said, like that made it better.

With that we lifted off and headed to New Vegas.

Chapter 16

The trip to New Vegas went smoothly, as smooth as a trip can for me while riding in a hover. I'm a macho guy, it's true. DOS, I have more attempts on my life in a day than 99.99 percent of the population has in their lifetimes. Therefore I'm not afraid to admit to my fears. My number one fear is heights. Well, not so much the heights but the falling from heights. Actually the falling isn't that bad (I have a strong heart), it's the sudden stops that are painful. Believe me—I experienced it once. I was lucky to survive the fall. Now on those rare occasions I get into a hover I feel I'm just taunting Death to take another crack at me. I may not be the brightest guy around but I'm smart enough to know one lady you don't want to taunt is Death.

Of course, going after Natasha was even more dangerous than flying in a hover. Gates, this is a woman who can wipe out an area just by being in a bad mood. In many ways this woman *was* death. Yet, somehow Natasha didn't scare me nearly as much as heights. Not sure why. I guess I understood Natasha had to be stopped.

Carol must have noticed me in deep thought. "We're almost there, *tío*," she said.

"Good," I told her.

"So, what's the plan?" she asked, trying to keep my mind off the fact we were hundreds of meters above the ground, flying faster than the speed of sound.

HARV appeared between us. "Please, Carol, how can you possibly think Zach would have a plan? We are still five minutes from the Nova Hollywood Towers. That means Zach is still five minutes from coming up with anything that can remotely be called a plan."

I shook my head. Nova Hollywood Towers had to be the most tacky place in a town overdosing on tacky. On the bright side, it was one of the few buildings in Vegas not owned by a big corporation. On the not so bright side, it was owned by a series of aging ex-HV and rock stars, which made it almost as bad. In fact, if I didn't know that an Elvis clone was a part owner the place would have no redeeming qualities at all. It would just be a graveyard for rock star memorabilia that nobody else wanted—at least at the prices they were selling it for.

Soon the Nova Hollywood Towers came into view. It was hard to miss. It was shaped like a giant drum with a star on top of it. Carol zoomed in over the parking lot. She started our descent. I looked away. I hate landings. I know if anything is going to go wrong, chances are it will be with the landing. The good thing about landings are once we settle on the ground it's over. Okay, so I have mixed emotions about them. We pulled up.

Turning to Carol I said, "Why are we going up?" Pointing down I said, "We have to go down to land."

"Sherlock Holmes has nothing on Zach," HARV said from the back of the hover.

"I agree!" GUS said proudly, obviously not detecting the sarcasm in HARV's voice.

"I was being sarcastic," HARV said to GUS, nose raised in disdain.

"I know," GUS told him. "I just choose to take your words at face value and ignore your tone."

HARV crossed his arms and turned away. "What do you know? You're just a weapon."

"Ah, back to the matter at hand," I said to Carol. "Why are we going up?"

"Look down at the parking lot, tió," Carol said.

I did. I've seen cans of sardines that had more room after they had been through a trash compactor. The parking lot below was a weird mosaic of cars and hovers all squeezed together. DOS, some of them were parked on top of others. There was no obvious spot to land.

HARV's eyes flickered, meaning he was calculating something. "I've accessed security cameras for this area. There are no parking places in a 2K radius."

"How can that be?" I asked.

"People keep checking in but nobody checks out," HARV said.

"Apparently, Natasha really knows how to throw a party," I said.

"We can't be certain this is because of Natasha. Security cameras inside the hotel are blocked. So I can't prove it is her," HARV told me.

I just looked at him.

HARV stood there for a moment. "They do have an excellent buffet." HARV paused for a nano. He hated the fact that I knew Natasha was in there without his confirmation. HARV might insist he doesn't need to be needed, but he does. HARV sighed. (Man, he has been connected to my brain for too long.) "I admit chances are great that Natasha is behind this."

"Thank you," I said.

I felt the hover descending again.

Turning back to Carol, I asked, "Did you find a spot to land?"

She shook her head. "Going to make my own."

Carol maneuvered our police hover over a spot close to the Nova Hollywood's entrance. The entrance was already blocked by far more cars than it could hold.

"I figure we'll get enough action when we meet Natasha," Carol said. "No need to do any extra walking."

Carol waved her right hand to the right. Half the cars blocking our way moved over to the right. Carol moved her left hand to the left. The other half of the cars scooted to the left. Not exactly parting the Red Sea, but impressive nonetheless.

Carol lowered the hover to the ground. The dome popped open. Carol made a little "ta da" gesture. We were less than two meters from the casino's entrance.

"What, you couldn't park in the lobby?" I asked, unstrapping myself.

"I could," Carol said, "but I didn't want to scratch the paint going through the doors. After all, this is borrowed."

I hopped out of the hover, Carol close behind. The big brass doors to the casino pushed open. Two Elvis impersonators wearing red bellhop suits came bounding toward us. They both had guitars strapped to their backs. That worried me.

"Sorry, brother," one of the Elvis impersonators said. "This party is by invite only."

"But we are invited," Carol said in her most hypnotic voice. I knew she was using her whammy on them.

Both of the impersonators removed the guitars from their backs and raised them over their heads. One of them rushed at me, the other at Carol. DOS, I have the worst luck with Elvis impersonators.

The Elvis attacking me smashed his guitar down at me. Dodging to my right I popped GUS into my hand. The guitar smashed on the ground, missing me.

"Dang it!" the Elvis said. "That's going to come out of my pay—"

He never got to finish that statement, as I clubbed him on the back of the head with GUS.

I turned my attention to the Elvis attacking Carol. Carol had him levitating up in the air. She was spinning her finger around and around, causing him to spin around and around.

Carol looked at me and winked. "Just because Natasha is blocking me from controlling their minds doesn't mean I can't control their bodies."

"Don't spin him around too much," I said. "Believe me, you do not want an Elvis to barf on you." Yes, I was speaking from experience.

"Good point," Carol said.

Waving her hand forward she sent her Elvis crashing into the casino just above the door. He groaned, then crumpled to the floor.

I headed toward the door. Apparently Natasha didn't want us at her private party. I wasn't sure if I should be honored or offended. I did know one thing—it was time for the party to end.

Chapter 17

Walking into Nova Hollywood, I remembered why I didn't come here more often. I like a good slice of cheese as much as the next guy, but this place would be too cheesy for a giant mutant rat who had been starving for a week. The reception area was lined with shiny gold carpeting that looked more radioactive than compelling. Making things worse was the fact that every step you took produced a musical note from the floor. I don't know who ever thought that would be a good idea.

Each of the pillars holding up the ceiling was a giant golden guitar. Looking over the area, I was forced to squint to block out some of the light. Between the glowing floor and the shiny guitars, you actually needed sunglasses to see anything. I didn't have sunglasses, but I had something even better.

"HARV, can you run a shade over my eyes to filter out some of this shine?"

"Done," HARV said.

Immediately things became dimmer and clearer and scarier. I could see the reception area and clear through to the main casino floor. The place was littered with bodies, female bodies, seemingly struck down while they were waiting on line. A couple of receptionists were slouched over their desks. Looking over the casino floor, it was the same thing. Cocktail waitresses, dealers, patrons were all spread out either on the tables or on the floor slumbering away next to the slot machines.

It was at that moment that the slot machines noticed us. As if it wasn't easy enough to gamble in these places, somebody somewhere had the bright idea of making the slot machines mobile and semi-intelligent. Not content to simply sit there and wait for customers, today's modern slot machine is built to pursue potential "clients" around the casino, coaxing them to play. The machines aren't happy unless they are being used.

This may only be a minor annoyance when a casino is loaded to the rafters with plenty of eager customers, but now, with everybody else either sleeping or otherwise occupied, there were a few hundred machines with nobody to play with. They spotted us and quickly started heading toward us buzzing like a swarm of electronic wheeled bees.

"Pick me!" one of the machines blared as it streaked toward us.

"No me!" another one said—then another, then another, then another.

Within nanos we were surrounded by a sea of moaning, groaning, begging, coaxing machines.

"Play me! I pay off a lot!"

"Can't lose that often with me!"

"Oh oh oh! Me me me!"

"I have great odds!"

"I haven't paid out for a while, I'm due!"

"Aren't my flashing lights pretty?"

All the noise and light blurred into one blinding combination of white noise and flash.

"Sorry, no time to play," I told all the machines.

"Always time to play," came one response.

"This is New Vegas, baby!" another machine shouted.

"What happens here stays and stays and stays here!" another said.

I shook my head. "Maybe later," I offered. "Now clear the way, we need to get through."

The machines stood their ground, blocking our way.

"Just one or two or three games!"

"We're fun fun fun!"

"Try it, you'll like it!"

"It's only money! Everybody knows you can't buy happiness, but by playing us you will be happy."

I drew GUS. I didn't really want to shoot them, but I couldn't have them slowing me down. "Move!" I ordered.

"Mr. Zach, I think you should honor their request," GUS said.

"Excuse me?" I said.

"These poor machines are only doing the jobs they are programmed to do. Natasha is not going anywhere. Just give them a play or two to make them happy." There was a slight pause. "Plus you might win!"

Before I even had a chance to consider what GUS was saying, the machines stopped their clamoring. They all lowered their frames and then quietly rolled backward to the spots they were in before they noticed us.

"I surmised the best course of action was for me to simply reprogram those simple machines to leave us alone," HARV said very smugly.

"Impressive," Carol said.

"It's not that impressive. I would hope HARV could control an army of simple machines," I said.

"I wasn't talking about the loco machines," Carol said. "I was talking about what Natasha has done to all these people."

"Oh. That's more like scary," I said.

I bent down to take the pulse of a woman who fallen by the door. I felt a faint beat. "This one isn't dead," I said.

"None of them are," Carol said.

"I concur," HARV said. "They are just comatose."

"Very comatose," Carol said. "Their brains have all been turned off except for basic life support functions. They aren't even dreaming."

Now that the slot machines had been silenced we heard music coming from across the casino floor. "I take it if we follow that music it will lead us to Natasha," I said, walking toward the sound.

"I concur," HARV said slowly.

"Me too," Carol said.

Noticing that I was the only one moving forward I stopped and turned to them. "Ah, are you two coming?"

"Zach, I'm a hologram, I don't need to walk someplace to be there."

Carol was silent.

"What's wrong, chica?"

"There are more than two thousand women on the floor here. Natasha put them all out easily. As an afterthought."

"Yeah, she's tough, I get that," I said. "I've taken on powerful babes before. It's all par for the course when you're me."

Carol took a step back. "This is different. I've never felt such power. It's like with less than single thought she could kill us all."

Over the last few years I've been through a lot with Carol. We've both seen a lot, but I've never seen her this scared. If was going to have any chance against Natasha, though, I was going to need Carol.

I took Carol by the hand. "Then we're just not going to give her time to think."

Carol was shaking ever so slightly, her skin a bit redder than normal and her hands were damp.

"We can stop her," I insisted.

"I've been studying the mental frequency Natasha broadcasts over," HARV said. "I believe I can block her out long enough for us to take her out."

Carol's eyes opened a bit. "Really?"

HARV nodded. "Believe me, Carol. I like being vulnerable even less than you do. She may be powerful but she has weaknesses."

"We can take her out quickly before she even knows what hit her," I said.

A weak smile crossed Carol's cheeks. She straightened her back. "Let's go get the bitch!"

Chapter 18

Carol, HARV, and I walked through the casino area toward the music. As all the women in the building were lying comatose on the ground it was clear to me that all the men had gotten up and left in a hurry. I was betting the men had all joined Natasha in the nightclub area that was adjacent to the casino.

On each side of the double doors leading to the night club were piles of more comatose women. They were all stacked up sort of neatly, more waitresses, dancers, and patrons. It appeared that Natasha had ordered them out of the dance area.

"Interesting," I said, looking at the piles of women.

"I've accessed the security tapes before the cameras went offline," HARV said. "The moment Natasha walked into the disco all these women stopped whatever they were doing, put their arms in front of their bodies and left like zombie sheep."

"Apparently, Natasha wants to be alone with her men," I said.

Pushing the doors to the disco open, we entered the dimly lit club. It was crammed full of men. Males from 18 to 118. Big guys, little guys, fat guys, skinny guys, all races, all nationalities—there were even some mutants and rock star clones. The place was so packed it was nearly impossible to move. Unlike their women, though, the men were anything but comatose. They were dancing and giggling and making general fools of themselves.

A floating platform above the dance floor contained a robotic band who were belting out electronic music versions of ancient hits. Currently they were playing "Heartbreak Hotel New California." Gazing through the crowd, I searched for Natasha. She wasn't hard to find; I just had to follow the glance of every man in the room. They were all focused on her. She was dancing away, arms flailing, to her heart's content. She seemed so happy she didn't even appear to notice we had come into the room.

"Shall I alert the proper authorities?" HARV asked.

"Why, so they can join Natasha in her dance?" I said, drawing GUS.

"No, of course not," HARV said. He thought about what I said. "Oh, right. You were being sarcastic. I understand now. Sorry, shielding us from Natasha has drained me some. It requires huge amounts of both energy and computing power. She is very strong. There are 2323 men in here and they are all totally under her control."

I popped GUS into my hand. Natasha was so enthralled with her dancing she wasn't paying any attention to us. That gave me a chance to take her out quickly and painlessly.

I aimed.

"Heavy, heavy stun, GUS," I thought.

"Will do, Mr. Zach," GUS whispered back in my mind.

I pulled the trigger. Nothing happened.

"Uh, GUS," I thought.

"Yes?"

"Nothing happened," I thought.

Silence.

"Uh, GUS," I prodded.

"Isn't that Natasha cute?" GUS said out loud. "She is far too cute to shoot. Besides, you have no need to shoot her."

"Uh, why?" I asked.

"Because she plans to harm no one," Natasha answered in my brain.

I turned back to HARV and Carol. HARV had disappeared. Carol had sunk back toward the door. She was now lying on the floor like all the other ladies who weren't Natasha. Oh, this was bad. I turned back toward Natasha. I didn't want to. I just had to. I popped GUS back up my sleeve. I won't be needing him, I thought, despite not wanting to think that.

I started jiving my way toward Natasha. The other men in place started parting to either side to let me through. Oh, this was so not good. Yet I so didn't care. As I cut a swath through the sea of men between me and Natasha, my brain was racing. How beautiful she was. How weird it was I was thinking that. No, it wasn't weird, it was just the truth. DOS, I had been through this type of manipulation before, you would think I would have some sort of immunity by now. Ah, but who would want to be immune to those eyes? HARV, are you with me? Spam! *Spam!* HARV was turned off so I was alone in my thoughts with Natasha. This was bad. Only bad was good. Right? Or was it? Damn, I so hate it when the psis aren't on my side.

When I reached Natasha, she held out her long slender hand to me. I wanted to take it. I didn't want to take it. I took it.

"Zach, how nice of you to join me," Natasha said.

"Thank you," I smiled. I frowned. "I am here to stop you," I said. I smiled again. "If you don't mind." DOS! This woman was making me bipolar and I loved it. No, I didn't. Yes, I did. DOS!

Natasha danced around me slowly. "There is no need to stop me, Zach. I am having fun."

"Fun is good," I said, shaking my hips in a way that

was still manly yet would have been embarrassing if I wasn't fighting Natasha's control. Natasha had me under her mental foot but not as tightly as the others. It may have had something to do with HARV and Carol protecting my brain. Or maybe I had built up defenses after all these years of dealing with psis? Or maybe she was just taking it easy on me?

Natasha took my other hand. I dipped her. I don't know why. It just felt right.

"What you are doing to these people is wrong," I told her.

She straightened her back and thrusted her chest toward me. "I'm just letting off a little steam. None of them will remember anything except that they had a great time!"

Dipping her again, I said, "I still think it's wrong!"

"You have some control of your thoughts because I want you to," Natasha said.

I pulled her back up. She removed my fedora and placed it on her own head with one hand while ruffling my hair with the other. "It's no fun if everybody is a mindless slave. I need somebody to talk to," she said playfully. "But if you keep questioning me . . ."

I'm not sure if it was the removing of the fedora. I'm not sure if it was the ruffling of my hair. I'm not sure if it was the cockiness of her thinking she had total control of the situation. Not sure if it was the not so veiled threat to turn me into her zombie. At that moment something inside of me snapped. I had to put this lady down, and fast.

Lunging forward I did the only thing I could do. I slammed my forehead down on hers. I'm blessed with a particularly thick skull. It comes in handy at times like this. When my forehead met hers, she dropped to the ground, stunned. I was lucky Randy and Earth Force at least had the foresight not to make Natasha nearly invulnerable, like the Thompson girls. I tried that move on Twoa once and my ears were ringing for a week after I came to.

Acting fast, I drew the old-fashioned gun I had been keeping tucked behind my back. It was Colt model 1908. Yes, it was well over a hundred years old. That meant no computer interface, which was a plus. It was small and easy to conceal, yet could still kill. I aimed at Natasha. This woman had proven she was a danger to all and had to be stopped. Still, I couldn't shoot her. Just not my style.

Moving forward I raised the gun over my head. I might not have been able to kill her but I could knock her out. Just to make sure she didn't try any mind tricks on me I started humming. I know psis hate humming. (Well, who doesn't?) I didn't hum anything in particular, just the "do do do do, do dooo do do" from Entercorp's *New Improved Jeopardy*. I hit her on the head with the barrel of my gun. She went unconscious.

That was easy. I've never taken out a mega-superhuman babe that easily. The powers that be don't like me that much. They just like testing me.

There was a tap on my shoulder. The music in the room stopped. I took both of those as bad signs. Yes, this was more my type of luck. The unconscious Natasha faded away. Turning toward the tap, gun ready, there was Natasha standing there holding her head.

"After you head butted me I teleported behind you, but created the illusion that I was in front of you. Just to see how you would react."

"I take it the fact that we're all still alive means you approve." Seeing I failed to put Natasha out of commission I was quite surprised I was still alive.

Natasha smiled. "Your actions weren't evil. You were doing what you could to protect the world you love. Yet you still couldn't kill me. You have morals."

"Yeah, I may be beginning to regret those right now," I told her.

Touching me gently on the shoulder, she said, "Zach, you give me hope. You give us all hope. That's why I would so hate for anything terminal to happen to you."

I waved my gun at her. "I have you in my sights," I said.

The gun melted in my hand.

"You know that was an antique gun!" I told her, kind of missing the big picture. If I survived the next couple of minutes I was going to have to look into my obsession with weapons.

"Zach, just be glad it was the gun and not you," Natasha said.

"I hear that a lot," I said.

"You do?" She said, eyebrow raised.

"You'd be surprised." I took a deep breath. "Any chance you're just going to surrender and come peacefully?" I asked.

She shook her head no and disappeared.

It became apparent that all the eyes in the room were now trained on me and they were angry. Yep, this is more like what I'm used to.

Chapter 19

Alone in a room with a little more than two thousand angry dudes. Those were bad odds, even for me. The good thing was, I wasn't really alone. I had HARV and Carol. They had just been forced to the sideline. I needed to get them into the game. I also had GUS—hopefully.

I popped GUS into my hand.

"GUS, are you ready?" I asked.

"A little dizzy, Mr. Zach, but I am functional."

"I need a wide stun blast fast!" I said.

I pointed GUS at my nearest assailants. A strange potpourri of men of all ages, shapes, and sizes. The only thing they had in common appeared to be a hatred of me.

"He made Natasha leave," they grunted in creepy unison. "We must hurt him a lot."

My initial salvo took out the five or six lead guys. They were just average joes under Natasha's spell, so I didn't want to hurt them. Of course, the feeling was far from mutual.

I felt a hand grab me from behind. Spinning around quickly I broke my attacker's hold. He was big guy, dressed in all black, with two-day old stubble on his face—probably a bouncer. Meaning he was an experienced brawler. He hit me with an uppercut to the solar plexus. If it wasn't for my underarmor that blow would have taken my breath away at the very least. Instead, it hurt his hand. He retracted his hand and starting rubbing it. The look of confusion on his face would have been entertaining if he was the only one trying to kill me. Thing was, in a room filled with enemies I didn't have time to savor the moment.

I just blasted him with GUS. He fell but was instantly replaced by two others.

I felt another hand grab me from behind. Then another. Then another. Oh, so not good. I felt myself being pulled backward—fast. I crashed to the ground and my armor once again took the brunt of the damage, but I was still in big trouble. I had more guys on me than I could count. They were using me as their personal piñata. Protecting my face with my arms, my armor would minimize the damage, but only for so long. If I was going to get out of this I was going to need help and fast. Of all the ways there might be to die, being pummeled by a mob of angry men was way down on my list of favorites.

Suddenly the pummeling stopped. Was this just a trick just to get me to expose my face or had Carol come back into play? I held my arms over my face a moment more.

"You can open up, tió," Carol said in my brain.

I spread my arms apart slowly. No punches fell. I looked up at the guys. They were all standing there dumbfounded. I stood up.

"I'm still weak. I can't hold this many people this long," Carol called. "I suggest we exit pronto."

I couldn't agree with her more. I headed toward Carol quickly. As I moved I tried to get HARV to reboot.

"HARV, are you with me yet?" I said, tapping the side of my head, like that would help.

HARV appeared alongside of me, projecting from my wrist communicator.

"I'm here," he said. "Sorry it took so long, I've been working on beefing up my defenses."

"No problem," I said as we drew closer to Carol. "HARV, you know you just said beefing up."

HARV sighed. "Yes, I am aware of the changes in my speech patterns and they don't alarm me. I chalk it up to being connected to you too long."

"HARV, you just said chalk it up," I said.

"Please, Zach, I feel bad enough as it is. Being in denial only gets me so far."

We reached Carol. She was already standing by the exit, so we were almost home free.

"Oh, no," HARV said.

"What is it? I don't like 'oh, no.' It's never good when you say that," I said.

"The women are awake," Carol said.

The door burst open. A mob of angry women, patrons, dancers, dealers, hookers, angry Elvis-clone fans, and more quickly filed in. Lucky for us (luck being a relative thing here), they were in such a hurry to get in they were all tripping over one another.

"And they are way mad!" HARV said.

"Why are they mad at us?" I said.

"Natasha has convinced them Carol put them to sleep in order to steal their men."

I nodded. "I can see why that would peeve them!"

We needed a course of action and we needed it fast. I looked at Carol.

She shook her head no. "Don't look at me. I can barely hold the guys at bay as it is."

With the women drawing nearer I looked at HARV. "Cloak us!"

He put his hands on his waist. "Fine, it's always up to the computer to save the day. But do I ever get the credit? No! Of course, while they may not see us, they can still feel us, since they are right in front us."

"Carol, lift us,'" I thought to her. *"We'll levitate out of here."*

As the angry mob of ladies closed in on us, I felt myself being lifted off the ground. The mob stopped, looking around.

"Where the Gates did they go?" one of them grumbled from below us.

We floated toward the door. Not the most elegant of escapes, but it worked.

Chapter 20

"Where to now?" Carol asked as we hurriedly got into the hover.

Fastening my seat belt, I asked, "Did you pick up any thoughts or vibes from Natasha?"

The hover lifted up. Carol thought for a nano or two. "I did look into her mind," she said. "I wanted to see how she thinks."

"HARV, you better drive the hover," I said.

"Check," HARV said, appearing from the hover's holo-projector wearing a scarf and leather driving gloves.

As the hover shot forward, Carol glanced off into space, seemingly looking at nothing in particular. "Her mind is very complicated. Like mine," she said. "I saw a lot of images, like a mosaic collage with all the pieces scrambled."

"Did you pick up anything?" I coaxed.

"I picked up everything, yet I understood nothing," Carol said. Her eyes lost the glazed-over look. She turned to me. "Why the DOS did I just say that?"

HARV and I both shrugged.

"Too much time in Natasha's brain?" I suggested.

"Too much time hanging around Zach," HARV suggested.

"A little of both," GUS piped in.

Ignoring HARV and GUS, I focused on Carol. "So, you picked up something?"

"So many images . . . I need something to help sift through them," Carol said slowly.

"Concentrate on the places in the posters: Niagara Falls, the Grand Canyon, Big Ben, Eiffel Tower, Pyramids . . ." I said trying to create a connection in Carol's brain

Carol closed her eyes and tipped her head back. She took a deep breath, exhaling loudly. Another breath, she held it. She exhaled louder. She opened her left eye slowly, then her right. "She's going to the Grand Canyon," Carol said.

"The UltraMegaHyperMart Grand Canyon," HARV corrected. "They purchased the sponsorship rights. It's new because they have added an observation tower and a new virtual experience. They call it 'the fall of your life, then death.' "

"Not really a whole lot of new in that," I said. "Still new or not it's where I have to go next." Pointing to the left I told HARV, "Make it so."

HARV just looked at me. "I assume that is some reference from some ancient television show I should know, but I don't care enough to access my ancient trivial database."

"That's trivia," I corrected.

"No, no it's not," HARV said.

"Just take us to the Grand Canyon," I said, pointing in the direction I thought it should be.

"We could get to the UltraMegaHyperMart Grand Canyon that way, but we would have to traverse several continents and an ocean or two. My huge virtual intellect tells me that is something you don't want to do."

I lowered my arm. "Just take us there."

HARV shook his head. "No can do. Electra's mom has arrived and Electra has very specifically stated she needs you home now."

The world or my love life. I suppose the world would have to take backseat. "Okay, send JJ and Fera to check it out."

"Already done," HARV smiled.

"If she is there make sure they do not engage her," I added.

HARV nodded in agreement. "Also already done. I don't know if they will listen, though."

"Put me through to them," I said.

HARV's holographic form morphed into JJ. *"Don't worry, I assure you I can fly and hologram at the same time,"* HARV's voice said in my head.

JJ looked up at me. "We're heading to the New Frisco teleport center now," JJ said. "HARV says you've already paid for our reservations."

"Yep, first class," I said.

JJ's image just looked at me. "I've never traveled first class teleporter before."

First class was actually just the same as regular class, only they let you sit in chairs while you wait in line. Still, it's an ego boost. "Only the best when you work with me," I told him.

"I guess you're not as big of an ass as I've heard," JJ said. I couldn't tell if he was kidding. He probably wasn't.

"Don't believe anything you hear and only about 30 percent of what you see," I said.

Fera looked in over JJ's shoulder. "How about taste and smell? How much of those can I believe?"

I couldn't tell if she was being serious, but I was pretty certain she was. I guess when you're part tiger, these things matter more. "About fifty-fifty," I said, no idea why. "The important thing is you know what to do if you run into Natasha. Correct?"

"Yes, we understand," JJ said. Fera nodded her

head in the background in agreement. "What do you do?" I quizzed, not sure if they really did understand what their roles here were.

"Stop her," JJ said.

Fera continued nodding away.

I pinched my nose with my hand, shaking my head. "No," I said.

The two of them just looked at me.

"Come on, Zach, we can stop her," JJ said.

Fera's head bobbed mindlessly in agreement all the while.

"HARV, play back for them what happened in Vegas."

JJ and Fera watched the playback hologram. JJ giggled. "Those guys are kicking your ass."

"Only because Natasha made them," I said. "HARV, show them the replay of the casino."

I watched as they watched.

"Are all those babes dead?" JJ asked his voice a bit higher than normal.

I hesitated, then said, "No, but they could have been. Natasha took a casino filled with ten thousand people, dropped half of them instantly, and turned the other half of them into her personal playthings."

"There weren't ten thousand people in there," HARV whispered in my brain, not quite getting where I was going with this.

JJ gulped and Fera stopped her head bobbing. "No psi is that powerful!"

"She is," I said, ice dripping from my words. (Literally. HARV helped out and created a hologram of my words with ice dripping off them.)

"Wow," JJ and Fera both said, stepping back.

"So what do you do if you find her?" I asked.

"Stay low and call you," JJ said.

"Exactly."

"We still get our share though. Right?" JJ asked.

"Of course," I said. I had to like the kid—he kept his mind on business.

"Then we understand," JJ said.

For their sakes I hoped they did.

Their image morphed back into HARV piloting the hover. I pointed forward. "Home, HARV."

"Home isn't really that way," HARV said.

"Just drive, buddy. Just drive."

Chapter 21

HARV dropped Carol and me off in front of my house, then drove away to return the hover to the police lot. Carol and I slowly walked up the sidewalk to my house. Actually, I walked slowly, Carol walked quite quickly. She was excited.

Turning back to me, she took my arm and started dragging me forward.

"Come on, *tió*," she coaxed. "I haven't seen my *abuela* in years."

"Yes, you've been a very bad granddaughter," I said, dropping my weight back some to slow Carol down. I'd been dating Electra for over eight years now. This would be the first time I actually met her mother in the flesh. Delaying a bit more couldn't hurt.

My dropping my weight back didn't slow Carol down in the least. She had to be telekinetically pulling me. "It's not my fault you keep me so busy and my grandma is so extra busy," Carol said as we approached the door.

"Yeah, she's a busy lady," I said. "Sponsoring the Anti Psi Proposition to the World Council," I said, drawing ever nearer to my door.

"I admit I'm not a fan of the APP," Carol said.

"I'm sure, though, she is doing it because she believes it is better for us, as it will eliminate much of the fear regular humans have of us. We may be powerful but we are vastly outnumbered."

The APP was a motion put in front of the World Council that would require all people with the psi gene to wear dampers that would monitor the use of their power as well as reduce it. Many people on Earth are uneasy with the way psis suddenly started popping up on Earth right after we made initial contact with our first race of aliens, the Gladians. Most of them just don't say it out loud because it wouldn't be politically correct. Plus we owe a lot of advances to the Gladians. So we can't really go around blaming them. We can, though, take steps to control our own people, limit their power. People in high places are afraid of what the psis can do. I'd dealt with a lot of psis in my day and I can't say I entirely blame them. Now that I'd seen what Natasha could do I might even be on their side.

Carol dragged me up my porch stairs. Carol reached for the door but it opened for her. Electra greeted us in the doorway.

"You're late," she said.

"Sorry," Carol said. "Busy saving the world." She saw her grandma then rushed up to her, giving her a big hug.

I walked in slowly. "What she said."

Electra looked at me, eyes squinting, forehead winkled. "You knew my mother was coming today."

"Yes, well, we had a few issues slowing us down and an angry mob of a few thousand people."

Electra studied me. She sighed. "Only you could use that as an excuse and have it be believable."

"Believe me, I'm well aware of that."

Electra turned to her mother. "Mother, I would like you to finally meet Zach." Electra turned to me, "Zach, my mother Helena."

Helena was a dignified looking woman in her mid-seventies. Her hair was gray, but she wore it well. Her eyes had the look of a woman who had seen a lot and taken most of it in.

"So, this is the man my daughter wants to marry," she said to me.

"And I want to marry her," I said, walking up to Helena.

I saw a figure moving in my kitchen. I popped GUS into my hand.

"What in the DOS are you doing, Zach?" Electra said.

I placed my body between my future mother-in-law and my kitchen, weapon ready. "There is somebody else in the house," I said. "HARV, how come you didn't detect them?"

HARV appeared from my home's holo-broadcaster. "I have detected them. It's just that they are not a threat."

"Because they are my mom's bodyguards, Liz Lazor and Greg Wombat," Electra said.

"Oh," I said lowering my gun.

Out from the kitchen came two forms, a redheaded woman with glasses and a big guy. He wasn't wearing the clown suit but I still recognized them both from before (plus he was still wearing the shoes). I raised GUS back up and blasted the ex-clown.

Electra rushed toward, "Zach! What the DOS are you doing?"

Looking at the redhead, I aimed GUS at her. "Don't try anything funny," I told her. Calling back to Electra, I said, "These two clowns attacked me yesterday."

"Zach, I told you they are my mother's bodyguards! You have nothing to . . ." Electra said. A wave of awareness swept over her face. She turned to her mother. "Mother?"

Helena shrugged. "I gave him a little test. I'm a mother. It's within my rights."

"To send professional killers after my fiancé?"

"They weren't supposed to engage him, just tempt him." Helena pointed at me. "He's the one who went all Manbo on them."

"It's Rambo," I corrected. I hated people using old trivia wrong nearly as much as I did having body-guards sicced on me.

"Whatever," Helena said. "It's just that I wasn't sure he was good enough for you."

"Mother, Zach has saved the world on a number of occasions."

Helena shrugged. "A mother never thinks any man is good enough for her daughter. I have friends on the World Council who don't speak highly of Zach at all. In fact, only Ona, Twoa, and Threa like him. To me that's just three more strikes against him."

I had to admit Helena may have had a point on that one. Still, I wasn't a big fan of my future mother-in-law testing me with her own personal muscle. On the other hand, she did it for the good of her daughter. So I couldn't be that angry. Besides when you're me, a thug in a clown suit and a girl with laser eyes is a kind of refreshing change of pace.

"No harm done," I said. Pointing at Greg, I asked, "Why were you wearing the clown suit?"

"I like floppy shoes," he answered pointing to his shoes.

Helena ignored us in favor of Electra. "You'll be happy to know he passed the test."

"So, you approve of him?" Electra asked her mom.

There was a knock on my door.

"Uh-oh," HARV said.

"This is Captain Rickey of New Frisco police force. Zach, I insist you open up your door now. You are wanted on over a hundred counts of assault in New Vegas."

I gulped. So much for "whatever happens in Vegas stays in Vegas."

"Let me withhold judgment for a bit," Helena said.

Chapter 22

My long-time bud Captain Tony Rickey marched into my house. Tony was backed by a dozen storm troopers all wearing white robotic exoskeleton armor topped by what appeared to be crash helmets.

"The armor the storm troopers are wearing makes each of them roughly equivalent to you when you are wearing your body armor and having me reinforce it," HARV said in my head.

"I can't pick up any thoughts from them without really pushing, so they must be using heavy psi blockers," Carol added in my brain.

This meant Tony and his men meant business.

"What's this about, Tony?" I asked.

Tony just looked at me. "Come on, Zach. Don't make this harder than it has to be. You know perfectly well what happened in New Vegas. The New Vegas police are not at all happy. They say New Vegas is a fun town, meant for sex, maybe, but not violence."

"I always thought the two went hand in hand with humans," HARV said.

I raised my arms in the universal (except on Glad-7) "I have no idea what you are talking about" position. "Tony, I don't know what you mean."

"Come on, Zach, we have video of you and Carol taking on over a thousand guys. Not to mention tampering with a lot of very costly slot machines."

"I thought you would have turned off all the security cameras," I thought to HARV.

"I thought I did," came his reply. *"Oops, my bad."*

Tony raised the arm he wore his communicator on. "I can show you the video replay if you like."

I waved my hand no. "That's okay, I lived it," I admitted.

"I knew it," Helena said under her breath, just loud enough so I could hear it.

I turned to Electra. "I was just defending myself from the mob." I thought for a nano. "And the slot machines had it coming!"

"Sí," Carol nodded.

"I believe you," Electra said.

"For what it's worth, Zach, I do, too," Tony said. "Thing is, we have over a thousand witnesses who say you started it."

I didn't know what to say. I certainly couldn't mention Natasha, at least, not here in public. I was going to have to let them bring us in. Maybe when I explained the situation to Tony in private he could pull some strings and get the Vegas cops to drop the charges.

I put my hands over my head. "Take me in."

Tony nodded, then pointed at Carol. "Carol, too. We need to hold you both for the New Vegas police."

Two of his men stepped forward, one carrying a headband which had to be a psi stopper. The other had neuro-restraints.

Carol looked at me.

"This is not the place or time to fight, chica," I thought to her.

Carol's eyes moved to her grandmother.

"This is exactly why I am proposing APP, to protect you and others," Helena said, the politician pushing the grandmother aside.

Tony snapped his fingers. Two more of his men stepped up. Tony held his hand out to me. "I need all your weapons, Zach."

I reached down and removed my knife and backup gun from their ankle holsters. I handed them to Tony. I put my hands behind my back. Tony left his hand out for me.

"Come on, Zach," Tony said.

I gave him the backup backup gun I had behind my back. Tony still wasn't sold.

"Come on, Zach, GUS too," he said.

I lifted my left arm up straight to make sure nobody got trigger happy. I popped GUS into my hand. I turned him around. I lowered him and handed him to Tony.

"Mr. Tony, sir, I assure you Mr. Zach and Carol are innocent," GUS said. "Well, maybe not innocent, as all humans have some guilt and flaws, but in this case they were so totally just defending themselves."

"Not for me to decide," Tony said.

Tony slapped the cuffs on me while his men put the cuffs and blocker on Carol. "You have the right to remain silent," Tony said. "Though I know you probably won't."

"He does know you well," HARV said, once again so not helping.

Chapter 23

On the ride over to police headquarters, I told Tony I couldn't really let him know what I was working on, but if hc contacted General Wall of Earth Force I was sure she could vouch for me. Tony rolled his eyes and mumbled something about with friends like me he didn't need enemies and how he didn't get paid nearly enough. The good news was Tony had been in the trenches with me before. We've fought side by side on occasion. I might drive him crazy but he understands most of what I do I do because the job requires it, not because I actually want to. He did know and trust me, at least to some extent, so he was willing to check out my story. Dealing with the police is never fun, but it's a whole lot easier dealing with the ones you know on your own home turf.

Tony left me alone in an interrogation room while he and the others went to see what they could find out from General Wall. Hopefully, she would be able override any claim the Vegas police had on me. I didn't have time to go back to Vegas. I needed to get back on the trail to Natasha as soon as possible.

Over the years I'd grown quite familiar with that interrogation room. Okay, maybe not that room exactly, as I'm sure the Frisco police had to have dozens of these kinds of rooms. But they all looked exactly alike. They made spartan look plush, with nothing in the room except a table with a bright light over it and a few very uncomfortable wooden chairs. One chair for the person being questioned, two others for questioners. Cops always liked to question in pairs. This way they could either play off each other with the good cop bad cop or bad cop worse cop. Or if they wanted they could back each other up. No matter what, I had seen them all.

Since I knew I was being recorded and watched, I communicated with HARV through thoughts only.

"Any word from JJ and Fera?" I asked.

Silence.

"Earth to HARV," I thought.

"Just your brain, not all of Earth," HARV said. *"Mr. Big Ego."*

"What's going on with JJ and Fera?" I prompted.

"They arrived successfully at UltraMegaHyperMart Grand Canyon," HARV said.

"And?"

"I have not heard from them since," HARV said. *"I have been trying to establish some sort of communication but everything there is out."*

"That means we've found Natasha again!" I thought.

"Not conclusively," HARV cautioned. *"This may be a bug."*

"She's there," I thought. I just knew it in my gut.

That meant I had to get out of here as quickly and as easily as possible. Hopefully, Tony would be able to help.

The door opened. Tony walked into the room, followed by one of his men, a big guy. Maybe not a mountain of a man, but no molehill either. The way he walked, the look in his eyes, he was the backup muscle. Tony was slouching, his eyes bloodshot. He was a guy with a tough job and it showed in the lines in his face. His once blond hair was now more gray than anything else. None of this boded well for a quick and easy release.

"HARV, where's Carol?" I thought.

"They tried blocking me from their security cameras," HARV said.

"I assume they failed," I thought.

"They did. I just felt like bragging a bit," HARV said. *"She's in the room next to us."*

Tony walked up to the desk, shaking his head. He dropped down into the seat across from me. The other guy stayed standing.

"Are you going to introduce me to your friend?" I asked.

"No," came Tony's only reply.

Okay, this really wasn't going to go well. If I was going to get out I was going to have to work my way out.

"HARV, we're going to need to get out of here. Can you communicate with Carol?"

"No," HARV thought back. *"Besides, with the new improved psi blocker on her she is powerless."*

"Work on it," I thought. *"We need to turn the tables . . ."*

I looked at Tony looking over me.

"So, Zach, are you going to tell me why you and Carol beat up a hotel full of people?"

I shook my head. "Tony, I wish I could but for matters of world security I can't."

"Zach, there is no record of this General Wall," Tony said slamming his fist on the table.

"Do you feel better?" I asked.

"A little," he said. "Now talk, Zach."

"Tony, it's not my fault that your clearance isn't high enough to get clearance to learn about General Wall," I said, arms crossed.

A message from HARV shot into my brain, *"Zach, if you can make eye contact with the blocker on Carol,*

I believe I can reverse its effects, making Carol a super psi, at least for a while. Long enough for us to get out of here."

Well, now we had some sort of chance.

Tony snapped his fingers in front of my face.

"Zach, I'm talking to you," he said, angrily. "You need to pay attention to me or else. Don't let your mind wander."

Tony knew I had HARV hooked to my brain. He must have surmised that I was distracted by HARV then, but he didn't let on. That meant that on some level he believed me. He just couldn't act that way in front of the cameras or his people. That meant that we had a better chance.

"Sorry, Tony, just thinking if the Mets had a chance at the series this year."

The man behind Tony snickered. I get that kind of reaction a lot. I'm used to it. I try not to take it personally.

"So, Zach, you're not going to give me anything else?" Tony said.

I shrugged. "I'm just doing what I somehow always end up doing," I said.

"Saving the world as we know it," Tony said.

"Yep. You gotta believe me, Tony, if I could say more I would, but I can't."

I stood up. "So, I'll be going now."

The big guy made a step toward me. Tony raised a hand to stop him from trying to stop me. "Sit," Tony ordered. "You aren't going anywhere. We're putting you in a holding cell until New Vegas comes for you."

I hesitated for a nano, just to judge Tony and the big guy's reaction. Tony remained calm, the big guy took another step forward. I sat back down, slowly, eyes on the big guy while talking to Tony.

"What about Carol?" I asked.

"We're holding her, too," Tony said. "I feel kind

of bad about that because I know she was only following orders."

"Yeah, she's a loyal friend," I said, coolly.

"She's your employee," Tony corrected.

"Still, she's loyal," I said.

"So loyal we're transferring her now," the guy in
back said.

I stood up again. The big guy took a step toward
me. I put my hands behind my head, showing him I
wouldn't be a threat.

"Well, I'm not going to talk, so no use holding up
the room," I said. "Take me to my cell. A room with
a view will be appreciated."

Tony motioned toward me with his head as he
talked to his man. "Take Zach to his cell. Don't worry,
I guarantee he won't cause you any trouble."

I smiled. Yep, Tony believed me. He just couldn't
say so.

The big officer drew his stun club and got behind
me and pushed me toward the door, club in my back.
"Move it, Johnson," he ordered.

I went as pushed. Normally I would have shown
some resentment, but I needed to pass Carol in the
hall.

I reached the door. It popped open. The officer behind me pushed me into the hall.

"Easy," Tony told his man.

"Why, because he's innocent until proven guilty?"
the man asked.

"Nah, because he has a really good memory and he
holds a grudge."

I saw Carol being walked out of the interrogation
room they had been holding her in. She was escorted
by two armored guards. They were a few meters ahead
of us, so I picked up my pace.

"Slow it down," the big cop ordered.

I didn't listen. I kept walking. "Sorry, I need to use
the facilities," I said. "If you know what I mean."

He eased off the club in my back. Nobody wants to get peed on. That one almost always works.

"How close do I have to be to Carol for you to reprogram the psi blocker?" I thought to HARV.

"I'll tell you when," HARV said.

I quickened my pace. I could clearly see the psi blocker now. Hopefully, we were in reprogramming distance.

"Slow down at least a bit, Johnson," the officer said.

"Take it easy on him," Captain Rickey told his man. "He's got a weak bladder."

So Tony was trying to help or, at least, not hinder. We had a chance here. Maybe not a good chance but I will take any chance I can get.

"HARV, any luck yet?" I thought.

"There is no luck involved here, Zach. Either I can make the calculations or I can't."

"Figure of speech, buddy," I thought, moving forward.

"You are thinking, not speaking," HARV corrected. *"And I have made contact successfully."*

"So, can you reprogram it?" I thought.

"Think something," HARV said.

"I think you're annoying."

"Think something useful to Carol," HARV said.

"Carol, HARV has reversed the psi blocker to make it a psi amplifier. You should be able to get us out of here."

"Groovy," I heard inside my head.

I walked a few more steps. I suddenly felt very sleepy. I yawned.

Next thing I knew Carol was standing over me slowly shaking me. "*Tió*, wake up."

I sat up slowly. I had been sleeping. I looked around. I was still in the hallway in police headquarters. Everybody around us was sleeping. I smiled.

"Impressive, niece."

"Thanks," she said.

"Hey, I helped," HARV said. "Not only did I soup up Carol's brain but I've temporarily turned off all the security bots."

"You did good, too, HARV," I said.

Carol handed me GUS, my knife, and my backup gun. "You're going to need these."

"Thanks."

Carol helped me to my feet. "Come on, I'm yearning for a rematch with Natasha."

We headed toward the door. We were anxious to get to the Grand Canyon and stop Natasha. I just hoped we weren't leaping from the frying pan into the fire.

Chapter 24

Carol and I "borrowed" another police hover and headed for the Grand Canyon. The trip was quiet, as Carol needed to concentrate to use her newly augmented abilities to push the hover to even greater speeds. Normally, I would have been worried both about traveling so fast and Carol's powers being revved up like they were. History has taught me no good can come of that. Still, this was a case where the she-devil I knew beat the one I didn't. At least I hoped it was.

We arrived at the canyon and quickly parked. Carol lost no time exiting the hover. Carol was a woman on a mission. The Grand Canyon (I refuse to call it by its full trademarked name) may have been a vast place (hence the name), but Carol seemed to know exactly where she was going. I followed close behind. I needed to walk fast just to keep pace.

"Carol, slow down," I pleaded. "We really should have some sort of plan of attack."

"I see her, I kick her tight little ass," Carol said without breaking stride.

"Wow, what is the world coming to when Zachary Nixon Johnson wants to have a plan?" HARV said.

"HARV, any contact with JJ and Fera?" I asked.

"None in the last forty-five minutes."

"Can you locate them?" I asked, figuring Natasha must be near where they were.

HARV nodded. "Yes, I can. We are heading right for them." HARV pointed ahead to a crowd of people. "They are in that mass of humanity."

Carol was bearing down on the same group of people.

"I'm assuming they are all watching Natasha," I said quickening my step.

"That would be logical."

Carol reached the mass of people right before us. They were all mesmerized, staring at the same thing. You didn't have to be me to figure what or, in this case, who that was.

Carol cut her way through the crowd, not touching anybody but still mentally pushing them aside like they were mannequins. I followed through the path Carol made. That's when I saw her.

There, floating midway over the canyon, was Natasha. She was in the lotus position, just sitting hovering, eyes closed above the vast drop-off. As vast and awe inspiring as the land around us was it still paled in comparison to Natasha.

"Time for payback, bitch!" Carol said to Natasha.

If Natasha noticed us on any level she didn't show us.

Carol clenched her fist and glared at Natasha. I was still a meter behind Carol when her mental attack began but I could feel the heat she was generating.

"Impressive," HARV said. "Carol is hitting Natasha with everything she has."

I drew even with Carol. She was now grinding her teeth, focusing all her powers on Natasha. The thing was, Natasha didn't seem to notice. If she did notice she didn't care.

"If Carol was directing this power at the crowd they'd all be dust now," HARV said. "Yet Natasha doesn't seem at all affected."

Natasha opened one eye. *This is so going to be trouble,* I thought. She tilted her head in our general direction. Carol froze in place, then fell flat to the ground. Natasha closed her eye, pretty much ignoring me.

Not being one to take being ignored quietly, I popped GUS into my hand. I didn't want to hurt Natasha but she was too dangerous to let roam free. I had to take her down so the government could deal with her. Once again going with the "better the devil I know" option.

"GUS, heavy missiles," I ordered reluctantly.

"Yes, sir, Mr. Zach," GUS said. I was surprised he didn't put up an argument. He, too, must have known the grave threat that Natasha posed.

I squeezed the trigger, not once, not twice, but three times. Three high-powered multiple MIRVing missiles launched from GUS. They went roaring over the canyon at Natasha. They hit her almost instantly. Yet no explosion came. Natasha just sat there, still like she didn't have a care in the world.

"What happened?" I asked.

"I made your silly toys disappear," Natasha said.

"I wasn't really talking to you," I said.

I was levitated off the ground, turned upside down then started floating over toward Natasha. Oh, this was so not good!

Natasha positioned me so my upside down head was even with hers. I could see exactly how great a drop it would be if she let me go.

"HARV, can my body armor let me survive a fall from this distance?" I thought.

"You're kidding, right? Is one plus one two in binary?" HARV answered.

"No, it's not," GUS said, managing to be overly helpful and completely unhelpful at the same time.

"Zach, you really are so trying to kill my mood," Natasha said.

I tipped my fedora to her. I was impressed it had stayed on. "Just doing my job."

"No, you were just trying to do the government's job for them."

"Whatever. Why don't you just turn me right side up and we'll talk about this on nice solid ground?"

"I'll give you one out of two," she said.

My feet and head slowly reversed position so I was still face-to-face with her but no longer floating upside down.

"Is that better?" Natasha asked me.

"Not reaaaaaaaaaaaaaaaaaaaaaaaaaaaaaaally," I shouted as I started plummeting toward the ground.

"You probably should have been more thankful," HARV suggested as I continued my freefall, the ground drawing ever nearer.

"HARV, can you help at all here?" I asked, spinning downward.

"I am writing your obituary. Well, not so much writing it as updating it," HARV told me.

If I lived, I was going to kill HARV. Of course, looking at the jagged ground beneath me but not so far beneath me, it didn't look like I'd be living for more than another few nanos. I knew this wasn't going to be pretty. I closed my eyes and waited for the end. I took a deep breath, figuring it would be my last. My rapid descent stopped on a dime. The funny thing was, I didn't feel a thing. Was I dead? Splattered across the Grand Canyon?

"You're not dead," HARV said.

Opening my eyes, I saw I was hovering horizontally less than a meter from the ground. I could reach down and touch it. I floated to a vertical position. Looking up, I saw Natasha drifting down to me.

"Are you looking up her dress?" HARV asked.

I turned my head to the side. "No, of course not." Natasha and I were eye to eye again.

"Was that better?" she repeated.

"Thanks for not killing me," I said.

"The day is still young." She smiled.

We both slowly started floating upward again.

"You don't get it, do you, Zach?"

I shrugged. It was kind of a strange sensation, shrugging with no ground supporting me. "I've been told on more than one occasion I can be quite dense."

"He's been told on 113 occasions he can be quite dense," HARV added.

Natasha smiled. "Zach, I just want to be free and happy. I don't want to be what they want me to be. I can be better without their influence."

I understood where she was coming from. I really did. I couldn't blame Natasha for not wanting to be a killing machine. She was just too dangerous to run around free, no matter what either of us thought. I felt bad but there are times when the job has to come before the feelings.

As we floated upward, Natasha's eyes opened wider. "You really think I'm worried about being a killing machine?" she asked me.

"I would hope you are," I said. "Or else I am going to have to try extra hard to put you down."

She gently reached over and touched me on the shoulder. "Silly Zach. They didn't really build me to kill. They built me to control."

"Excuse me?"

"Zach, they have thousands of different weapons they can use to kill people. But they don't want to kill people. Well, not most people. They just want to influence and control them. And they didn't have any weapons to do that. Until me."

I thought about what she said. It had its own twisted government-meets-military logic. Therefore it was probably true.

"I'm the ultimate control device. I was designed to be able to bend the masses to the will of the people who designed me. The death thing is just a bad side effect. One that shows they really had no idea what they were doing."

"Not surprising," I said.

"Of course when you think about it, death is the

ultimate form of control. That's why I'm running, Zach. I don't want to be forced to be a control device. It makes me sad and when I am sad, everything around me dies. You have no idea how depressing that can be for me."

"Not to mention the lives you snuff out," I told her.

She lowered her head. "Yes, I try not to think of them. At least they never suffer. When I kill someone, it's instantaneous and painless." She looked up again, locking eyes with me. "They were smart to send you after me."

"I am very good at what I do," I said.

"And so modest," HARV added.

She laughed, at me, not with me. "No, that's not it. It's because you are a test subject, too."

I kind of knew what she was getting at but I played dumb. "I don't understand."

"Don't play dumb with me," she said. Reaching over, she touched me on the forehead. "The computer in your brain makes you a test model, too."

"I suppose so. I am the first human to share my brain with an intelligent machine."

"As I am the first machine to share my brain with a not-so-intelligent human," HARV added.

"But the government didn't do this to me. A friend did. To help me do what I do and for the good of science."

A moment of silence as we continued floating upward. "Zach, your friend's work was funded by the military, the World Council, and UltraMegaHyperMart."

"Excuse me?"

Natasha gazed at me like she was looking at a poor lost child who had just banged his head. "You don't know. Do you?"

"I don't know a lot of stuff," I said. "I just don't let it slow me down."

She tilted her head. She was sad for me. I was kind of surprised she didn't pat me on the head.

"What I am missing?" I asked, against my better judgment.

"Your interface with HARV, it was a prototype."

"Not surprised by that," I told her. "It's annoying!"

"Hey, I can hear you!" HARV said.

"But it does have its practical applications," I finished.

"That's more like it," HARV said.

"It allows you near instant access to the world's information," Natasha said.

"I can't argue with you there."

"Plus HARV can modify your body and interact with your armor," Natasha said.

I nodded. "That part takes a little getting us to."

"And if people know the frequency HARV uses to broadcast to your brain, they can use him to control your actions," Natasha said.

"Impossible," I said.

HARV projected himself through my eye lens that binds us together. Normally we both prefer that HARV project himself from either my wrist communicator or a nearby holo-projector, saving the eye lens for emergency use. The fact that he was using it now meant he was angry. "I don't often totally agree with Zach, but in this case I do," he said, getting right in Natasha's face.

Natasha locked gazes with HARV.

"Make Zach kick himself in the butt," she told HARV.

"Okay," HARV said, without processing.

My right leg kicked upwards into my butt. It didn't hurt that much, but the point was made.

"Hey!" I said, rubbing my butt cheek. "What gives?"

"Ooops," HARV said. "I knew it was a bad sign when we agreed . . ."

Pointing at HARV, I shouted, "Why'd you make me kick me?"

HARV stood there, dumbfounded. It's never ever a good sign when the mega-supercomputer stuck in your brain is stuck. "Um," was all he said.

"He didn't mean to do it. I made him do it!" Natasha said.

Oh, this now went way past really bad to possibly quite tragic, if the powers that be had been planning what I thought they might be planning. It was so bad I actually forgot I was hovering a kilometer or two off the ground.

Natasha reached over and gently placed her hand on my shoulder. "Once they figured they couldn't control me, a living breathing entity, they moved on to another possible option."

"A programmable electronic one," I said.

"Me," HARV gulped.

"Yes they approached Dr. Pool about modifying you," Natasha said.

"Wow, that really sucks spam," GUS added.

"But I, too, have my own free will," HARV protested. "You caught me off guard that time. I have rewritten and rerouted my subroutines so I would not make Zach kick himself again." A pause, a sly smile. "Unless, of course, I wanted him to."

Natasha reached over touched HARV on his shoulder. "Oh, silly HARV. As advanced as you may be, I could figure out a way around your reprogramming. I'm sure others could, too."

HARV threw his hands on his hips. Leaning forward, he shouted, "Maybe, but I could make it really hard."

Natasha removed her hand from HARV's virtual shoulder. She opened her eyes and looked at both of us with a knowing smile. "Yes, you would. That's why they decided a highly intelligent machine wasn't the way to go either. You were just another step in the chain."

"A step above you," HARV said, thrusting an unnaturally extended finger in her face.

Natasha turned away from the finger, concentrating on me. "Only in that HARV's actions were easier to predict than mine."

"But that's a good thing. I'm consistent. Not wishy-washy like you humans." HARV slapped himself on the head. "DOS! They used me."

Now that she had gotten through to him. Natasha turned back to HARV. "Don't worry. Like I said, they also concluded you were too difficult to deal with."

"I can attest to that," I said.

"Amen," GUS added.

"Hey, no comments needed from the peanut gallery," HARV said. He thought for a moment. "The PIHI-Pods," he said.

Natasha smiled. Touching her index finger to her nose she said, "Vingo."

"They can transmit subliminal messages into people's brains using the P-Pods," HARV said.

"They figure that since they can't control me directly, they can use me to broadcast to the P-Pods. I would be their beacon. Not only was I bred and created to have the power, they thought they could condition me to do what they wanted. That's why I left. I want nothing to do with controlling the masses or being controlled. Plus if they force me, well, then I get angry and everything just drops dead. I don't want that either. It's a real bummer."

We floated over to where Natasha had frozen the crowd. This was a dilemma. I didn't like the fact that I was used as more of a test dummy than I had originally thought. I also didn't like the fact that P-Pods could be used to send subliminal messages to people. I liked it even less that Natasha could be the broadcaster of those messages. Maybe I should just let her go and let that be that? Nope, I couldn't do it. Like it or not, I was hired to do a job. Like it or not, Natasha was just too damn powerful to let wander around on her own. I knew it wasn't her fault, but I had to bring her in. I'd worry about the mass subliminal message thing later. Sure, that was potentially bad, but the media had been programming us for about a century now. Who's to say this would be any different? It wasn't my call. At least not yet. Right now I had to take down the clear and very present danger, a woman who could simply think us all dead. She was the direct threat. The one I could see and touch and hopefully clobber.

We landed on the ground. I was going to have to play it coy, like I was on her side. I started humming old TV theme songs just to keep her out of my mind as much as possible. Get her to drop her guard and take her out with GUS. It almost worked in Vegas. I just made the mistake of going too easy on her there.

Natasha looked up to the sky, giving me my chance to take a shot.

"They will be here soon," she said.

"Who?" I said, holding back for a moment.

"Earth Force special unit."

"I didn't call them," I said.

She pointed to my link in my eye. "No need to. They've been watching through that."

"That's impossible," HARV told her. "I do not let people tap into me!"

"Just like I can't make you kick Zach?" Natasha said, concentrating on HARV.

With Natasha distracted I figured this was my chance. I popped GUS into my hand. I aimed. Natasha was gone. What the . . . ?

"I've just given you a little taste of how they envisioned me using my power. See how you like being the most wanted person on the planet!" Natasha said inside my brain.

I so did not like the way that sounded.

Chapter 25

The second Natasha disappeared the crowd around us reanimated. DOS, the woman was powerful. I nudged Carol.

"Come on, chica, Natasha is gone, we need to find her, pronto."

Carol looked at me, her eyes squinted. What I could see of them showed nothing but contempt. She raised her arm slowly, pointing at me, nearly trembling with absolute disdain. Oh, this was going to be so far past way bad!

"Surrender now, scumbag!" she ordered.

"Ah, Carol, it's me, your—"

I never got to finish that statement as Carol sent me flying a good hundred meters away from her. Hitting the ground with a thud, I was lucky my body armor was so strong. I propped myself up on one knee. I examined the crowd's faces. They all had the same look as Carol's.

One of the onlookers pointed at me. "Get him!" he shouted.

"He's an enemy of the nation of man!" another shouted.

They rushed toward me. Before I had a chance to

react, I was grabbed from behind and pulled back to the ground. My attacker was Fera. She was slashing at me in a feral rage.

"Surrender, you scum of the scum!" she shouted as she clawed.

"I'm guessing this is what Natasha was talking about," HARV said. "She must have broadcast a 'You hate Zachary Nixon Johnson' message on the P-Pod network. This entire site is wired."

"Great deduction there, Brainiac," I said rolling to my back with Fera still on top of me.

"You have to be patient with me, Zach. I'm having a bad day," HARV said. "Just as I am finally starting to come to terms with being connected to your brain I learn I may not be as invulnerable to outside influences as I had computed. I'm sure that has something to do with me being connected to your brain . . ."

I didn't have time to deal with HARV right now. Fera was slashing away at me I had to get her off soon. *"GUS, are you still on my side?"* I asked.

"Always at your side and on your side," GUS answered.

"A simple yes was I all I needed there, buddy."

"Yes." A pause then, *"Sorry."*

"Good."

I popped GUS into my hand. *"Heavy concussion blast,"* I thought to GUS.

"Check."

Positioning GUS between myself and Fera, I pulled the trigger. I admit I took some pleasure watching Fera go flying off of me.

"Stealth mode, now!" I ordered HARV.

From the confused looks on the faces of the attacking mob I knew they couldn't see me. I smiled.

"What, no please or thank you? I understand you too were under a bit of stress but politeness never hurts," HARV lectured.

"Thanks," I thought.

"See, that wasn't so hard!" HARV said.

Chapter 26

Earth Force special squadrons had arrived and they, too, were much more interested in me than they were in Natasha. The good news was, now that HARV knew he could be used as a tracking device or a Zach-locating device, he scrambled his signal, telling them I was everywhere. HARV hated being used almost as much as I did.

Walking invisibly through the crowd I knew I needed a plan. I decided the best course of action would be to return home. When in doubt, return to base, regroup, and hope for the best. Of course, taking the hover was out of the question. I was going to have to teleport back home. Of course, they would be looking for me so I was going to have to be extra careful.

The good news was the Canyon had its own tele-port station for tourists and it was less than two kilo-meters away. An easy walk in stealth mode. I still didn't think that adding a teleport station was enough to classify the Grand Canyon as new and improved but I had to admit it was handy to have right now.

Reaching the domed teleport center, I saw the bad news. Guards posted at the door.

In stealth mode, getting by the guards wasn't going to be a problem. The trick was getting on a transporter and getting back to Frisco. The way public transporters work is every time they are activated, every pad is activated whether it has a person on it or not. That makes for fewer calculations. Of course, it's also less passenger-friendly that way, as porting stations are loath to send to a port when they have less than 91 percent capacity. The teleporter here had twelve pads, so that meant there would only be one open pad at most.

I easily walked past the guards at the door. The port center was crowded, but not overly so. Most people were still trying to figure out what had happened and why they couldn't remember much of the last hour. Scanning the joint, I saw two additional guards standing on each side of the check-in desk. There were also a couple of roving guards checking the IDs of travelers on the transport pads.

"It might be easier to steal a car," HARV said.

"I'm a good guy, I don't steal cars," I thought back.

"Then maybe borrow one," GUS suggested.

"Nope."

"It's a long walk home," HARV told me.

"When is the next scheduled transport to Frisco?" I asked.

No reply.

"HARV?"

"I'm here, Zach. These schedules are so complicated even I have problems with them. The next port is to New New York. That one is full. The next one is to New Cleveland. It has an opening."

I wasn't all that surprised Cleveland had an open spot. Cleveland was the spot the Gladians originally landed when they first made contact with Earth. Despite that, or maybe because of it, Cleveland gave peo-

ple a lot of people a bad vibe. I've actually never been
there. Looks like I would be going now. Cleveland
wasn't Frisco, but it wasn't here. That was a good
thing.

I hung out by the door until right before the port
to Cleveland was scheduled to take off. I had HARV
identify all the passengers who came in. I wasn't sure
what I'd do if another Cleveland passenger arrived. I
figured I'd deal with it if it came up. There are times
in life (many more then most of us realize) when in
order to be successful we have to be lucky. This was
one of those moments. My fate was coming down to
the luck of the draw that not enough people from
Cleveland would show up at this time.

Time passed without any other Joe or Jane Cleve-
lands showing up. I breathed a little sigh of relief.

*"Mr. Zach, what do we do when we get to New
Cleveland?"* GUS asked. *"I'm sure it's a lovely town
but it's actually farther from Frisco than here."*

*"I'll worry about that when I get there. There will
be less police and military around. It should be easier
to get back to Frisco from any place that isn't here."*

Drawing closer to the teleporter, inspiration struck.
"HARV, can you reprogram a teleporter?"

"Can you tie your shoes?"

"I assume that's a yes."

HARV just sighed. *"You won't steal a car but you'd
have me reprogram a teleporter . . ."*

HARV wouldn't understand, so I didn't bother explaining. I believe a car is a part of a person, therefore
stealing (or even borrowing) their car is like taking a
little piece of their soul. Sure, most cars are alike these
days, so it may not be a very big piece of their soul.
But it's still enough to bug me. A car is personal. A
teleporter ride is not.

*"The people will just take a little extra trip to New
Frisco,"* I thought. *"Who could complain about spending time in Frisco?"*

Even the aliens preferred Frisco. They may have

landed in Cleveland, but they established their first embassy in New Frisco. Today, not many aliens actually come to Earth. (Most aliens think we smell funky.) But if you are to see one, chances are it will be in Frisco. Frisco is the cultural and cool capital of the New New World.

"Surely the police and Earth Force will be looking closely at any arrivals from here to Frisco," HARV cautioned.

"True, if they are scheduled," I said. *"I'm betting an unscheduled one will cause enough commotion to allow us to escape."* I walked over and stood on the open teleporter pad. Two guards were still checking all the other passengers' IDs. A couple of them griped and commented on what a weird day it had been. Yet they all cooperated, so the check only took a minute or two.

Once the guards were satisfied I wasn't on the transporter, they gave the operator the okay signal. The operator pressed a button. The countdown started. Three, two, one . . . Have a nice . . .

"You know teleporting disrupts cloaking," HARV warned. *"Once it's activated the guards may see you."*

I did not know that and he could have told me sooner. It wasn't that bad a problem, though.

"That's okay. It will be too late to stop me and they'll be expecting me to arrive in New Cleveland. Before they figure it out, we'll be long gone."

"I also won't be able to cloak you for thirty minutes and fifty-two seconds and twelve nanoseconds after our arrival," HARV told me.

"Can you throw a holo-disguise over me?"

"Yes . . ."

The next thing I knew, I was standing on a port pad. It seemed like the one at the canyon, but it wasn't. It was in a much larger area. This port pad was one of many in the area. Looking up, I saw a big neon hologram that read: WELCOME TO NEW FRISCO. I smiled.

". . . I can," HARV finished saying.

"Do it now."

The other passengers started to grumble.

I made a quick exit. I needed to get out of there before anybody put two and two together and came up with me.

Chapter 27

I exited the building just as a couple of police bots rolled in to try to calm the crowd and figure out what had happened. The Frisco teleporter station was only ten kilometers from my house. Not an easy walk, but a doable one. I figured exercise would do me good, so I started hoofing it. Sure, I get a lot of exercise when people are trying to kill or maim me, but this was different. This was exercise that allowed me to relax and collect my thoughts.

Of course, collecting those thoughts wasn't that comforting. I was up against one of the most powerful minds, if not the most powerful mind, in the world. Natasha was a woman who could kill all around her as an afterthought—or by accident for that matter. As if that wasn't daunting enough, I was also now the most wanted man on the planet. And by wanted I mean as a criminal, a shoot-first-ask-questions-later criminal. I was being hunted by the government agency who had hired me to track Natasha. And all my usual allies had also been turned against me. To make matters really complicated, according to Natasha I was being used as much as a lab rat as she was. That part probably pissed me off more than anything. I don't

mind bad guys trying to kill me. They're bad guys—
it's what they do. But if one of the people I trusted
had intentionally inserted HARV into my brain knowing he might be used a means to control the masses . . .
Not sure how I was going to handle that.

Walking toward, my house it occurred to me that I
had no idea what I currently looked like.

*"HARV, what kind of holographic disguise am I
wearing?"*

*"You are currently a little old Mexican woman
named Lila Gomez,"* HARV said.

*"Ah, HARV, I don't really need a name for my holo-
graphic cover . . ."*

*"Sure you do, Lila. It helps make the cover more
believable,"* HARV said.

"I like the name Lila Gomez," GUS said.

"First intelligent thing you've ever said," HARV
told GUS.

"Thanks!" GUS said.

I walked in silence. Then GUS added, *"I like the
name Zach, too."*

"Suck-up," HARV said.

I continued walking, all the while thinking what a
truly bizarre life I led.

Coming within viewing distance of my house, I
quickly noticed that there were at least three plain-
clothes officers on the street. One was posing as a
satellite tower worker. Another was going door to
door, supposedly looking for his lost dog. The third
was just walking up and down the street pretending
to be lost. There was a hover van marked Speedy Web
Service parked across the street. I was betting they
were also keeping my house under electronic
surveillance.

"HARV, can you scramble sounds?" I thought,
walking up my sidewalk.

"Just like you scramble eggs," HARV answered.

"Can you make me talk just like a little Mexican lady?" I thought.

"No," HARV answered.

"Well, then great, if I can't—"

"Zach, I can't do it just like that, but I can make it so close nobody will notice."

"You couldn't just say that?"

I was sure somewhere HARV was all smiles. *"Sure, I could have."*

I strolled up to the door and knocked on it. The door cracked open. Electra peered through the crack.

"Yes?" she asked.

I needed to say something so Electra would know it was me without letting anybody else know it was me. I had to come up with some sort of reference only I would come up. Yet it couldn't be so obtuse that Electra wouldn't figure out it was me.

"Avon calling," I said.

The door opened much wider. Electra motioned to me. The nano I got through the doorway, Electra closed the door. Pushing a switch above the door, she activated the house's external security system.

"Zach?" she whispered.

I smiled. "In person."

She hugged me. Of course, to everybody else in the room, it looked like she was hugging a little Mexican woman.

"The whole world is after you," Electra told me.

"Hence the disguise," I said.

"What happened?" Electra asked.

I, well, the little Mexican lady shrugged. "No idea. That Natasha lady just put some sort of whammy on me or everybody else. Underneath I'm still the same loveable Zach I've always been."

Liz Lazor, Greg the clown guy, and Helena had all been watching closely. I was keeping one eye on them. I saw their mouths dropping open. They were confused.

Until Liz said, "That's got to be Zach!"

One of her eyes started to glow red. Laser force beams shot from her eye. By instinct I popped GUS into my hand and used him to reflect the beams back. One beam hit Liz, taking her out. The other hit Greg the clown in the midsection, taking him down. I looked at GUS. I was really impressed by what I had just done.

"Wow, watching all those old *Star Wars* movies really paid off," I said.

HARV appeared. "Hardly. I took control of your hands. The Force has nothing on the latest technology."

"Oh," I said, a bit disappointed. The hologram around me peeled away.

Helena glared at me. She turned to Electra. "Call the police immediately."

Electra shook her head. "Mother, no. Zach is being framed."

Helena touched the P-Pod she was wearing on her ear. She looked into Electra's eyes. Lowering her arm, she said, "You trust this man, *hija?*"

Electra put her hand over her chest. "With all my heart." Electra turned to me. "So, what happened, chico?"

"Carol and I found Natasha at the Grand Canyon."

"You mean the New Improved UltraMegaHyper-Mart Grand Canyon," Helena corrected.

"Like I said, Carol and I found Natasha floating over the Grand Canyon and we engaged her."

"I take it you lost," Helena said.

I shook my head. "I wouldn't say that."

"I would," HARV said.

"Me, too!" GUS added.

"We ran away very fast. If we had had tails they would have been between our legs," HARV continued.

"I made a strategic withdrawal," I claimed. I figured if I said it enough, I would believe it. "Natasha wiped the floor with us. Well, she could have but she chose not to. Instead she decided to send most of the world after me. She either wanted to let them do her dirty work or she truly didn't want me dead and just wanted to teach me a lesson."

"Speaking of Carol," Helena asked. "Where is she?"

"I don't really know," I said.

"She's coming up the walkway now," HARV said. "And she doesn't look happy."

"Does she know I'm in here?"

"Well, all the undercover police on the street have suddenly packed up and left."

I took that as a yes. Carol wanted to take me down all by herself.

Chapter 28

Carol came barreling into the house. Under normal circumstances Carol was a formidable foe, not to be taken lightly. When she was mad she became scary dangerous. When she got really angry she could go nuclear.

"Where is he?" Carol shouted.

Electra and Helena each took a step backward, meekly pointing at me standing between them.

"Step back, *tiá* and *abuela*," Carol ordered. "I don't want to hurt you in the crossfire!"

Electra and Helena backed away quickly, taking cover behind my sofa.

Carol locked her glare on me. "Time to give up, *tió!*" she spat.

I shattered into millions of pieces like a jigsaw puzzle. Carol took a step backward. *"Dios!"* she said, hand on heart, "I just wanted to stun him, not shatter him!"

I was glad to see my niece really didn't want to kill me. I was even gladder that I had had HARV project an image of me in the middle of the room while I stood in stealth mode behind the door.

Moving forward quickly, I gave Carol a chop to the back of the neck. Caught totally off guard, she fell to the ground.

Everything around me shimmered as HARV took me out of stealth mode.

"This stealth mode is really handy," I told HARV. "Why don't we use it more often?"

HARV appeared in front of me, arms crossed, head tilted. "You really should read your e-mails from Randy more carefully," he lectured.

"I skim them," I protested.

"Well, if you skimmed them more carefully you would know that prolonged exposure to stealth mode may lead to side effects."

"I can handle . . ."

"Impotence." HARV smiled.

"Oh," I said.

"Randy hasn't really tested it on humans. It's extra tough to get volunteers for those types of experiments," HARV said. "Though he has computer simulated it and the results tend to support this conclusion."

"Let's try to limit our use of stealth mode from now on," I said.

HARV just smiled.

By now Electra and Helena were already tending to Carol.

"I didn't hit her that hard," I said.

"I know," Electra told me, examining Carol's pupils with a small flashlight. "She'll be fine."

Helena stood up and walked over to me. I didn't know what to expect here. I was the most wanted man on the planet who had just taken out her bodyguards and her niece.

"So, Zachary, what's the next step?" she asked.

I didn't have to think hard on that one. "I'm going pay another visit to Randy. I've got some questions that only he can answer."

"What can we do?" Electra asked.

"Bring Carol around and try to convince her I am not public enemy numero uno. If I'm going to stop Natasha I'm going to need her."

I walked up to Electra and gave her a kiss—hard. "Wish me luck," I said.

"Good luck." She smiled.

"Man, are we ever going to need it," HARV said.

Chapter 29

Since Carol had psionically removed the police watching me, I was able to at least borrow Electra's car to drive to Randy's. I still couldn't be myself, since the police or their cameras could be anywhere. So I picked a new holo-disguise. I told HARV I wanted a plumber's disguise. Nobody would question a plumber making a house call.

HARV, to his credit, went all out with the disguise. Checking myself out in one of the car's mirrors, I was a good half-meter shorter, so much shorter it was obvious even though I was sitting. I was dressed in blue jeans with suspenders and a red top complete with a little red cap and white gloves. My normally Roman nose was now rounded, with a big cheesy mustache underneath. I didn't look anything like the ruggedly handsome, slightly graying PI.

"Nice job," I told HARV. I was surprised to hear I talked with an exaggerated Italian accent.

"I figured you'd appreciate the look," HARV said.

"I don't get it," GUS said.

"You're lucky," HARV told him.

We pulled up next to Randy's lab. I looked around. There didn't appear to be a police presence. I didn't know if I should take that as a good sign or an especially bad sign. I decided to be optimistic.

I got out of the car and started walking toward the door. *"HARV, I'm going to need an old-fashioned monkey wrench. A big one."*

"Is this phallic?"

"Just do it, HARV."

I was carrying a big holographic monkey wrench. The weird thing was, even though I knew the wrench wasn't really there, I could still feel its weight in my hand.

"I'm making your brain think it's actually carrying the wrench," HARV said in my brain.

"Uh, why?"

"Realism, Zach, realism. It helps you sell the disguise. I didn't go through all this trouble to have you blow your cover with a poor performance."

Ignoring HARV, I walked up and knocked on the door. Randy's holographic image appeared on the door. "Yes?"

Showing the image the big monkey wrench, I said, "Hello, sir. I'm Zario from Zario Brothers plumbing. I understand you have a leak?"

The image shook its head no. "Sorry, I don't. Even if I did, I would fix it myself. Plumbing is like a hobby to me. I find it relaxing." Randy thought for a bit longer. "Actually, it's more like a passion. A relaxing passion. Yes, that's it."

I held the wrench up again so the image could see it.

"I understand you are a collector of old tools. Perhaps we could make some sort of deal?"

Randy's image's eyes grew wider. The door popped open.

"Come in! Come in!"

I smiled and entered.

Randy had been in the back part of the lab, but came rushing up to meet me. I knew of his love for tools and had played to it. "I haven't seen a classic monkey wrench in decades. Can I touch it?"

I grabbed Randy and quickly pulled him toward the outside door. If I got him outside his security system wouldn't kick in when I kicked his ass.

"Where we going?" Randy asked.

"I have more tools like this in my car," I said in my accent.

"Oh, megacool," Randy said. He stopped resisting and walked outside with me.

I pointed to my, well, Electra's car. "I have more tools just like this in the trunk."

"This is so exciting!" Randy said, hands clasped together. He looked at the car. "Doesn't look like a plumber's vehicle."

"My brother has the business car. I'm using my wife's."

"Oh," Randy said.

For a smart guy, Randy could be a real sucker sometimes. We reached the car.

"Can I hold that wrench?" Randy asked.

I grabbed him and threw him against the car.

"Ouch! A simple no would have been sufficient," Randy said, rubbing his shoulder.

Grabbing Randy by the lab coat, I said, "Listen, buddy, we have to talk."

"You know, I've always had the utmost respect for the working man, but if you don't release me I'm afraid I will have to call my security. Now, can I hold that wrench or not?"

For a smart guy, Randy could be really dense. "HARV, remove the hologram," I said.

Randy looked at me. "Zach!"

"Smart man."

"Zach, what are you doing here? I'm fighting every urge I have to call the police. Do you know you're the most wanted man on the planet right now?"

Ignoring Randy's question I asked, "Are you using me as a guinea pig?"

Randy nodded. "Yes, of course. I've always been quite open about you and HARV."

Putting a finger in Randy's face, I asked, "Does HARV have more potentially nefarious uses?"

Randy was mum. I gave him a little push to unglue his mouth. "Well?"

"Zach, everything can be misused! I saw an old HV show once where a guy used a pen to kill somebody. Does that make a pen a nefarious weapon?"

Randy may have been naïve, but he wasn't stupid.

"Was HARV a test model for devices you wanted to stick in everybody's brains?"

"No, of course not," Randy said.

"Really?"

HARV appeared next to me. "Yeah, really?"

Randy looked down. "Um, well, uh, that wasn't ever my intent. I really designed HARV to be a completely useful, totally interactive interface and assistant."

"Did the military fund HARV?"

More silence from Randy. "Define fund."

"Give you credits that you used to design and build him," I said.

Randy looked up, but still not at me. "Well, Earth Force gives me credits for many of my projects. Yes, so HARV was probably one of them." Another slight pause then he said, quickly, "But they swore to me that it's all purely for humanitarian reasons."

"Randy, you had to suspect that there was something more afoot," I insisted.

Randy simply shrugged. "My credo has always been don't look a gift investor in the morals. I invent things for the greater good. I can't be responsible if people pervert or misuse my ideas."

"Pretty simplistic, don't you think?"

"Don't go raising your eyebrows to me, Zach!" Randy said loudly. "Until now you've never questioned any of this. You've been perfectly happy to test drive whatever I gave you. All you cared about was how it helped you get the job done."

"Yeah, well, my job is saving the world," I said.

Randy rolled his eyes. "And mine is improving the world. Face it, Zach, you're as guilty as I am!"

I stomped down on Randy's foot. Hard.

"DOS, Zach!" Randy yelped, hopping on his good foot while rubbing the bad. "Why'd you do that?"

"Because I'm pissed at both of us and I thought it would be silly to stomp on my own foot!"

"Oh, okay, I guess that makes sense," Randy said. "The really strange thing is, I no longer have the urge to turn you over to the police."

Well, at least something was going right.

"Uh-oh, Zach," HARV told me. "Randy's security is onto us."

"So, I've dealt with his security before, I'll do it again."

"This is different," HARV said.

"Why?"

"Because I'm not some bloody bot," a sexy British accent said.

Randy pointed toward the accent. "Zach, I'd like you to meet my new personal bodyguard, Eleanor Ash."

I turned to see a shapely auburn-haired woman coming toward me. Then everything went black.

Chapter 30

I came to and looked around. First thing I noticed was that I was in a chair in Randy's lab. Second thing I noticed was Randy in the chair next me. Trying to move, I then noticed my arms were tied to the chair arms and my legs to the chair legs by old-fashioned rope. I probably should have noticed this sooner, but I was bit groggy from whatever Eleanor had done to me. Next I noticed Randy was also roped into to his chair. Not sure why a high-tech man like Randy had so much low-tech rope around, figured it was best not to ponder over that one at all. Finally, I noticed Eleanor hovering over both of us. Since she was dressed in a tight-fitting leather catsuit that would have made Catwoman blush, I really should have noticed her sooner.

"Ah, nice to see you're awake," Eleanor said to me.

Randy lifted his head up, his long red hair covering most of his face. "I'm awake, too!" he said, as if this should warrant a medal.

Turning as far as I could toward Randy, I said, "Isn't she your bodyguard?"

"Yep," he said proudly. "I got tired of just bots.

Science can be so lonely so often. So I hired Eleanor. She's hot and deadly.''

Yes, quite the combo, I thought. I ran into it a lot in my line of work. The hot was nice but it was distracting, making an already dangerous woman even more so. I guess that's why it worked so well.

Eleanor strutted toward us. "I used to work exclusively for rock stars and politicians, but now I've moved to the geek sector. They may not shower as much, but the work is less taxing. And I love playing with gadgets," she said with a wink. "Of course, it also pays less. Hence the reason I'm so anxious to collect the ten million credit award for Zach."

Randy shook his head. "Eleanor, Zach's not really a wanted man. Well, he is, but he shouldn't be. He's innocent."

"They all say that," Eleanor insisted.

Randy nodded in agreement. "True, but in Zach's case he's not lying, at least, not about this. Some mega-superpowerful psi has zapped everybody's minds to think Zach is a bad guy."

"Oh please, that old story!" Eleanor said.

"So, Randy, you see me as me now?"

"Yes, the moment after you stomped on my foot I knew the truth."

That must be key. Pain must break Natasha's hold. At least, in this case when she needed to broadcast to so many. I had to tell HARV to relay the information to Electra so she could pull Carol back to our side.

"I've already told Electra," HARV told me. *"Carol is on her way over."*

"Can Carol take Eleanor?" I thought.

"That's the least of your worries right now," HARV answered.

I so did not like the sound of that. I hesitated, figuring that maybe if I didn't ask HARV about the bad news the bad news wouldn't happen. Desperate, I know.

"Zach, not asking is not going to make it not happen," HARV said.

"I think you need to be penalized for use of the triple negative," I thought to HARV.

"Delaying me isn't going to delay it either."

I took a deep slow breath. I took another one. I had put it off as long as I could. *"Okay, what's going down?"* I asked HARV.

"Wait for it," came HARV's reply.

I hated it when he did that.

Twoa came crashing down through the ceiling. Oh, yes, this was just what I didn't need now. Being tied up while a mad omega superwoman working for the government shows up, thinking I'm public enemy number one.

"Oh, hi, Twoa," I said. "Nice to see you again."

Twoa shot a finger at me. "Shut it or lose it!" she ordered.

Twoa patted Eleanor on the back. "Excellent job, citizen. We will have the ten million credits forwarded to your account."

"Thank you," Eleanor smiled.

"Carol and Electra are on their way," HARV told me.

I was less than thrilled to have Carol and Electra messing with these two superbabes, but if I was going to have any chance they were my only chance. I had an idea to give my ladies a better chance.

"Is that ten million tax-free?" I asked Twoa, trying to stir a pot of trouble

"No, of course not," Twoa said.

"Why not?" I asked.

"Yeah, why not?" Eleanor asked.

"Because the government needs its share, too," Twoa insisted. "We provide a lot for the people. It's not cheap. So every citizen has to pay her fair share."

"Oh please, Twoa. We are all adults here. We know the government can do whatever it wants when it wants and find a way to justify it. So you could easily make Eleanor's bounty tax free,"'" I said.

"I agree!" Eleanor said.

Twoa stopped and put a finger to her mouth. "I'm just a small representative of the government."

"But you can still do whatever you want."

"Well, maybe," Twoa said. "But everybody can't do that or it would be anarchy. We can't have that."

Eleanor grabbed Twoa by the shoulder, twisting her toward her. "I deserve just as much as you do."

"No, you don't," Twoa said. "I've dedicated my life to fighting crime and righting wrongs. Plus, I've spent the last year in the public sector. I deserve a lot."

Hard to believe my ploy had worked. I might not have had them fighting yet, but they were distracted. Hopefully that would be enough to give Carol and Electra a one up. At least, long enough to make Twoa realize I wasn't the bad guy here.

There was a loud explosion. Turning toward the explosion, we saw Carol and Electra entering the far end of the lab through a wall. Carol's hair was standing on end, alive with energy. She got that way when she was really channeling power. Electra was wrapped from head to toe in tight-fitting battle armor. It looked like it was made out of leather but it was nano-enforced, making it much stronger than any natural metal. She was also wielding a heavy duty energy rifle.

Randy was loving the anticipation of the action, but dreading it was going to take place in his precious lab.

"This has the makings of a great brawl! Way better than anything I get on credit-for-view," Randy said, nearly hyperventilating with excitement. "I just hope either they or my insurance pay for the damages."

Randy had the magic combination of being horny and cheap.

Electra opened fire, hitting both the distracted Eleanor and Twoa with powerful blasts of energy, knocking them both to the ground. Eleanor was out for the count. Twoa, though, wouldn't be put down that easily. She was already pushing herself up off the ground.

Carol decided to help her up by telekinetically flinging her into the ceiling. Twoa smashed into the ceiling—doing the building's structure more harm than Twoa. Carol mentally locked onto Twoa, drilling her to the floor.

Electra and Carol ran toward Randy and me. Twoa just lay there for a nano. Was that it? Had they taken her out?

"Okay, now I'm pissed," Twoa said, separating her face from the floor.

Carol and Electra each took a step backward. Electra pointed her weapon at Twoa. Carol took a ready stance.

"The pain should have caused Twoa to realize I'm not the real enemy here," I muttered.

"Oh, it did," Twoa said. "But I'm still going to put some hurt on somebody."

"Quick, cut me free," I said.

Electra pulled a knife from her boot (another reason why I love her). She cut the ropes from my arms and then my legs, all the while never taking one eye off the slowly rising Twoa.

Twoa stood up. She twisted her neck one way, it cracked. She twisted her neck the other way, it crackled. She smiled. "Ah, that's better."

Carol and Electra had hit Twoa with all the force they had, yet it still hadn't been enough to stop her. You couldn't beat Twoa by force. You needed to outthink her. I noticed Carol was still wearing the HARV enhanced headband. That gave me an idea.

"Carol, we can't outpower Twoa, but she's not as confident as she seems. You have to convince her she's weak."

"Uh, sure. I'll try," Carol thought back.

Twoa zoomed past me at Carol and Electra. She yanked the gun away from Electra and broke it over her knee.

"True warriors don't need weapons!" she said.

"Yes, they do!" Electra insisted, smacking Twoa dead in the nose with a left jab.

Electra pulled back her hand in pain. *"Dios!"* she shouted.

Twoa flicked Electra on the nose with her index finger, knocking her out cold. Twoa turned her attention to Carol, who was channeling all her mental energy.

"Now for you, little girl," Twoa said, making a fist.

"You are too weak to take me on," Carol insisted.

"No, I'm not," Twoa insisted, drawing closer.

Carol was straining. I could see her physically trying to bore her thoughts into Twoa's subconscious.

"You are weak," Carol said.

"You're going to feel so much pain," Twoa said.

"You are weak," Carol repeated, the headband starting to smoke.

"HARV, you've got to increase the power to Carol," I said.

"But it'll overload the reversed neutralizer," HARV said.

"It's our only chance."

"You are weak," Carol insisted.

Twoa stopped her approach. She shook her head. "I don't like this feeling . . ." she said.

Carol collapsed to the ground. She was out. The good news was Twoa was confused. Springing up from the chair, I headed toward Twoa. I don't believe in hitting ladies. But I've dealt with Twoa enough to know she's not much of a lady.

I tapped Twoa on the shoulder. She turned toward me. I hit her with a HARV-enhanced uppercut right to the chin. Her head rocked back. I hit her right between the eyes with a left. She went down like a sack of bricks on Jupiter.

That had felt way better than it should have.

I turned toward Randy. He had fainted with all the excitement.

HARV appeared and looked over the room. "Wow, not often you're the only one left standing in a room."

HARV was right. Usually I was the one taking the lumps. Maybe that meant that this case was finally turning around.

Chapter 31

It didn't take long for all the ladies to come to. (Actually, Randy was the last one to wake up.) Nobody was worse for the wear, though Twoa was very ashamed that I, a mere normal human, had been able to knock her out. She offered HARV (and me) a million credits just to destroy any video recording HARV may have made. As tempting as the offer was, I turned it down. I did promise Twoa (and so did HARV) that the video would never see the glare of the world media. Just as long as Twoa didn't get too pushy. She agreed. Twoa realized that if she ever pushed me too hard I might end up suffering from amnesia. If that happened, the video might accidentally end up being broadcast worldwide over the P-Pod network. (True, it may have not been the ideal good guy thing to do, but this woman had tossed me around pretty good for the last five years. It felt nice to have some leverage for once.)

The good news was Twoa and Eleanor now both realized once again that Natasha was the one who had to be found and stopped. My hunch was, the finding wouldn't be that tough. Stopping her, though, that was an entirely different story, a story I wasn't sure I wanted to experience.

"Time to collect all our assets," I said. "We need to figure out the best way to go after and stop Natasha."

We quickly organized a meeting of minds. Electra, Carol, Twoa, Helena, Eleanor, Liz, Greg—in full clown bodyguard armor—JJ, Fera, and I were all crammed around a small table in a back cubicle of Randy's lab that he called a conference room. With Carol back to normal and Twoa back to what passed as normal, they could erase or minimize Natasha's influence over this group, making sure none of them hated me more than normal.

Randy didn't have enough chairs for everybody so JJ and Fera had to sit on robots. Randy was walking around the room, carrying a tray and serving drinks and cheese. (Of course, he also had a cleanbot following him around making sure nobody made a mess.)

"We need to find Natasha, sooner than sooner than possible," Twoa said, taking charge of the meeting.

"We?" I said.

"Yes, Zach, it is obvious you can't handle her alone, so next time we will be going with you," Twoa said.

"Well, not all of us," Helena said. "In my youth I would have gladly donned battle armor and butted heads with her. Today, though, my skills are better lent to other tasks. I will send one of my bodyguards, Liz Lazor."

Liz acknowledged her name with a bow.

"I'm also much better way in the background," Randy said, slicing a piece of cheese for Eleanor. "Though I will gladly offer Eleanor to the fight if she wishes to go."

"I do wish to kick the bitch's ass," Eleanor said. It sounded so classy because of her accent.

"I think I have a pretty good idea where Natasha is," I said. "Niagara Falls."

"Why there?" Helena asked.

"Just one of my PI hunches," I said.

Truthfully it was more than a hunch. Niagara Falls

was the next closest spot from the posters on Natasha's wall. She may have a lot of Carol's genes but Natasha was raised in a strict and ordered military way. It made sense that she would do her vacation in the most efficient way.

"So we have to go on one of your hunches?" Helena said. "I'm not comfortable with that."

HARV appeared, standing on the middle of the table. He cleared his throat. "I, not being big on hunches, have data to collaborate Zach's deduction." HARV's image morphed into one of a waterfall—a very big waterfall. The image was so real I had to fight the urge to go to the bathroom. Looking at the waterfall were hundreds if not thousands of tourists.

"This was Entercorp's Niagara Falls fifteen minutes ago," came HARV's voiceover.

The image of waterfall and onlookers sped up. Taking my eyes off the falls and watching the crowd, I saw what HARV wanted us to see. They were all leaving.

"This is how the falls look now," HARV said.

Same waterfalls, only there was nobody there. Yet the sun was shining, the sky was blue.

"Maybe it got really really cold," Twoa suggested.

"It's unseasonably warm," HARV told her. "Sixteen Celsius . . . ."

"Any sign of the bitch?" Carol asked.

"I assume you mean Natasha?" HARV said.

"Smart computer."

HARV's face superimposed itself onto the waterfall. The head shook no. "Nope."

"I'm not surprised she can shield herself from cameras and scanners," Twoa said. "She is a cunning one."

"She could be just trying to throw us off track," somebody, I think it was Fera, suggested.

I stood up just to make sure I was noticed. "She's there all right. I'm sure of it," I said sternly.

Everybody nodded in agreement. Well, almost everybody.

"You're sure you're sure?" Helena said.

"A hundred and ten percent sure!" I said, pounding my fist into the table for more effect.

"Zach, even you know there's no such thing as one hundred and ten percent," HARV whispered in my brain.

"Yeah, HARV's right. Sorry," GUS added.

"I know that, guys. Just trying to make a point," I thought.

"Oh," GUS said.

"There's never a good reason to use improper math," HARV lectured.

"The point is we have to get there and we have to stop her," I said.

"Trust him, Mother," Electra said. "Zach knows what he's talking about."

Helena looked across the table at Twoa. "Will Earth Force send reinforcements?"

"Not until we confirm it is her," Twoa said. "We can't spend money sending high paid special units off on wild superhuman chases."

Yep, you could tell Twoa had spent some time on the World Council.

"I understand," Helena said.

Yep, you could tell my future mother-in-law was planning a run at the Council.

"We should have enough firepower in this room to stop Natasha," Liz said.

Everybody in the room nodded in agreement. Everybody except for Carol and me. Carol and I had gone up against Natasha. We knew what she was capable of. Frankly, I wasn't sure if we could stop her if we had ten times the man- or womanpower.

"You have five minutes to collect your thoughts and any items you might need, then I'll teleport us there," Twoa said.

Randy meekly raised an arm. "Ah, remember, my talents are better utilized here," he said.

"I remember and I agree," Twoa said.

"I don't think JJ should go either," I said.

"What?" JJ shouted, leaping up from the robot he was sitting on.

"If we fail, we're going to need somebody else to rally the next round of troops," I said, looking JJ in the eyes. "I want that to be you."

JJ became a bit less rigid. "Oh, okay, that makes sense," he said.

I turned to Electra. "You shouldn't go either," I told her.

"*Mi amor,* I can handle myself with the best of them. I've proven myself on many occasions."

"True, but you're also the best doctor I know. We're bringing a lot of firepower down on Natasha. You're the only healer we've got."

Electra sat there thinking.

"When the man is right, he's right," Helena told her. "I didn't put you through medical school to have you going off on wild superhuman chases."

Electra nodded. "Very well."

"So it's agreed," Twoa said. "Ladies and Zach, we'll meet outside in three minutes."

The others got up and left. Only Electra and I held back. Electra took my hand, eyes open wide, she said, "Now, you are going to be careful. Correct, *amor?*"

"Like always," I said.

She just looked at me. "Zach, my mother is finally starting to learn to tolerate you. Don't go getting yourself killed."

I kissed her and left.

Chapter 32

After a few minutes of bathroom breaks and collecting our thoughts, we gathered outside of Randy's lab. It surely was an interesting crew. Carol, Liz Lazor, Fera, Eleanor, Twoa, and I were set for travel. Electra, Helena, Greg the clown, Randy, and JJ were there for moral support. Well, at least, Electra was there for support. Randy and JJ were mostly there to ogle the women. Helena was probably there to make sure I didn't screw things up too badly. In true politician form, she wanted to be in charge without ever doing anything.

Those of us that were making the trip to the falls gathered in a tight circle maybe six meters from the lab. Twoa stood inside the circle giving last minute instructions.

"Okay, when we get to the falls, our first goal is to confirm Natasha's presence. Once we are sure she's there, I call in backup and we take her out. Simple as pie." She paused for a nano, then added, "Any questions?"

I was the only one to raise my hand.

"Zach, don't embarrass me," HARV whispered in my brain.

"Yes, Zach?" Twoa asked.

"How do you call that simple?"

Twoa shrugged. "Okay, maybe not simple as eating pie, but simple as making pie." She paused for a moment. "Any other questions?"

I looked around. It didn't seem like anybody else was going to raise this question. So I popped my hand up again. I knew teleporting from teleporter pad to teleporter pad was reasonably safe. The thing was, here we were using a personal teleporter to teleport seven people from one place without a teleporter pad to another place without a teleport pad. That didn't seem easy.

"Yes, Zach?" Twoa said, anxious, but trying to maintain patience.

"I thought personal teleporting over long distances was still dangerous," I said.

"Zach, that's a statement not a question," Twoa said.

Liz, Fera, and Eleanor all nodded behind her in agreement. Apparently we were playing Jeopardy in more ways than one. I didn't mention that reference because it would have been lost on this crowd.

"How can we use your personal teleporter to teleport such large distances safely?" I asked.

"Just watch," Twoa said.

Twoa pushed a button on her wrist.

The next thing I knew, Carol, Eleanor, Fera, Liz, Twoa, and I were all standing on teleport pads. Looking around, it seemed that we were now all in a small spaceship.

Twoa saw the looks of confusion on our faces.

Fera scratched her head. "If this is Niagara Falls, then their promos have way overstated the place . . ."

"We are on my personal spacecraft which is constantly orbiting the Earth," Twoa told us.

Now we all just looked at her.

"It's one of the perks that come from being a billionaire, ex-superhero, ex-World Council member, current freedom fighter."

"Wow, nice work if you can get it," Eleanor whispered to Liz.

"Zach may be a bit of a coward and a chicken when it comes to teleporting, but he's right. You need a full blown teleport pad to port more than a few k."

I wasn't thrilled with being called a cowardly chicken, but it was nice to know I was right.

"So, you're going to teleport us to the falls from here?" I said.

"Yes." Twoa nodded. "My computer system and HARV are working together. They have tapped into security cameras at the falls so they cannot only get us near to where HARV believes Natasha is, but also assure that we materialize in open space."

Everybody nodded that that was a good thing.

"Why couldn't you just say that while we were on the ground?" I asked.

"Why, Zach, I'm both a woman and a high-ranking Earth Force official. Surely I get to keep some secrets."

"Surely," I said.

"All right, team, look alive," Twoa ordered. "We're transporting . . . now!"

First thing I felt was my feet back on solid ground. Nice, soft, green, solid ground. I saw grass and wide open spaces in front of me. Looking up, I saw clear blue sky. There were birds singing in the background, though you could only just make them out over the crashing sound of running waters. Lots of running water. We were at the falls.

Turning toward the sound of the water, I could see the falls. I hadn't been here in years, but the massive constant cascade of the crystal clear falling wall of water was still an impressive sight. As much progress as man has made, we still can't build anything near as awe-inspiring as this.

Looking over the area once more, it was devoid of

any humans besides my team and me. It was a beautiful day, clear blue sky with the sun shining high and bright. There may have been a slight nip in the air, but this was Niagara Falls in December. There was supposed to be a nip in the air.

"Any sign of Natasha?" Twoa asked anxiously. Apparently she wasn't into sightseeing.

The rest of the team shook their heads no. I pointed toward the falls. "I'm guessing she's hovering over the water," I said.

Carol nodded in agreement. "That does sound like fun."

Twoa pointed forward. "Move it, troops," she ordered.

"Somebody has been watching way too many old war flicks," HARV smirked.

"I heard that, soldier," Twoa said.

"I'm a cognitive information processor, not a soldier," HARV corrected.

"Whatever you are, be prepared!" Twoa ordered.

Walking toward the falls, the others were at least trying to take in the scenery. I moved alongside Carol.

"Nice place, huh?"

Carol nodded. "It is lovely and so peaceful. We have to come back here sometime when we're not hunting a power-mad, evil superwoman."

Hard to believe the number of times I've heard that statement in my life.

We reached the railing overlooking the falls. We all peered over it. No Natasha. At least, at first. Then Twoa pointed a bit down from the main area of the falls. There she was, hovering peacefully over the water.

"There!" Twoa said loudly. "That must be her!"

HARV zoomed in so I could see her more clearly. But he didn't need to. I knew it was Natasha. It had to be. "Let's hope it's not some other ultra-powered superwoman," I said.

Moving quickly toward Natasha, Twoa said, "Don't worry, I've used my super-vision to confirm it is her. Let's get in position."

We hurried down until we were nearly parallel to Natasha's position. She didn't seem to notice us or care that we were here.

"Let's take her out now, while she's doing her meditating crap," Fera said.

Twoa held up one finger. "Hold on. I've called for reinforcements."

Twoa pointed behind us. We all turned. One ANABEL android/cyborg appeared. Then another, and another and another appeared, until there were eleven of them.

"I thought there were at least twelve ANABELs," I said.

"There are," Twoa told me. "We're holding one back just in case."

The ANABELs marched up to us in formation. They reached Twoa. All saluting at once, the lead one said, "ANABELs reporting for duty, ma'am!"

Twoa had a wide smile on her face as she returned the salute. She spun toward Natasha and pointed at her dramatically. "That is our target! Hit her hard and fast."

Waving my hands in front of the anxious mob, I shouted, "Hold on! Hold on!"

They all looked at me.

"Yes, Zach, what are you worried about now?" Twoa asked. Looking over her shoulder to the ANABELs, she mumbled, "Zach likes to worry."

"I don't like to worry," I told them. "It just comes with the job." Holding my hands up flat in the "slow down" position, I continued, "I just don't think we should be too anxious to piss Natasha off."

"I only wish to be left alone," Natasha said in my mind.

I looked at the others. "Did you all hear that too?"

"Yes," they all said.

"Maybe we should try talking to her?" I suggested, though Twoa seemed set for battle, so chances were grand that she wouldn't listen.

"Zach has a point," Twoa said.

"I do?"

"Yes. She probably has a mental force field around herself, so we need to have a plan. Zach, you distract her with conversation. You're good at distracting people. It's your one true talent. Then when she is distracted all psis attack her mentally. All ANABELs and people or near-people with energy weapons hit her with those. Long range attacks are best!"

"I don't think any attacks are best," I said.

Twoa patted me on the head. "Oh, Zach, you can't be right all the time."

"I wouldn't make me angry. You won't like me when I'm angry!" Natasha broadcast to our brains. I was impressed by her reference to the ancient TV show. I doubt the others were. It was interesting that Natasha would use a quote from a character originally created for comic books. She certainly had her strong geek tendencies. I found that one of her more interesting features.

Twoa pointed at Natasha. "Aim!"

I drew GUS and pointed him at Natasha. I had lots of reservations about opening fire. For one thing, she wasn't doing any harm. For another, I didn't think it would do any good. For another, I didn't want to make her mad. No good could come from that.

But Twoa had her mind made up that this was the only way. I had to pray that this was one of those rare times when the violence first approach worked. Too bad I wasn't a religious man.

"Fire! Think!" Twoa ordered.

The ANABELs fired away. I only assumed the psis were thinking away. I withheld my fire. It wasn't going to make much difference one way or another. If it looked like it would make a difference, I'd chip in.

Natasha was still just hovering over the water, peacefully. The energy attacks just bounced harmlessly off what I assume was her mental shield. The mental attacks may have been doing something, but if they were I couldn't tell.

"Keep hitting her, team!" Twoa shouted. "We're bound to break through!"

"NO!" Natasha cried out in all our brains.

That's the last thing I remembered . . .

Chapter 33

"Zach, Zach, get up!" I heard faintly inside my head.

I just lay there on the ground, eyes closed. It felt like a dump truck had hit me, then rolled over me a couple of times, then dropped its load on me.

"Ah, how long was I out for?" I mumbled.

"Less than a minute," HARV said.

"Ah, I feel dead," I said.

"Well, you were," HARV answered.

"What?"

"Zach, you weren't sleeping. Well, sleeping with the fishes maybe, but not sleeping in the traditional sense."

"So, she killed me," I said, forcing my eyes to open.

"Yes. Luckily I was able to restart your brain and use GUS to shock you."

"Why'd she kill me? I didn't even fire . . ."

"It wasn't just you, Zach, she killed everybody . . . I don't think she did it on purpose."

"What?" My eyes shot open as I sat up quickly.

Looking around my team and the ANABELs were strewn across the ground, lying there lifeless. All the grass in the area was dead. No birds singing. No signs of life at all. So this is what happens when Natasha actually gets mad . . .

"Damn, damn, damn," I said pushing myself up. No time to ponder what my death meant and what it didn't mean. I had to bring back the others.

"The Earth Force med vac ship is still two minutes away, Zach," HARV told me.

I needed an idea and I needed it two minutes ago. Well, if HARV could use GUS to revive me, I should be able to revive everybody else with GUS.

I lifted GUS up into the air.

"HARV and GUS, I need you guys to work this out. Fire balls of electricity into Carol, Eleanor, Liz, Fera, and Twoa. We need to at least get their hearts pumping. Then we'll worry about the ANA-BELs."

HARV appeared before me. "I understand," he said solemnly.

I squeezed the trigger. Five bolts of electricity flew from my gun. One each into Carol, Liz, Eleanor, Fera, and Twoa. Each of the bodies jerked up and down.

I quickly moved to Carol. I bent over to check her carotid pulse. It was there.

"They are all showing signs of life," HARV told me.

"Okay, now for the androids," I said.

Lifting GUS into the air, I fired again. This time eleven bolts of electricity went streaking into the air. Each hit one of the androids. There was no reaction.

HARV looked at me, looked at them. "Apparently not only was Earth Force wrong about being psi proof, but whatever they thought made them psi proof makes them harder to revive."

A giant shadow appeared over us. Looking up, I saw the bottom side of a huge Earth Force air cruiser.

General Wall's voice came booming over the PA system. "Prepare to be evacuated . . ."

A large door opened on the bottom of the ship. Rescue pods started falling to the ground.

Well, they weren't here in time to stop Natasha. Probably better they weren't. They all would have been dead, too. At least they'd be able to save the ladies.

Chapter 34

Medbots, battlebots, and human soldiers in full battle armor rolled out of the pods that fell to the ground. The battlebots and soldiers took up positions along the perimeter. The medbot teams rolled to their patients, one team of bots on each of the fallen ladies. As I watched with great anticipation, General Wall strode up to me, assessing the situation.

Wall shook her head. "Too bad my rapid emergency squad and I couldn't get here quicker from Earth Orbit Base-I."

"Yeah, well, lucky you guys aren't any more rapid or you all would be dead now, too," I said.

The general could tell from the sound of my voice, which I wasn't trying to mask at all, that I wasn't happy with their response time. "We got here as fast as we could. The base is ultra-secure; the only way up or down is by space elevator. Then to move this much firepower we needed a big high speed transport. It's impressive we responded as quickly as we did."

I pointed out the fallen ladies and all the dead fauna in the area. "Yes, impressive."

"We were monitoring the situation over the sat feed. That was too impressive," the general said.

"Was impressive on your word of the day calendar today, General? Yes, it is quite impressive that Natasha could so easily kill such a powerful group."

The general glared at me. "Yes, that was impress—remarkable, but I was talking about your performance."

Now I knew the general had lost it. "General, all I did was die, too."

"Yes, but not many people can spring back to life on their own."

Okay, she had me on that one. The general was sharper than I gave her credit for. She knew something was going on with my resurrection. I wasn't sure how much General Wall knew about HARV. Obviously now the World Council knows that he is connected to me. I assume therefore that some higher-up generals know too. This may have been another of those matters that were above General Wall's pay grade. Therefore I made up a story. Making up stories is something else I'm good at. When you're a PI, being able to bluff or tell a good (false) anecdote is almost as important as being able to tell when someone is bluffing or telling you a tall tale. That's why I always wrote off my poker losses as business training.

"My body armor has a built-in fibrillation unit," I told her. "When you are me, that's kind of standard equipment."

The general summed me up with her eyes. "Yes, I've read your record. I can see where that would be true." Apparently she bought my story. "The interesting thing is, you disappeared from the sat feed after the initial death strike."

"I went into auto stealth mode," HARV whispered in my brain.

"Another one of my armor's little tricks," I said. "Auto-stealth mode while I am—rebooting . . ."

"Impressive—I mean ingenious," the general said. "It was also fast thinking on your part to use your weapon to revive the ladies." The general put her hand to her headpiece and smiled. "They are all going to live. My med teams say your fast actions are what saved them."

"Just doing my job, General."

"Actually, your job was to find Natasha," she said. "And you have done that three times. It's my team that hasn't been doing its job. I'm ashamed at how easily she turned us all against you. Now you see how grave of a danger Natasha represents. You, Zach, must use all of your resources to help us bring her in before she can kill again."

It was just then I realized that apparently I wasn't public enemy number one any longer. Sure, I was a little slow to come around, but I had been dead. All I could guess was that after Natasha killed me, she figured there was no use making everybody want to kill me since I was already dead. Either that or she knew I was no threat at all. Or quite simply with me being dead the world no longer had me to hate. Whatever. I would take that fact that the government wasn't hunting me down any longer as one good event in a day of really terrible events.

"So you and your men have no urge to arrest or shoot me?" I asked General Wall.

She shook her head no. "No. Not really sure what came over us," she said.

"Oh come on, General, you must realize that Natasha zapped all your minds."

The general looked at me. I swore I detected the slight crack of a smile. "Now that would truly be an impressive feat if she could do that."

"No ifs about it," I told her. "And what you call impressive I call scary."

General Wall looked me square in the eyes. She pondered her words. Before she could say anything though, we both noticed two balls of energy appear a few meters from our position.

"Oh, shit . . ." the general said.

I had the feeling my terrible day was going to get even worse.

Chapter 35

The two balls of energy took shape. They were as the general and I had suspected, Twoa's sisters: Ona and Threa Thompson. Both of them looked more worried than I had ever seen them. (And I have seen them both facing the world being annihilated by a brown hole.)

Ona stormed up to the general and me while Threa headed over to the medbots tending the fallen.

"General, how could you have let this happen?" Ona asked sternly.

The general showed surprising backbone standing toe-to-toe with Ona. (Not head-to-head since Ona was a good head higher.) "I did not LET anything happen, Madam Council Woman Ona." She drew a breath to strengthen her nerves and steady her next words. "The subject is just far more powerful than any of you surmised." Looking Ona as square in the eye as she could, she repeated, "ANY OF YOU . . ."

Ona showed more restraint than I thought she was capable of by not squishing the general right there on the spot. She finally seemed to notice, or got around to acknowledging, me. "Oh. Hi, Zach. Just once I wish we could meet when the world isn't in grave danger, but I guess my lot in life is to bear the responsibility that comes with great power."

I've dealt with superwomen and politicians enough to know the best course of action when it comes to handling them is to compliment and agree with them. Giving Ona a comforting pat on the shoulder, I said, "Yes, it must be terrible being a billionaire superbabe World Council member."

"I knew you'd understand," she told me.

Threa came running over to us. "Good news," she said. "The med teams say everybody should completely recover. They are stable and ready to be evacuated to our facility in New Frisco."

"Yes, that is good news," Ona said.

Threa noticed I was there. Giving me a little wave, she said, "Hi, Zach, thanks for saving Twoa."

"Just doing my job," I said.

Ona put her arm around the general. "Speaking of doing their job, General, we need to talk . . ."

Chapter 36

Ona and Threa were nice enough to let me tag along back to New Frisco in the medical transport ship they had arranged. I was glad they understood the importance of me sticking with Carol (and the others) for the trip back. I was lucky that they both remembered how I hate teleporting.

The med ship was a flying full-service hospital. All the previously dead ladies were in med recoup beds in a long medical dormitory. Each of them had one medical doctor and two medbots at their side, except for Twoa, who had twice as much staff on her. Plus, Threa was constantly at her side.

Ona, though, was suspiciously missing and so was General Wall. Since the docs and the bots assured me Carol was stable, I walked over to see Threa.

"Zach, how nice of you to come and check on Twoa," Threa told me.

"How's she doing?" I asked.

"She is strong. She will be back to pounding people in no time," Threa told me.

"That's good," I said, looking around, though I knew I wouldn't see who I was looking for. "Where's Ona?" I asked.

Threa hesitated. She wanted to choose her words carefully here. "She's about to chew General Wall's and General Chen's asses off," Threa said.

Okay, maybe she wasn't going to be that careful with her words.

"Oh?" I prompted. "You World Council folks aren't happy with the military's approach to Natasha?"

"I've said too much already," Threa said, putting a finger to her mouth.

She knew she shouldn't tell me, but she still wanted to tell me.

"Come on, Threa. I've been to your realm. We fought side by side."

"The Council deemed the project too dangerous five years ago. The members ordered them to scrap the project, but they continued it in secret, secret even from us."

"Bad military," I said.

"The accountants probably should have caught it," Threa said. "But somehow they didn't notice when the Area 51b spent over a billion credits on staples."

Before Threa could utter another word, Ona stormed into the room. And when I say stormed, I mean it. She actually had a brown cloud over her that was generating mini-lightning bolts.

"I can always tell when Ona is in a bad mood," Threa said.

"Yeah, you have a keen sense of people," I said, "True."

"Threa, no need to tell Zach much more about our little mistake. He knows the pertinent facts. Natasha is out and must be stopped at all costs."

I didn't like the sound of that. Natasha may have been the deadliest being in the world, but she hadn't asked to be made that way. It wasn't her fault that when she got angry people died. *That* was the government's fault.

I found it hard to believe that I was defending Na-

tasha, especially since she had just, well, killed me.
The powers that be may have made her, but I didn't
think they had the right to kill her. Funny thing was,
even though she did kill me and everybody else
around, I got the feeling Natasha had taken it easy on
us. She'd been in my mind, so she could figure out
HARV and GUS would resct mc and I'd savc thc
others. All Natasha wanted was to be able to live her
life. My brain was telling my gut that she might have
killed us just a little to prevent us from making her
so angry that she killed us beyond medical repair.

Ona and Threa must have seen the look of determination on my face.

"I think he is worried," Threa said.

"Are you sure it's not just gas?" Ona asked.

"It's not gas," I said.

Ona walked forward and patted me on the head,
making it clear that she was the one in charge. "Oh,
silly Zach, when we said stopped at all costs, we
weren't talking about killing her."

Taking a step back, I said, "You weren't?"

Ona shook her head and smiled at me like I was
daft kid. "Of course not. She is only to be frozen until
we find a way to cut down on her power, bring her
under control."

Threa took a step forward. "Yes. We appreciate the
rights of superhuman women more than most people.
We didn't want Natasha harmed."

"Okay," I said cautiously.

"Unfortunately, Major Wall and one-star General
Chen disagreed. They thought we needed her to com-
bat the growing threat of people like her."

"Wasn't it General Wall and five-diamond General
Chen?" I asked.

"Think about it," HARV said in my head.

*"Believe it or not, I caught it, HARV. I just need to
see the Thompsons' reaction."*

"Zach," Ona told me, "they are lucky they have
only been demoted. If I had my way, I would have

Threa turn them into chickens, but we understand that may be bad for morale and for our image."

"They are just fortunate Ona and I weren't on the Council when the initial orders were given or else I would get nasty with them."

"The thing is, Zach, the genie is out of the bottle . . ."

". . . and now I have to get her to go back in," I finished.

Ona looked at me. "You?"

"Ona, I know this sounds crazy but I think I can talk Natasha into giving herself up. Letting herself be frozen. We have a sort of a bond."

"Uh, Zach, she killed you," Ona said.

"And apparently made everybody hate you," Threa said.

"Yeah, I'd hate to see how she treated you if she didn't like you," HARV said. He was so not helping.

"I think she did all those things to test me. To make me stronger. Like they say, whatever doesn't kill you and then keep you dead makes you stronger."

"I don't think that's quite right," HARV said.

Ona and Threa nodded in agreement.

"The point is I'm not dead now. I came back. She knew HARV would revive me."

"It's not a very good point," Ona said.

"I agree," Threa said.

"I don't think you can safely conclude that," HARV said. He turned to Ona and Threa. "I'm constantly amazed he's not killed more often."

I actually couldn't blame them for thinking like they were. DOS, I saw no reason to think like I was thinking. Still, my mind was made up, I wasn't giving up.

"I can find her and stuff the genie back in the bottle," I insisted.

"We're kind of killing that phrase," HARV said.

The two superwomen just looked at me. They smiled.

"He certainly is persistent," Ona said to Threa.

"Like a bad rash," Threa said.

"Okay, Zach, you can stay on the case," Ona told me.

"Now that's what I call a rash decision," HARV said.

I shuddered. Yep, HARV was spending too much time in my mind.

"Of course, if you can't convince her to turn herself in and submit to being frozen, then we will have to take matters into our own hands," Ona said. "You have forty-eight hours to find her."

Chapter 37

When we arrived in Frisco, the medical staff escorted the wounded down to the special military hospital, and I escorted them. I was glad to see Electra and Randy in the hospital, waiting for us. Even the government was smart enough to recognize the value of those two being here. Electra and Randy were moving from patient to patient, making sure they were all okay. Once satisfied, Electra came over to me.

"How are you feeling?" she asked.

"I've been worse," I told her.

"They told me you were dead," she said.

"I got better," I shrugged.

We kissed.

"You got better?" Electra asked.

"HARV saved me," I said without thinking. For the first time it occurred to me that HARV had saved my life. He was being surprisingly discreet about it.

HARV appeared projecting himself from the room's holo-projector. "Just doing my job," he said. "If I wasn't built into your brain I am sure Randy would have really have had some sort of back up defibrillator attached to your armor." Looking down he said, "Of course you could have said thanks . . ."

Yep, HARV was becoming more human.

"Thanks," I said, patting him on his projected shoulder.

"I couldn't have you dying. As strange as you may be I have a feeling my life wouldn't be as challenging if I was attached to any other human's brain. I'm a cognitive processor. I live for the challenges."

"Glad to know I keep it exciting for you and that you always have my back."

"I have more than your back," HARV said. "I have your front, top, bottom, sides, and all your internal and external organs covered."

Of course while become more human he still had a way to go.

Getting back to the matters at hand I pointed at the super ladies laying prone in their medical beds. I asked, "Are they all going to be okay?"

"Yes, thanks to you, HARV, and the others. In a few days, they will all be up and around."

I felt better about that. Now it was time to focus on finding Natasha again.

Electra must have seen the look of determination on my face. "So, you're not giving up on this case yet?"

"No, can't do it."

"You have to die twice before you quit a case?" she asked.

"Three times. Four max."

"Ha-ha," Electra said. She looked at me then lowered her eyes. "Zach, I'm serious. You died and in the medical field we always consider that to be a bad outcome. Obviously there are some deaths we can't prevent and just need to accept, but you running off to battle some megabitch isn't one of them."

I took Electra's hand, gently caressing it in my own. I lifted her hand to chest and placed it over my heart.

"See? Still beating," I told her.

Maybe I should have been more concerned with death, however brief it may have been. The fact that it came and I lived through some how made me more determined than ever I had to find and stop Natasha. The fact that she had killed me was just one of the ever-growing list of things in my life that it was better not to think too much about. A wise man knows what to think about and what to ignore. Of course Electra was going to need more than that.

"Look, the fact that she killed me and I didn't stay dead should make you feel more secure," I told Electra.

"If nothing else this is going to be interesting," she replied.

"Whatever the reason, my love, be it sheer dumb luck, a stubborn constitution, or being equipped with all the best science has to offer I think I've proven I'm harder to kill than most."

"I believe it's mostly because of the first and third factors," HARV said. "Mainly the third but luck somehow plays a role."

Ignoring HARV I continued. "Whatever the reasons I am the one most suited for the job of stopping Natasha. If I don't do it soon I just know things are going to get way worse way fast for everybody," I told Electra.

Electra tilted her head up at me, "What's the next step, then?"

"Not sure yet."

"So, business as usual," Electra said.

"Story of my life," HARV said.

General, well, Major Wall walked into the room. She stormed up to me and saluted. I found it strange, but I kind of dug it.

"I understand you are in command of this operation for now," the major told me, albeit begrudgingly.

"Uh, that's news to me," I told her.

"Zach is easily confused," HARV said.

"I am," I admitted. "At least when it comes to the ways of Earth Force and the World Council."

Wall looked down at the floor, apparently making

sure the maidbots were keeping the floors spic and span. "I don't blame you. Damn World Council sticking their noses and asses in business they know nothing about."

Okay, sure, Wall was a bitter employee now, having just been dropped a couple pay grades, but being bitter doesn't mean you can't be right.

"Ona and Threa are just trying to do what's best for the world," I said, surprised those words of defense came out of my mouth.

"I'm doing the same thing, keeping the world ordered and therefore safe," Wall said.

"Keeping the world safe from whom?" I asked. "After all, we're all the same world now. The other planets leave us alone. They share technology with us, and all they ask in return is that we give them our dirt and chocolate chip cookies."

"I'm keeping the world safe from them," the general said with venom dripping off her words.

"Them?"

"The people who don't agree with us," Wall said.

"Us?" I asked.

"The people we agree with. The ones who want what is best," Wall said.

"In other words, people who think like you."

"It's not that simple," the major said. "My job is to maintain order and I believe the best way to maintain order is to follow orders." She thought about what she said. A slight smile crossed her lips. "Maybe it is that simple."

"Sounds more like a credo than a job," I noted.

"Semantics," Wall said. "When the spam hits the fan it is my job to maintain that order at all costs."

"That's nice to know," I said.

"Is it?" HARV said.

"Sounds kind of scary to me!" GUS added.

Scary as it may have been that statement told me a lot. You can't take the general out of the soldier no matter what her current rank is. Wall was the type of person who would do *whatever* she needed to get the job done.

"I've got a question for you, Major," I said.

She looked at me, hands behind her back in at ease position. "Yes?"

"Why'd you put the kid on the job?" I asked.

There was silence followed by a wee smile. "He was always bugging me for something to do. I figured this would keep him busy and he might actually be helpful."

"Surely you knew Natasha would be too much for him," I told her.

The major went into her spiel. "Yes, but he works cheap. I was betting he wouldn't be able to track her down on his own, but that he would go after you. He's young and hotheaded. He'd want the bonus I promised for himself. I leaked the fact that you were also on the case. I knew he couldn't take you but you being the sucker you are would probably take him on. That is what happened. Isn't it?"

"I'm impressed, Major," I told her.

"I do my homework before I make my plans," she said. "I knew he'd turn into a useful aide for you. Giving you another tool to help you track down Natasha."

"See," HARV told me. "Planning is good."

"So, what's YOUR plan, Johnson?" Major Wall asked.

"Is that the question of the day?"

"How do you plan on finding and stopping Natasha?" the major pushed.

I could give her a nice vague answer. I could tell her to back off, she's only a major now, this was none of her concern. That would really cheese her off.

"Zach, remember it's never good, well, hardly ever good to kick a person when she is down, especially a heavily armed person," HARV reminded me.

HARV was right. If this was going to work out we were all going to have cooperate and work together.

She had told the truth about JJ. Hopefully he would turn out to be an asset. The major deserved the truth from me. Taking a step back and relaxing my posture, I told her, "Frankly, I don't know yet."

A faint trace of a smile cracked the major's stony facade. I wasn't sure if she was laughing at me or just happy I had told her the truth.

"You are totally baffled and have no plan of attack," she said.

"Totally baffled is a bit strong," I said, "but yes."

The major gave me a pat on the shoulder. "Thank you for being honest with me," she said. She turned and walked away mumbling, "We're doomed . . ."

HARV appeared next to me. "She is quite perceptive for a military person."

"Shut up, HARV!"

Yes, the major and HARV may have been right, but now wasn't the time for negative thinking. This was the time for creative thinking. I needed to figure out where Natasha was going and fast. There was only one course of action to take. I went home to take a nap.

Chapter 38

HARV, of course, chastised me about wasting hours sleeping when I only had forty-seven of them left to track down Natasha. I assured him he shouldn't worry. I would only rest for a couple of hours to let my mind regroup.

I got home, tossed my hat toward the coat rack (and missed). Heading toward my bedroom, I dropped my trench coat to the ground. What good were having maidbots if I didn't give them a little work? I didn't have much time and I wanted to optimize it.

Reaching the bedroom, I plopped down on the bed. I didn't have the time or the energy to take my clothing off. I was exhausted. I would have said I felt dead but now I knew what dead feels like and it didn't feel the same. Death may get a bad rap, but at least there's no stress.

"How long do you wish to sleep for?" HARV asked.

"I'm not going to sleep, just close my eyes and think."

"How long do you wish to sleep for?" HARV repeated.

"Three hours—no, four," I said.

"That will only give you forty-two hours to track Natasha down," HARV told me, looking at his watch.

"Nice to know my computer can do math," I said, closing my eyes.

My main thought was that the first time I saw Natasha I was sleeping. Maybe I could find her that way again? Or maybe she would find me? Whatever, it worked once, sort of. And I was desperate. I wasn't sure if Natasha and I really did have some kind of bond, but I thought we did. Of course, even if I was right, that still didn't mean the bond would be strong enough to give me a clue to her whereabouts.

Thinking of the bond reminded me of something.

"HARV, is Randy still at the hospital?"

"He's having his car drive him home now," HARV told me.

"Great. Patch me through to him."

"Zach, I thought you were going to sleep."

"HARV, I thought I was the one in charge here."

"You thought incorrectly."

"Just connect me with Randy, HARV!"

"Coming up."

Randy's holographic image appeared in the middle of the room. He was in the backseat of his car, reclining. He opened his eyes, "Oh, hi, Zach. Not every day a person dies and comes back to life."

"Randy, when I left we had some unfinished business."

Randy looked down. "You're talking about the P-Pod and HARV connection."

"Yes."

Randy thought carefully about his choice of words. "Zach, HARV was, in a sense, the precursor to the P-Pods. I learned a lot from him. The most important thing I learned was most people don't want or need a computer that is smarter than they are wired to their brain. People just want access to entertainment and information without either they or their computer thinking too much about it. Hence, the P-Pods were born. All the information without all the headache."

HARV turned to me and asked, "I give you headaches?"

"Not just headaches," I told him.

"Not to mention that with the P-Pods there is no searing pain from boring into the brain. The marketing consultants I hired told me that would make it a tough sell, no matter what the price."

"So, can you use the P-Pods to program people?" I asked.

Silence. Then more silence.

"Well?"

"It depends on how you define 'program,' " Randy said. "It is quite possible for advertisers to send specialized subliminal messages into people's brains via the link."

Randy stopped to see how I would react. Now I was the one to let silence and a grimace do my talking.

"Really, Zach, trust me, this is a good thing. We just help people know what they want. It saves them time and stuff."

I stayed silent for a few more nanos just to convey my feelings.

"Wanting what they can get is a win for everybody," Randy insisted.

"You know, after this is all over, I'm going to have to go to the press about this," I told Randy. "Let public opinion be the judge."

"I won't stop you," he said. "You, of course, realize, though, if people poke around enough HARV may become very public knowledge too."

If anybody else had said it I would have taken that as a threat. In Randy's case, I think he meant it as a statement of fact. He was probably right, the world would find about HARV. After all these years of keeping him secretly locked in my brain, coming clean might be best for all of us.

I could be fairly certain the World Council already

knew about HARV. There were obviously higher-ups
in the military who had funded Randy's initial research who were aware of HARV's and my connection. In fact the club "we know HARV and Zach are
connected" was growing with every case I had. So sure
it would annoying if the press started poking around.
Sure I might lose some of the element of surprise if
people knew HARV and I were connected and augmenting each other. Thing is, I could deal with it if I
had to.

"So be it," I said. "Let the chips fall where they
may."

"Anything else?" Randy asked.

"Not for now," I told him.

"Then I think we both better get some rest."

Randy's image faded away.

I closed my eyes. I figured I needed to get some
sleep. I had died today, yet something told me tomorrow was going to be even tougher.

Of course I couldn't sleep, at least not soundly. My
mind was filled with images, images of people. There
they were, wall to wall people of all shapes and sizes.
Big people, little people, medium sized people, slim
people, fat people, sexy people, people whose own
moms probably didn't find them attractive. People of
all races and colors. People dressed as cowboys, space-
men, workers, strippers (I kind of liked those), doc-
tors, nurses, sexy nurses (this was my subconscious
after all), businesspeople, soldiers, salesmen—the
works. People of all ages from crawling babies to tod-
dlers, from tweens to teens, from young adults to the
middle aged, from seniors to centenarians to the way
way old.

Concentrating my search through the myriad people, I tried to spot Natasha. The faces of each of the
people before me came into focus, some very familiar:
Electra, Carol, Randy, Captain Rickey, Ona, Twoa,
Threa. Some mildly familiar: that officer who tried to
rough me up, that other officer who tried to rough me

up, various thugs who tried to do worse than rough me up, my date for the junior prom, my date for the junior prom's angry dad. Some faces I would have preferred to forget but couldn't, many those of people who have tried to kill me, a couple of ex-girlfriends, and a tax collector or two. It seems my mind was going through a replay of every single person I had ever known. There was my mom, sitting at her desk. There was my dad, standing by a canvas, painting away. There was my first grade teacher explaining to every kid in my class the proper protocol for addressing her was not, "hey you, lady, like Zach said." My aunts, my uncles, my nieces, my nephews. If I knew you, you were there. DOS, if I didn't know you but had seen you, you were there.

My mind was stuffed with everybody and anybody I had ever seen, except for one very blaring absence. There was no Natasha. I tried focusing more on the crowd. She had to be there. She had been popping into and out of my dreams for the last couple of days. Now was no time for her to get shy. All the variety of body shapes and faces suddenly became the same generic body and face. Wave after wave of the same exact person who was kind of an amalgam of all the other people I had known. No clear features, nothing distinguishing. They were all the same. Then one face became clear through the masses. It was a very familiar face—it was me. Just then I caught a glimpse of another face. She was trying to blend in with others, ducking behind one of them. But I knew who it was. It was Natasha.

"Zach, your sleep time is up!" HARV said.

Opening my eyes, I sat up in bed. "Oh, DOS!" I said.

"I see you were dreaming," HARV said, appearing next to me.

"I might have had her if you'd let me sleep a few minutes more," I said, rubbing my eyes.

"By dreaming?" HARV said. "Zach, even you know you can't solve a case by dreaming."

I sat up in bed. "HARV, even you know that this isn't your ordinary case."

A maidbot rolled into the room with a cup of coffee on a tray. A clawlike hand extended from the maidbot's body, grabbing the cup. The arm extended upward to me. I took the coffee. Taking a sip I said, "Thanks, I needed that."

HARV shooed the bot away. "You've done your job, now get out so I can do mine."

The bot rolled out of the room. I was kind of surprised it didn't flip HARV off.

"You had a call from Threa while you were asleep," HARV told me.

"Lovely . . ."

"She said she thinks she has a way to stop Natasha once you find her. She didn't say what it was. I asked, but she said I wouldn't understand because I was just a machine."

"I wouldn't take it personally," I told HARV as I stood up and stretched.

"You wouldn't, but I would," HARV said. "Imagine her thinking you could understand something that I couldn't."

"Can you connect me to her?" I asked.

HARV shook his head, "Gladly, no. Her realm is out of contact range. She can call us but we can't call her."

"That's not very useful," I said.

"I also took the liberty of telling Comic-Con you won't be there," HARV said. "I figure saving the world takes precedence over addressing groups of geeks."

That's when it hit me. "HARV, can I still get into Comic-Con?"

HARV looked at me, eyes open wide. "Zach, this is no time for you to get caught up by the small fan base you have . . . I am sure I can find a way to get you in. But why?"

"Don't you get it, HARV?" I said.

"I get almost everything but not what you are getting at," HARV said.

"Natasha is a high-powered superhuman just looking to fit in and be accepted," I said.

"So?"

"Where do you find the most accepting people in world? Especially when dealing with superbeings?" I asked.

HARV processed for a nano or three.

"Comic-Con," he said.

I touched my finger to my nose, "Vingo." It made perfect sense. The Supergirl poster and comics in her room. The quote from the old *Hulk* 2-D show. She not only was an actual superbeing but more importantly she was a fan. She had to be there.

Chapter 39

It was now clear as day. Natasha was either at or heading to ComicCon. That meant that's where I was going. The question was, did I alert Ona and Threa? I decided to hold off on telling them. After all, with their personal teleporters they could be there in minutes if I determined Natasha actually was there. This way I saved them from going on a super wild-goose chase on the off chance that I was wrong.

I rolled out of bed and stretched. I would have loved to drive to San Diego but speed was of the essence here. As much as I hated it, I had to port there.

"HARV, book me a port reservation for San Diego, pronto," I said.

HARV shook his head. "Sorry, Zach, all ports into New San Diego are overbooked solid for the next four days."

"Well, that's not . . ." I started to stay.

". . . good," I finished saying, only now I was somewhere else.

I was standing on a single person port pad. Looking

around, I saw space all around me. Turning to the right, there were three short, silver-skinned, humanoid creatures with big foreheads and eyes to match, no noses, and small mouths. They all had albino white complexions. They were Gladians. I just wasn't sure which of the Gladian planets they were from.

I hopped off the port. I have dealt with the Gladians a couple of times in the past. Most humans have never even met an actual Gladian. I didn't know if that meant I was lucky or cursed.

"To what do I owe this pleasure?" I asked.

"Zachary Nixon Johnson, we need your help," the three of them said without moving their lips.

"Yeah, I assumed this wasn't a social chat." Walking over near one of the transparent walls, I peered out. There was Earth in all its glory.

"How far up are we?"

"Just a thousand miles or so," the Gladians said. "We are cloaked, but your government knows we are here, observing."

"Observing what?"

"Observing who," they corrected.

"Observing who?" I asked.

"Observing whom," HARV corrected.

"What the DOS are you doing here?" I said.

From the way their eyes widened even more, I saw the aliens were surprised by my reaction.

"Why, Zachary Nixon Johnson," they said, "You should know we are interested in the one called Carol Gevada. She has acted as our liaison in the past."

I nodded. "Yeah, I remember the incident quite clearly. It's hard to forget Carol being redhead and radioactive. So, you are upset she's in the hospital. Don't worry, I assure you I've been assured that she is fine."

The three of them shook their heads no in unison. "While we of course as passionate creatures care

about the one called Carol Gevada, we are fascinated
by the possibilities presented by altering her DNA and
creating the one called Natasha."

"Fascinated in a good way or a bad way?" I asked.

"Time will tell," the Gladian in the middle answered.

"They do say time heals all wounds," I said. A bit
non sequitur, but with aliens it helps to be a bit obtuse. Turning away and looking out the wall again, I
asked, "So, why bring me here?"

"We figure you are a friend of the Gladians. You
have worked with us in the past."

"I'm friends with lots of people and aliens and
bots," I said. "Come on, guys."

"I am a female," the one in the middle said.

"Come on, guys and female," I corrected.

"We are females, too," the other two said in my
brain.

"Come on, gals," I said. "There is more to it than
this."

"We think this Natasha may be dangerous," the
middle Gladian said.

"Yeah, I've been here done that with you guys before, with Foraa Thompson. She was a threat to all
that was and I had to stop her at all costs. If I recall
correctly, and I know I do, you threatened and tried
to crash a spaceship into Earth when you didn't think
I could stop her."

They shrugged. "Bygones will be bygones," the
middle one said. She raised both of her hands to show
me she had three fingers and a thumb on each hand.
"Besides, those were our brothers from Glad-7. We
are from Glad-8, the more rational of the Glads."

The other two nodded in agreement.

"So, then what are you proposing I do?"

"We are excited about the possibility Natasha pres-
ents while at the same time leery that she may simply
kill us all."

"Yeah, that would be a bummer. I've been dead and I can tell you it's a drag."

"We want you to, as you say, take Natasha out, but leave her alive so we can study her along with your Earth scientists. She is an amazing being, just too dangerous to roam free."

"Why bring me here?"

"We just wanted you to know we are interested, too. You need to realize how important the stakes are here for your people and our people. Natasha could be a bond between us."

"How so?"

"You would not understand," they all said.

"Any helpful hints?"

"Don't make her mad," one of them said.

"Sneak up on her," another added.

"Buy low, sell high," the third said.

"So, this was just a pep talk," I said.

Their three heads bobbed back and forth.

"And also to let you know our services are available if there is anything we can do that won't attract attention to ourselves. Your government is funny. They took our knowledge but don't want our advice. Anything we do they see as meddling."

"Well, you are aliens and you're fighting against a hundred years or so of bad popular press. We depicted you guys as bad guys a lot," I said.

"We never invaded," said one of the aliens.

"No, but you did poke and prod a fair number of humans in your day," I pointed out.

"Science," one of them said.

"Research," another said.

"We need our fun, too," the third said.

I didn't push it anymore. I figure it didn't hurt to have aliens on my side.

"Can you at least drop me off in San Diego?" I asked.

"We cannot travel through time," the middle Gladian said.

"New San Diego, I need to be dropped off in New San Diego . . ."

"Of course," they said. "Maybe you can pick us up some *Star Trek* memorabilia. We love that crap!" The alien pointed to the transport pad. "Now please stand on the pad and be prepared for transfer."

Chapter 40

I re-formed in the middle of a park in New San Diego. I was close enough to the convention center that I could see the building, but still far enough away that it was a nice walk.

"Wow, that meet and greet with aliens was more useless than most meet and greets with aliens," I told HARV as I started heading toward the convention center.

"Not so," HARV told me.

"True, at least I got free transportation to San Diego," I said.

HARV started walking along side of me. He was in shades and a T-shirt that read GEEKS DO IT DIGITALLY. I guess it was his version of cover. "Wrong again, Zach. The Gladians requested a one thousand credit transport energy fee."

DOS, I forgot how cheap the Gladians are. "And you paid it?"

"I had to, in the interest of human and alien relations."

"So this was even more useless than I thought."

"Do you ever get tired of being so wrong?" HARV asked.

"Do you ever get tired of driving me so crazy?" I asked back.

"Do you even have to ask?"

"HARV!" I shouted.

"Zach, quiet, I am in disguise," HARV whispered. "And so are you. You are wearing holo-sunglasses, a cowboy hat, and boots."

I didn't even question the choice of disguise. "HARV, what I am missing?"

"A sense of style and grace for two things."

"HARV, what else?"

"The Gladians were involved in the initial tweaking of the human genome to create psis," HARV said in my head.

I always had suspected that, but it had never been confirmed until now. "Go on?"

"They sold us the original specs they based the first psis on," HARV said.

"Why?"

"So I might be able to find a weakness in Natasha and take advantage of it."

"Why didn't they tell me this?"

"They don't want humans to know, Zach. I wasn't supposed to mention it."

"Then why are you telling me?"

"Since when do I do what carbon-based creatures tell me to do?" HARV said.

"Good point."

"Besides, I just love showing you how wrong you are!" HARV added.

"And?"

"I think I have done my job."

"In proving me wrong?"

"Yes," HARV answered.

"And finding a weakness," GUS added.

I stopped walking. My gun and my holo-assistant were brainstorming for solutions without me. I wasn't sure if I should be happy or worried.

"What did you come up with?"

"Bright light," HARV said.

"And high frequency sounds," GUS said. "I have modified myself so I can generate them both."

"Good for you, GUS," I said.

"Good for all of us," HARV said. "We have deduced that if you hit Natasha with a burst of bright light and then high pitched sound there is a likelihood you will incapacitate her at least for a short time."

"Can you be more specific?"

"Between ten seconds and ten minutes," HARV said. "Our data was a bit sketchy. And you're only as good as your data."

"Just curious, how much did all this info cost me?" I asked.

"I haggled," HARV said.

"How much?" I persisted.

"Let's put it this way, we better catch Natasha."

I started walking again. Heading toward the building that was the New San Diego New Convention Center (or the NSDNCC for short), I couldn't help reminiscing about the old days. Back when I was a kid, my dad, a bit of geek, would take me to Comic-Con. In those days it wasn't quite the media Cirque du Soleil that it is today. Sure, it was big, bulky and congested with fans, media, writers, current stars, wannabe stars, ex-stars trying to relive their glory . . . you get the idea.

Back in the early days they had only added two floors to the original convention center and the con was attended by only around three hundred thousand people. Comic-Con had actually suffered a lull in attendance around the 2020s. Two events, one major and one not so major, contributed to this dip.

The not so major one was the comic book companies deciding they could replace human artists and writers with bot artists and writers. After all, bot artists work cheaper, smell better, need less pampering, don't sleep, don't take vacations or spend work time looking at porn on the Web—the list goes on. This was so appealing to the money people and the suits at the big comic book companies that they hired a team of consultants and programmers to create a database of images and ideas that these bots would draw from. Their point was all the good ideas have been done already and we're just recycling ideas from a hundred years ago and calling them "rebranding" or modernizing. DOS, machines can do that. The end result was hundreds of artists and writers replaced by three bots who just cranked out material.

For a while, the small independent publishers stayed organic with actual human creators, insisting that's what the people wanted. Soon, though, the lure of a cheap and endless supply of material caused even them to switch to bot-driven material. (A few underground human-drawn comics still existed, some artists even doing their comics on real paper. Problem was, without a marketing budget, hardly anybody heard of them.)

At first, bot-created comics sold well simply because they were all first issues and buyers naturally assumed they would all be collectors' items. The comic book companies helped perpetuate this by creating many different (but still mostly the same) storylines, so they could all be first issue collectors' editions.

The result for Comic-Con was that it wasn't nearly as fun interacting with a few bot creators as it was meeting human creators. So, not only were there fewer creators at the con but fewer fans.

The really major change, though, was the arrival of actual real aliens on Earth in 2020. Once aliens made it known they really existed, pretending to be aliens at cons wasn't nearly as fun or attractive. Not only that, but the first aliens to arrive said they were quite offended by how they were depicted in our media. They were always either overly evil, bent on just destroying the world or they were overly sweet and loveable, just eating pieces of peanut butter candy and looking to make long distance calls. The aliens pointed out that their personalities come in many shades of gray. They are as different and as varied as people. And most annoying to them was that they really preferred chocolate candy.

Defenders of aliens in popular culture pointed out that many popular shows had featured aliens of different types showing a vast array of personalities. The aliens countered by saying real aliens never say anything as hokey as "May the force be with you" or "Live long and prosper."

The·end result was that Comic-Con wasn't that fun a place to be for a few years after 2020. Then two things happened to revive comics and popular culture. First, the movie and HV industry figured they could save tons of credits by replacing human actors with holographically-simulated actors and computer-driven (i.e., written) stories. Luckily for those of us who are fans of human created organic entertainment, the actors' and writers' unions were very powerful and influential. DOS, these days the best way into politics is as an an actor or a rock star. The union convinced the viewing public that shows created by machines for humans just weren't fun enough. They started an entire campaign stating that entertainment is as much mysticism as anything else and humans can create works that machines can't.

The viewing public bought it and demanded more organic programming. Now the entertainment and comic industry is a mix of humans and bots working together to provide better (i.e., more profitable) entertainment for all.

As for the aliens, after a few years they decided their protests were just "darn silly." (Yes, those are the exact words they used.) They had now decided that their depiction in popular media was actually just good fun and good for human and alien relationships. They could see why humans enjoyed blowing off steam by showing up at these conventions dressed as aliens. They would no longer protest. Today some claim aliens come to these conventions dressed as humans. Based on many of the attendees I've seen, I wouldn't rule that out.

All this meant that Comic-Con became more popular then ever. So popular that some people felt the convention was outgrowing the convention center and that they'd need to move it from New San Diego. Of course the popular masses wouldn't hear of it based on the very simple logic, it's always been here, let's keep it here. Some people then suggested building a new convention center. Once again the it's always been here, let's keep it here argument prevailed. So, instead of building a new convention center, every few years they add a new floor to the existing one. When I was just out of college, there were six floors. Now there are twelve.

By the time I was done waxing poetic about the past I'd reached the crowd of people lining up to attend the convention. The doors had been open to the public for a couple of hours now, but the line still extended at least a kilometer.

"I do have a pass to get in. Correct?" I said to HARV as I walked past the tail end of the crowd.

"Yes. Obviously they would have let you in as Zachary Nixon Johnson since some people here look at you as a real life comic book," HARV said with a mix of disdain and amusement.

"Such is my lot in life," I said.

"But I knew you would be better served coming incognito so you could get around more freely. I have obtained for you a media/government pass," HARV said, "Granting you all access."

"How'd you swing that?"

"It's best you don't ask," HARV said.

"I already did," I said.

"Just don't be surprised if you hear about some of your old underwear on sale at eBay."

"What? You sold my underwear?"

"Not all of it. Just some old pieces you really

shouldn't wear any longer. It's embarrassing for both myself and Electra, as well it should be for you."

"You sold my underwear?" I repeated.

"Yes, I sold the pair you were wearing the day you first saved Sexy Sprockets' life," HARV said.

"You keep track of that stuff?"

"I could easily," HARV insisted.

"Yes, but do you?"

"No, of course not. Even I, with megapowerful cognitive processors, who can do a billion things at once, don't want to waste any processing power on that."

"Oh . . ."

"The main point here is that the buyer thinks that's the underwear and in advertising and marketing perception is all that matters."

"If you say so," I said.

We had now walked past at least half the crowd. I could now see the door that the main crowd was being herded into. I also saw the Media/Politicians door just a few hundred meters past that. (The stars and talent had their own entrance on the roof. DOS, some of them were so popular they had to be ported into the building.)

"Truthfully, it never ceases to amaze me that other humans would be interested in your underwear as a collectable. I know it's not a high number, but the fact that there is any demand is kind of scary."

"I do save the world from time to time," I noted.

"Yes, but it's usually due to sheer luck and persistence and having me by your side. I swear, Zach, a chimp could be trained to do what you do. And not an especially bright one."

"Yeah, but they wouldn't look nearly as good in the fedora and trench coat as I do. Like you said it's all marketing and perception."

We had now passed the fan entrance. In a minute or two, I would be in the building and hopefully there would be something to distract HARV from rambling on about the value of my underwear.

"I don't think a chimp could ever replace you, Mr. Zach," GUS said.

"Thanks, GUS. That's why you are my favorite."

I couldn't see HARV, but I knew, somewhere, he was rolling his eyes.

Strolling up to the media and politicians' gate, I was happy to see that while the line was long it wasn't as intimidating as the fans' line. I took my position behind a human reporter and her bot camera crew. The bots were branded WNN, so I knew they were from World News Now. The pretty young blonde reporter smiled at me, took one look at my badge, frowned, and turned around.

"HARV, who the spam am I pretending to be?" I asked.

"You're a blogger from blogs without spam dot news."

Ah, that would explain the look of contempt. Even today, after nearly seventy years of being around, the mainstream news media still looks down on bloggers. No problem. I could use that to my advantage. The less attention paid to me the better.

Moving closer to the entrance as the crowd inched up, I had to get my mind back on the case. Where in this mass of humanity and geekdom would Natasha be?

"HARV, show me today's schedule."

"Zach, there are over five thousand events going on."

"Just do it, HARV!"

"Yeah!" GUS added. *"I have faith in Mr. Zach's deductive abilities."*

The list of events scrolled across my eyes, almost too fast to comprehend. Still, somehow I was able to. I sorted out the ones I knew she wouldn't be interested in. Signings and promotional events, no way. Live action role-playing games, no way. Virtual role-playing games, even less of a chance. Fifteen different seminars on How You Too Can Write for Comics,

Interactive Comics, and HV. Nope. The story of the Marvel versus DC Wars, interesting but no. A five minute advance trailer for *Kangarooman 22*. Sorry, even I think that series lost something after the tenth movie.

There had to be something on this list that would interest a superpowerful killer babe who really didn't want to be a killer. A discussion of the twentieth anniversary of the sixth retelling of the Dark Phoenix saga. That was it. They were going to have a panel discussing its merits on the seventh floor at 1 p.m. That had to be where she'd be.

"She'll be at the Dark Phoenix retelling discussion," I thought.

"How can you be so certain?" HARV asked.

"Dark Phoenix was a vastly powerful beautiful woman who both reveled in her power and had trouble dealing with her it," I said. *"Does that tell you anything?"*

"That you're a geek . . ."

I may be a macho guy but like most people I do have some geek tendencies. (DOS, I have a computer wired to my brain!) So there was a lot of classic comic book reading in my past. Even today, on occasion, I will still glance through one.

"Your pass, buddy," the guard at the door said, bringing me back to the matters at hand. The guard was a big man who hadn't shaven in a day or two. I guess he thought it made him look tough. To me he just looked lazy.

"Oh, sure," I said, pointing to the holographic badge on my chest.

The guard bent over toward me, eyeing the badge. He pulled out a monocle and placed it in his right eye. Squinting, he said, "This badge is a fake."

"No, that can't be," I insisted.

The guard just shook his head. "You bought this from Charlie. Didn't you?"

I shrugged.

"Yes, I did," HARV said in my brain.

"Guess so," I said.

The guard shook his head. "They fired Charlie a couple of hours ago. He was selling fake tickets for crazo prices."

DOS! I said to myself as I saw two guardbots rolling toward us.

"I'm afraid you'll have to go with the bots for a while," the guard told me.

"Why? I didn't know the ticket was fake . . ."

"Dude, ignorance is no excuse!"

Before I could comment on ignorance is actually a perfectly legitimate excuse, two guardbots were now on top of me. They were the ten-armed, heavily armored type. Basically, they were small tanks with arms and little robo-head-human-interface screens on top. They meant business.

"Come with us peacefully, sir," one of the guardbots said, grabbing my right arm with a clawlike hand.

"Yes, we do not wish to hurt you, but we are quite capable of doing so," the second bot said, grabbing my left arm.

They yanked me off the ground and started rolling backward. Yep, it's true, bloggers just don't get any respect.

"Where are we going?" I asked.

"We have cooling off cells in the basement where we keep troublemakers."

"Uh, for how long?"

"Until you calm down or the police come and take you away. They usually send a paddy wagon hover over around midnight," the guard answered.

Chapter 41

The bots tossed me into a holding cell. Pushing myself off the ground, I heard a voice say, "Hey, look, a new guy is here."

That was followed by a mock cheer from maybe five or ten other people. Looking around I saw my cell mates, about fifty people, all guys, dressed in assorted costumes from space explorers to superheroes to ninjas to princes.

"I have good news for you," HARV said.

"HARV, I'm locked in a cell with a bunch of costumed megageeks."

"I think they prefer to call themselves pop and electronic culture connoisseurs," HARV corrected.

"So, what's the good news?" I thought.

"I managed to maintain your holo-disguise even though the guardbots had some holo-detecting software!" HARV said proudly.

"Great, so I'm locked up but nobody knows I'm me," I said.

"Yes. Your image doesn't need any more negative marks," HARV said.

A man dressed as a wizard with a long purple robe walked over to me. He was a short man, probably in his early twenties. His only discernable feature was a long nose that seemed to take up over half his face. If he really was a wizard, he would have made that disappear long ago.

Putting on a hand on my shoulder, he asked, "What are you in for, my brother?"

I tried to think of an answer the guy might like.

"Using an illegal ticket," GUS whispered in my brain. I was glad the guardbots didn't notice GUS while they were rolling me here. While I may not have needed GUS to help me make up excuses I would need him when I faced Natasha.

"Trying to get in with an illegal ticket," I said, trying out the truth.

The man's face dropped. He removed his hand from my shoulder and slowly backed away. If he was braver, he would have spit on me.

"What gives with him?" I asked HARV.

"Zach, you know Comic-Con is a really big deal in New San Diego. It's the one thing they feel separates them from the rest of the world. It's what they do best."

"Though I understand the zoo and aquarium are also lovely," GUS added. There was something about a high-powered superweapon saying lovely that I didn't want to think about.

"True," HARV said. *"But the Con gives them less hassle from animal rights activists and, more importantly makes more money than anything else. So, people who sneak in are really despised, as it not only hurts the economy but robs the Con itself."*

"The city also has the world's largest shrine to Ted Williams, which I think is subzero!" GUS said, really impressing the baseball fan in me.

Out of the corner of my eye I saw the fake wizard talking to a man dressed in an ogre costume. I know it was a costume because I've met real ogres and they don't look nearly as silly as the man did. The wizard was pointing at me and the ogre was grunting.

The ogre listened to the wizard talk for a few more nanos, glaring at me and nodding his head. Yep, this guy was the cell muscle. The one who ran the show. Or at least thought he did. Once the wizard was done speaking, I knew the ogre would be over to teach me a lesson.

Sure enough, he started lumbering over toward me, pounding one of his hands into the other. The bad news was, I was about to get into a brawl. The good news was I hadn't been in a brawl all day and I was kind of starting to miss the action. The really good news was this guy wasn't a real ogre, so this would be a short fight. Thrusting a finger into my chest, the ogre said, "I understand you tried ripping the con off!"

While he might not have been a real ogre, he did have the ogre smell down. His breath reeked of cheap beer.

I grabbed the finger he was jabbing me with and pulled it backward. He yelped in pain.

"I'm just a poor blogger trying to make a living," I said, forcing the guy down to his knees. "Do you have any complaints about that?" I asked him.

"Actually, I do," he said through a grimace. "Hence the reason I came over. We don't like people trying to rip off the Con!"

He swung his free hand at me wildly, actually trying to hit me in the groin. Seeing the move coming I simply pulled him forward, dodging the blow and driving his face into the floor. I stepped over him, never releasing the finger. Instead I twisted his arm behind his back while placing my left leg on top of his shoulder.

"Let me rephrase that," I said.

"Fine," he groaned.

In a way I gave the guy some cred, he was standing up for what he thought was right. I needed to give him a way out. "If I say it won't happen again can we decide to call this a draw?" I asked.

"Sounds fair. We all make mistakes," he moaned.

I released his arm and let it drop to the floor. Walking away from him, I said, "Good, I'm glad we could be reasonable about this."

"He's going to rush you. Isn't he?" HARV said.

I had hoped not, especially after I had given him a break. Still people who are drunk and in costumes do things they would never do sober and in their daily clothing and probably wouldn't do if they were just one or the other. The combination, though, was dangerous. It was probably compounded by the fact that I had put him down on the turf he thought he ruled.

"Tell me when he's coming," I thought to HARV, slowly continuing to walk away.

"Now!" HARV shouted in my head.

Spinning around, I clocked him right between the eyes with a left jab. Ah, the look of surprise on his face the nano before he blacked out was priceless. It probably felt much better than it should have as I watched him crash backward to the ground out cold.

Turning to my cell mates, I said, "Anybody else have any problems with me?"

They all shook their heads no.

Now it was time to get out of this joint. The crowd would give me space, which allowed me to concentrate on the room. The cage was a couple of hundred meters long with doors on each end.

I was actually surprised a high-tech place like this used old-fashioned metal bars. Then I realized there was probably no better way to keep a high-tech crowd in jail than using the lowest-tech solution.

Getting close to the barred door, I bent over to give HARV a good look at the lock mechanism.

"What do you think?" I thought.

"Zach, I don't need a closer look. It's double lock, one electronic, one old-fashioned key sprung."

Chances were none of this crowd could pick an old-fashioned lock. They could probably find out how to do it on the Web, but looking around I saw that all their P-Pods and computer links had been removed.

There are times when having your computer interface drilled into your brain can be quite helpful. For anybody to get out of here, they'd have to be able to deal with two very different kinds of locks. Kind of clever, actually.

"HARV, can you pick the locks?" I thought.

"I can, but it would take time," HARV said. *"The Con has great encryption software. It would be a lot faster just to use GUS to shoot one of the doors open."*

"Yay for me," GUS said.

"HARV, it's big of you to admit that."

"Zach, when it comes to the safety of the world, I can put my pride aside. I am a machine, not a human. Nothing fancy needed here. This door wasn't built to keep in an armed man."

"Or woman," GUS added. *"Women can use weapons, too!"*

"Occasionally it is helpful to have a weapon that looks like a joystick," HARV said.

There are times when the best solution is the easiest, simplest, and most obvious. It's funny how sometimes that can be the hardest one to see. Luckily, I had HARV to point out the obvious for me. Of course, I would never admit that to him. His ego was giga-sized already.

"How many guardbots are on duty?" I thought.

"In all of the world or just this building or on this floor?" HARV answered.

"Ah, for now let's just concern ourselves with this floor."

"Two," HARV said. *"Most of these guys are actually pretty docile."*

Having GUS with me, I could easily shoot out a door and probably take out the guardbots. The thing was, that wasn't exactly the smooth good guy way of handling things. Much better if I caused a distraction and then slipped out during the chaos.

"You have that look in your eye," HARV said.

"How can you tell?"

"I'm looking at you from the jail's security camera feed."

"What time is it?" I asked.

"Five p.m.," HARV said.

"How could it be so late? I missed the panel Natasha will be at!"

"Zach, that's five Greenwich Mean Time," HARV said.

"Which means?"

"Zach, do I have to explain GMT to you again?"

"No, I just need to know what time it is here in New San Diego."

"Oh, why didn't you just say so? Just subtract seven, Zach."

"Ten a.m.," GUS said.

"Thanks," I thought to GUS. *"HARV, why are you being extra thick and stubborn now?"* I thought.

"I hadn't noticed."

"I have," GUS said.

"Who asked you?" HARV said to GUS.

"What's going on, buddy?"

"I'm fine thank you, Mr. Zach," GUS said.

"Was talking to HARV, GUS."

"Oops, sorry . . ."

"Silly weapon," HARV said.

"The point still stands, HARV."

There was silence.

"Well, HARV?"

"I am running diagnostics now."

More silence.

"Well?"

"Be patient. Halo wasn't programmed in a day, you know."

I waited a nano or two longer, tapping my foot. I didn't have a lot of time to kill here. *"Ah, HARV!"*

"Apparently the pressure of maintaining the holo-disguise after being dead put extra stress on my processors," HARV said. *"I am running repair routines now."*

"That's good."

Now it was time to turn my attention back to getting out of this joint. Since I was armed, that wouldn't be much of a problem. I just needed to figure out the best possible diversion. Shouldn't be too hard, after all, diversions were one of my specialties.

"HARV, how many people are in this cell?"

"Including you?"

"Sure."

"Fifty-three. Of course, one of them is you and one of them has been knocked out by you. So that makes . . ."

"Fifty two . . ." I thought.

"Very good, Mr. Zach!" GUS said.

"Yes, you did that without taking off your shoes to help you count," HARV sputtered.

"You are working on correction subroutines. Correct?" I said to HARV.

"Yes . . ." he sighed.

Now that I was de facto cell block leader, I was going to use some of my newfound power to my advantage. I walked over and leaned on one of the cell doors. I was acting cool, but not too cool. After all, I had to remember I was a blogger now, not a PI.

I pointed at the guy dressed as a wizard. He pointed back at himself, amazed that I would point at him. I pointed at him again and nodded. He looked at me, still not sure that I wanted to actually see him. I motioned toward myself. He slowly started walking toward me. I pointed at a couple of other guys, one dressed as some sort of ratman and another dressed as a fairy. Nope, not making that up.

They also looked at me with a mix of surprise and admiration. Actually, the fairy guy headed right over. The ratman character seemed a bit more apprehensive. I spun my finger around rapidly, letting him know I was in a hurry. Which I was.

The fairy guy reached me first, followed by the wizard, followed by ratman.

"How can we help you?" the fairy asked, waving his wand up and down.

I grabbed the wand from his hand. I broke it over my knee. I handed the pieces back to him .

"For one thing, you can stop waving that wand around," I said, after the fact.

"Oh, okay," he said, not quite as enthusiastic as before.

"What can we do for you, brave blogger?" the wizard asked.

"Yes, that was a nice hurt you put down on the ogre," the ratman said.

"Yeah, when you make your living blogging, you learn to be tough," I said.

They all nodded in agreement. By now, a few other of the caged geeks had noticed our formation and had slinked over. They weren't quite part of the group, but they were within earshot and that's what I wanted.

"So, who was the best *Star Trek* captain ever?" I asked loudly.

"Kirk," the wizard said.

"Easy, Janeway," the fairy said.

"Ah, come on, guys, Sulu rocked," the ratman said.

"You're all crazy!" a chubby man dressed as a Greek warrior shouted. "The classic characters can't hold an old-fashioned wax candle to the new incarnations! Spock the Third rocks!"

"No way!" another voice shouted. "Torak from the house of Torath was the greatest! After all, he was the first Klingon to captain the *Enterprise*."

"You're crazo!" the wizard shouted. "You can't go against the best!"

"Janeway could have kicked all their fairy asses," the fairy shouted, pushing the ratman.

The ratman grabbed the fairy by the neck, trying to pull him to the ground. A couple of other bystanders became participants by jumping in. Vingo! This was going exactly how I wanted it to. Now that the fire was starting, I just needed to toss some more fuel onto it. I needed this to be an all out brawl.

Pointing to another group that had congregated away from ours, I said, "Look at those losers. I heard they are *Spaceship 7-Eleven* fans!" I said.

The wizard put his hand to his heart. *"SS 7-Eleven!"* he spat. "How can anybody watch that crap! Really! It's a show about a spaceship that travels the galaxies selling junk food! It is so derivative of what came before it!"

"Kind of hard to be derivative of what came after it," HARV said.

"Unless the writers had a time machine," GUS added.

I ignored the electronic voices in my head. "I hear they think it's the finest example of SF in the last twenty years!" I goaded.

"Are they nutso?" somebody else growled.

Those who weren't scrapping over *Star Trek* captains leaped at the other unsuspecting group. A grand clash erupted. I smiled for a moment.

"Are you proud of yourself?" HARV asked, not even bothering to communicate silently.

"Don't worry, nobody will get too hurt," I said. "The boys are just letting off some steam. It's good for them." It was good for me to watch other people do the fighting for once. Hugging the bars I moved down the cell to the other door. Freedom was now in my grasp. I watched the two guardbots. They had rolled to the other door. They were both yelling orders for the others to calm down. The orders were falling on deaf ears, which was great for me. The only way the bots could have been able to quell this crowd was if they had a mint condition *Superman* number 1 in their claws and threatened to destroy it if they didn't calm down.

Popping GUS into my hand, I casually aimed him at the lock of the other door.

"Silencer mode, GUS," I said.

"Check," GUS whispered.

I pulled the trigger. The door jarred open. Slipping out the door, I thought to HARV, *"Okay, change my cover."*

"Please," HARV said.

"Please," I added.

The foreground shimmered in front of me, indicating that my disguise had changed. Quickly walking out of the cell, I noticed my reflection in one of the incoming guardbots. I looked like a little old lady, gray hair, a cane, the works.

"Won't I stand out in a place like this?" I asked HARV.

"Of course not. You're an original fan of the Ratman *series,"* HARV told me.

Before I totally slipped out of the basement area, one of the patrol guardbots rolled up to me.

"What are you doing in this area?" the guardbot asked.

"Ah, HARV?"

"Don't worry, Zach, I've got you covered."

"Ah, I was coming to down here to check in on my little, uh, Jay," I said in an old lady's voice. I put my hands over my heart and feigned a move backward. "But then this terrible scuffle broke out. I got so scared."

"Very good, ma'am!" the bot said. "Proceed to the main floors and let us handle this."

Walking past the bot, I couldn't help cracking a smile.

Chapter 42

I actually couldn't complain that much about my little time in the pokey. I had some time to kill anyhow, waiting for Natasha, so I didn't lose much. I'm not sure why, but I was now very confident that Natasha was not only here, but that she would be at the Dark Phoenix panel. So confident that I had HARV contact both Captain Rickey and Ona and Threa. In a couple of hours it was going to be time to end this once and for all.

Natasha was a danger and I was determined to put her out of commission. But I was just as resolute not to let anybody harm her. Sure this may have been a case of wanting my cake after I had eaten it. Like my old mentor used to say, "If you want to have your cake and eat it too, just order two pieces of cake." I decided my best course of action would be to head up to the seventh floor and stake out the room until Natasha showed up. Hopefully, the early panels would be entertaining.

I started working my way through the thick crowd toward the escalator to the seventh floor. I'm not a big fan of escalators. Yeah, I know I'm a macho guy. I'm not suppose to admit my fears, but I do. I don't think it makes me any less of a man to confess that I don't like heights in any form. The only good thing I can say about escalators is that they probably aren't as bad as teleporters. (To me, teleporting up floors was not only a waste of energy and computing power, it was also bad karma.)

Making my way through the crowd, though, something strange happened, and when I say strange I mean by normal standards. For me, it was pretty much just another average run-in with a superpowered being. The mass of people suddenly froze in place, then parted to the side, clearing a path in front of me. Turning back, I noticed the path behind me was also void of the masses. Strutting through the opening was Threa Thompson in all her fairy princess glory. I paused for Threa to catch up with me. I may not be the brightest bulb in the box, but I'm smart enough to know life is easier when you don't piss off Threa.

"Dear, brave, Zach," Threa said, extending her arm to me. "How nice of you to summon me."

I shook Threa's hand.

"You were supposed to kiss it, you clod," HARV said from the recesses of my brain.

I knew that. The thing was, while I wanted Threa on my side, I didn't want her to think she had total control of the situation and I would simply bow to her every whim. Yeah, she was a stunning superpowered mutant fairy princess, but I brought my unique skill set to the party. Threa wouldn't be all set to pounce on Natasha if it weren't for me.

"Threa, I'm glad you could get here so quickly," I told her. Looking over her shoulder, I asked, "Where's Ona?"

Threa pointed to the escalator. "Walk with me," she said. It was more of an order than a statement. She walked, I followed. Sure I didn't want her to think she had total control of the situation, but I wasn't stupid either. When the bio-waste hit the fan I wanted as many superbeings on my side as I could muster.

"Where's Ona?" I repeated as we reached the escalator.

"She's around," Threa said.

We started climbing up the escalator.

"What floor is this event on?" Threa asked.

"The seventh," I said.

"And this moving stair device will take us to the second?" she asked.

"Yes, then we get on another to the third and another to the fourth . . ."

"I get the pattern," she said. "It's too slow."

I looked at my wrist communicator. "Well, we do have a couple of hours to kill," I said.

"Still, I don't want to waste it simply traveling upward," she said.

Threa snapped her fingers.

Next thing I knew we were off the escalator, in the middle of a different crowd of people.

"We are now on the proper floor," Threa said.

"Thanks," I said, though I didn't really mean it.

"I will bask in the accolades of the crowd while you seek out the one you seek," Threa told me.

"I repeat, where's Ona?" I asked.

Threa smiled. "Don't worry, little Zach. She will be ready when we are ready."

"Are you going to tell me what the plan is?" I asked.

Threa just stood there smiling at me.

"I take it that's a no," I said.

She nodded. "You are quite perceptive. You chose the proper line of work."

"How come?"

"Zach, being perceptive must help when being a PI," she said.

"No, how come you won't tell me?"

Threa just looked at me like I was a small daft child.

"Well?"

"Because you're a blabber mind," she finally said.

"What?"

"A blabber mind," she repeated.

"A blabber mind," GUS repeated.

"A blabber mind," HARV echoed.

"A blabber mind?" I wasn't really sure what one was, but I was reasonably certain I wasn't one. "I am not a blabber mind."

Threa patted me on the head. "Oh, poor, silly Zach. You are, you just don't know it."

"Can you at least tell me what it is?"

"A blabber mind. You wear your thoughts on your sleeve. If I told you our plan, Natasha would glean it from your mind. Our plan is foolproof, but we don't want to take any chances."

"Yeah, fools can be a lot a more ingenious or harder to proof against than people think."

Threa then dismissed me with another pat on the head. "Go entertain yourself for a while. I'll be here mingling with the little people. When you spot Natasha, let me know and I'll swing our plan into action."

At that instant, the crowd suddenly noticed that Threa was there.

"Hey, it's Threa Thompson!" a couple of people of yelled.

I went the opposite way as the crowd migrated toward Threa. For all the many attractions of Comic-Con, none of them beat being in the actual presence of a true fairy princess.

"Can you turn my math teacher into a toad for me?" I heard a kid ask.

"Hey, turn me into a poodle!" another requested.

"What happened to the pixies who used to hang around you? I liked the pixies."

I just got as far away from the crowd as possible. Then is occurred to me. "HARV, am I still wearing the old lady disguise?"

"Yes."

"How did Threa find me?" I asked.

"She says she can tell you by scent."

That wasn't all that reassuring. I decided not to think too much more about that. "Just drop the cover, HARV. With Threa here, nobody will care about me."

"Yes, but what about Natasha?"

"If Threa knows it's me, I'm betting credits to soy donuts Natasha does, too," I said.

The scenery in front of me glimmered for a moment. I assumed that meant HARV had dropped the holo-disguise. HARV appeared next to me.

"What do we do now?" he asked.

"Hang out and wait," I said.

"Ah, the story of our lives," HARV said.

Yep, that's the thing with being a PI. People are either trying to kill you or you're bored to death waiting around. There's not a lot of middle ground.

"By the way, I'm not a blabber mind," I stated.

"If you say so," HARV said.

Wandering over to a corner, I starting admiring some of the animated holographic posters on the wall. There was the original Spiderman swinging from building to building. I always wondered what the heck he connected his web to when he did that. Then there was Spiderman Junior climbing up a building to take on Professor Squid. Ah, those were the good old days of comics, when everything seemed so much purer. Next to Spidcy was an old Fantastic Four hologram. I barely remembered the days when there were just four of them. Now they are the Really Fantastic Forty-four. I picked up a holographic issue once, all action, no character development. Next was the X-People poster. I had to confess, I didn't really follow the series once they gave into political correctness and changed the name to X-People. There, though, right next to the X-People holographic poster, was the quintessential poster. It was so old it wasn't animated. It wasn't even in 3-D. In fact, I was betting that that was real paper under the hermetic seal. It was a simple poster, it had to be nearly a hundred years old. That made it sweeter. All it was was the old X-Man Jean

Grey rising out of the water, surrounded by a Phoenix halo. Underneath, all it said was "Phoenix Reborn (Yet Again)." It was simple, yet elegant. They don't make posters like that anymore.

"They don't make posters like that anymore, do they?" a voice behind me said.

"Nope," I said, without even thinking about it.

Turning toward that voice, I realized it was Natasha. (I also realized I really was a blabber brain.) Natasha just smiled at me. She looked stunning as always, hair dancing playfully around her shoulders. She was dressed in a short shimmering silver dress that was reflecting the light around us giving it a sort of hypnotic effect, just not as powerful as the woman in the dress.

"Zach, you came. I don't know if I should be honored or scared," she said with a weak grin.

"Probably a little of both."

"I have alerted Threa," HARV said in my head.

DOS! I wasn't ready for that yet. I wanted to try to talk Natasha in before Threa and Ona and whoever tried roping her in.

"Natasha, you need to turn yourself in," I said, part demanding, part pleading.

"Not going to happen," she told me. "Why do you think it would so much better for me if I did?"

Truthfully, I wasn't sure. I had internalized about this problem over and over. I wasn't sure she would be better off giving herself up. I just thought, well, I hoped they would work with her, teach her how to use her power.

"Zach, you know they won't teach me anything. They will either find a way to use me or kill me."

I could see where she was coming from. I really was being forced to choose between the lesser of two evils. I had to believe the best possible outcome for all was bringing Natasha in and teaching her to harness her powers. I truly thought that with all the resources and minds the government had at their disposal they could do something for her.

"You are assuming they want to do something for me," Natasha said. "That they just don't want me to be a killing or brainwashing machine."

DOS, I was a huge blabber brain. "I have to believe that, Natasha," I said. Shaking my head, I added, "I see no other way."

Sadly, that was the truth. I knew the World Council and Earth Force certainly were capable of some nasty deeds. I knew she had to be controlled or, well . . .

"Eliminated," Natasha said.

"Yes," I said, looking her square in the eyes. "I hope it doesn't come to that, but if it comes down to you or you versus the world as we know it, I go for the world."

"Ah, the last noble man," she said.

"Not the last, but we are getting harder to find," I said, drawing GUS. "Now if you come quietly this will be easier on everybody."

"Zach, while you may still, on some level, trust the people who run this world, I don't. So I am afraid I choose to remain free."

I was afraid she was going to say that. Can't say I blamed her. DOS, I would do the same in her shoes.

"HARV, time to get Threa over here," I thought as quietly as I could.

"They let the Thompson sisters roam free," Natasha said. "In fact, they even help run this world you work so hard to protect."

"People don't all die when the Thompsons are in a bad mood," I told her.

"True, but is it my fault that I am so powerful? I didn't ask for this power. I just ask for my freedom. Given my freedom and space I will learn to control my power."

"Zach, there's a problem," HARV told me, appearing in between Natasha and me.

"What?" I asked.

HARV pointed behind me. Turning, I saw that Threa's mob of fans had turned into an angry mob.

"Zach, you of all people should know I can do other things beside make everybody drop dead," Natasha said.

The mob had encircled Threa and wrestled her to the ground. I knew this wouldn't last and that it wouldn't turn out good for the mob. There was bright burst of energy from Threa. It was so bright I had to turn away.

"You can look now," Natasha told me. "It's over."

Turning back toward where the once angry mob had been, I saw Threa standing up, straightening her back. She was glowing with power. Everybody around her, though, was still vibrating from it. They were lying prone, legs in the air, hands crossed over their chests, eyes shut. They weren't dead, just knocked into unconsciousness.

"Now how is that different from what I do?" Natasha said.

Frankly, I wasn't all that sure anymore.

"Because we can control our power!" a very familiar voice said. Ona appeared behind Natasha. "Here, let me show you," she said, hitting Natasha with an uppercut to the jaw.

Much to both my and Ona's surprise, the blow bounced harmlessly off Natasha's chin.

"Please, I saw you thinking that before you even thought it!" Natasha taunted. "It was so easy to mentally parry your blow."

Ona wasn't one to give up without a fight. You don't become the richest being on Earth by giving up if something doesn't work the first time. She unleashed a fury of blows on Natasha. A left to the head. A right to the body. A kick to the midsection. A head butt to the, well, head. A stomp on the instep. Even a well-placed knee between the legs. That one made me shudder. Natasha, though, was taking it all in stride. She didn't have the pure physical power that Ona had, but her mental power more than made up for that.

The only thing I really couldn't wrap my mind around (well, not the only thing) was why Natasha hadn't unleashed her death aura yet. Not that I'm complaining, mind you, but I found it puzzling. Maybe she really was learning to reel it in some?

"See, Zach, I am learning how to control my emotions and my power," she told me, answering my question. "Plus, I have to admit I am more than a little amused by Ona's efforts. To think she is the second most powerful woman in the world and I deflect her attacks like she is a little mosquito."

It was pretty impressive.

"Are you through yet?" Threa asked Ona.

"I am," Ona admitted.

"But I'm not!" Threa said, leaping into the air toward Natasha.

As they crashed together, we were all consumed by a ball of energy.

The next thing I knew Natasha, Ona, Threa, and I were standing alone in a lush thick jungle. Exotic bird and animal noises filled the air. Looking up at the clear blue sky, I swore I saw a red dragon circling overhead. It was so humid I removed my jacket. I had been here before. Maybe. I was hoping this wasn't where I thought it was.

"Welcome to my realm," Threa said to Natasha.

DOS! Sometimes I hate it when I'm right.

Chapter 43

I have been to Threa's realm on two separate occasions, both of them memorable, but not for reasons I care to remember. The first time, I ended up fighting a dragon and an ogre and getting mooned by pixies. Who would have thought that would have been my more subtle trip? The second time, more recently, I journeyed here with Ona to talk with Threa. We ended up fighting swarm after swarm of shadow beings made out of everybody's worst fears. Then I got stuck in the middle of Ona and Threa duking it out, superbabe on superbabe. An event that would have been fun to watch, if I hadn't been caught in the middle of it. Some guys might think it's never bad to be stuck between two broads fighting. I'll wager those guys have never met any of the Thompson gals.

I turned to Ona and Threa, "So, this is your big plan? Take Natasha to your realm?"

"Zach, in my realm, I am queen. What I want to happen happens."

"Um, didn't Ona and I kind of kick your butt here once?" I pressed.

"Well, that's because you are my friend and my

sister. I took it easy on you." Threa pointed very dramatically at Natasha, "Not like her! See I have already taken some of the fight out of her. She will let her guard down while Ona recharges."

For her part, Natasha was sitting by a sparkling pond, soaking her feet. Looking over her shoulder, she casually said, "I like it here, Threa."

A fawn walked over to Natasha and started nuzzling her with her nose.

Turning to Ona and Threa I said, "Ah, this isn't at all how I remember this place . . ."

Threa put a hand to her mouth and whispered, "We're making her comfortable."

Natasha now was surrounded by bluebirds, smiling squirrels, and happy hippy hoppy bunnies. It looked like a scene out of an Entercorp animated kid's flick.

"I think I liked this place better when it was brimming over with trolls, ogres, dragons, and shadow creatures," I said.

"Oh, Zach, you're so cynical," Ona told me.

Maybe I *was* cynical. But while the mythological monsters may have defied logic, they just fit Threa's world better. These sugar- and honey-coated animals just didn't sit right with me. I had to give Ona and Threa props though, Natasha seemed happy. A happy Natasha is the best kind of Natasha to have. I suddenly saw the logic in their plan. I hadn't been giving them enough credit.

"Excellent plan," I said. "Keeping Natasha nice and calm and letting her stay here where she can't and won't hurt anybody is pure genius!"

The two superladies looked at each other and smiled. Their smiles made me frown and shake my head. DOS, this wasn't going to be that simple, was it? They both shook their heads no.

I held my arms forward, stopping them from making any moves. Well, at least trying to get them to think before they made their moves.

"Wait, ladies. Why can't she stay here?" I asked.

"Because it's my private realm," Threa said. "It wouldn't be private if I let another human stay here."

"But you have thousands of minions," I said. Yes, I actually used the word "minions."

"That's different," Threa said. "Minions are here to serve and make me feel good. Besides, they aren't humans."

"But here Natasha is happy and everybody is safe," I said, though I knew despite the ladies' superhearing it was falling on deaf ears.

"Don't worry, we're going to make sure everybody stays safe!" Ona said.

I so did not like hearing that. I knew the odds were against me, but I had to try reasoning with Ona and Threa.

"Ladies, there are times when force isn't the best solution," I said.

They both nodded in agreement, though they weren't paying any attention to me. They were locked in on Natasha, who was now surrounded by a virtual sea of cute and cuddly animals: squirrels with cymbals, chipmunks in furry hats, mice with bells on. Fish were jumping out of the pond almost like aquaworks. Butterflies were floating around her. One landed on her nose. She smiled, then giggled softly. Birds were chirping chipper songs. It was all nice calm and relaxing.

"Ladies why can't we just leave well enough alone?" I asked.

They shook their heads. "Zach, we're politicians and businesswomen. Well enough is never good enough. We need better, new and improved. That's our only goal, to make the world a better place," Ona said.

"And to turn a profit," I added.

Ona shrugged. "That's kind of an unstated goal. That's a given, so it doesn't count."

"Besides, who's counting?" Threa said.

"Good point," Ona said to her sister. They both turned back to me. "The thing is, Zach, it befalls us to make the world safer for the little people like you."

Pointing at Natasha I said, "Things look pretty safe now."

"Yes, our plan is going exactly as planned," Threa said.

This wasn't good. I could see the flaws a kilometer away. Biggest flaw was, Ona and Threa were so caught up in tooting their own horns and basking in their own brilliance, they didn't see the flaws. Either they were going to fail, meaning Natasha was going shove those horns up their tight butts, thus extinguishing the horns' brilliance. Or Ona and Threa were going to take out a perfectly harmless (for the moment) Natasha. I didn't like either of those selections. I decided to try adding another option.

"Why not find her another place to live?" I asked.

They both looked at me. They didn't say anything, so I kept going.

"Find a place without people. A place she can stay, be happy, only she doesn't hurt anybody and nobody hurts her. Like an island . . ."

"Islands are expensive, Zach," Ona said.

"Yeah, they just don't pop out of the ground," Threa said. She pondered her words for a moment, then added, "At least not anymore." She thought some more. "At least, not without investing a lot of credits." She thought a little longer, then decided she had said all she needed to say. She smiled.

"Look, with the resources available to you ladies, I'm sure we can find a suitable solution."

"We?" Ona said.

"Well, mostly you two," I conceded.

"We already have a solution," Ona said. "It's much more fiscally responsible. We're politicians now, Zach, we have to think about staying within a budget."

"Since when?" I asked.

"Zach, just watch and learn," Ona told me.

"Hey, she sounds exactly like Electra when you first started going out," HARV said.

"Shut up, HARV."

"Just trying to lighten the mood a bit. Things are about to get UltraMegaUgly."

Even HARV could see it. Sad really, that a supercomputer could catch the bugs in the plan that the superbeings couldn't. Like they say, live and learn. Hopefully, we would all get a chance to do both.

"Ladies, don't you see it? Finding a place for Natasha to stay where she is happy is everybody's best chance."

"Zach, we'd love to teach her how to use her powers," Threa said.

"You mean you want to teach her to use her powers in the way you want her to," I said.

Threa nodded. "Yes, of course. That last part was implied." She smiled. "I'm glad you picked up on that. Thing is, first we have to beat the stuffing out of her, to make her more ready to accept our help."

"What if she doesn't accept it then?" I asked.

"Best not to go there, Zach," Threa said.

Okay, this was frustrating. Dealing with politicians is worse than dealing with mutant hitmen. At least with hitmen it's easier to determine their goals and end game. I had made a snap judgment. I was now convinced the best possible outcome for this whole affair was to find a place where Natasha could live in peace and be happy. And the World Council would also have access to her, so they would be happy. I wasn't loving this idea, but it could work. In a pinch, you go with workable, not perfect.

"You could find a nice island for her and send consultants and trainers to help her learn to deal with her powers."

Ona glared at me. "We have a perfectly good base for her to stay at. We've already allocated a budget and everything."

"But . . ."

"Zach, we have our minds made up! Don't try confusing us with more options and information," Ona said, cutting me off.

"Zach, you'd have better luck trying to row up Niagara Falls without a paddle than you would getting these two to change their minds," HARV said.

"I agree," GUS said.

I sighed. "So, what's my role in your little scheme? Why am I here?"

"Zach, Threa and I are two of the most powerful beings on the planet. We don't have little schemes. We have huge grandiose plans."

"So, what peon role do I play?" I asked.

Ona patted me on head. "Now that's the spirit."

"Natasha seems to kind of trust you. She's calmer when you are around," Threa said.

"So, I'm like a pacifier?"

"Well put," Threa said.

"Plus, you have a really powerful weapon that may come in handy once we lay the hammer down," Ona said.

"That, too!" Threa agreed.

HARV decided this was his cue to appear. He didn't like being upstaged by GUS.

"And what about me?" he asked the ladies, hands on hips, head tilted forward.

"Oh, you're important, too," Ona told HARV meekly.

"How?" he pushed.

"When the time comes, we'll tell you," Ona said.

Ona had only been a politician for around a year now, but she really had the game down. She had become a master of answering a question without answering the question. Making it look like everything that turned out right was her idea. I was sure that anything that went wrong she would blame on others.

Ona pointed at Natasha. "Pay attention," she ordered us. "The fun is about to begin."

I popped GUS into my hand (out of habit). I turned to face Natasha.

Natasha was now surrounded by a whirlwind of the cutest animals you'd ever want to see. A couple of squirrels were giving her a pedicure. A bunny was slowly massaging her back. Two blue birds were braiding her hair. Another swarm of birds were serenading her with Top 100 hits from the past century. A couple of mice were feeding her grapes. Gross, who'd let mice feed them grapes? Dolphins were whizzing back and forth in the water. Three gophers and a few fawns had made a makeshift band. The gophers were using hollowed-out logs as wind instruments while the fawns beat on rocks like drums playing what I believed was a version of the ancient song "Rock Me Gently." Many, many other animals were just hanging around her, generally having a good time just doing whatever it is made-up animals do. I've seen a lot of surreal events in my time. This one certainly ranked in the top twelve.

I focused on Natasha's face. She had a wide content smile, her eyes open and relaxed. She was clearly enjoying herself. She was no fool, though, she had to suspect this was all a ruse, a setup to lull her into a false sense of security before Ona and Threa pounced. Natasha put her arms behind her head, sank back on the ground, and closed her eyes. Okay, maybe she didn't know? Maybe she trusted that this was Ona and Threa's plan, to keep her here, nice and happy. Nah, she knew they were politicians. She knew this wasn't the end game. If that was the case then she was extremely confident that she could handle anything Ona and Threa might throw at her.

It was at that moment that I finally realized how powerful Natasha truly was. Here she was totally off her own turf, surrounded by potential enemy troops, yet she was calm, peaceful, even serene. She knew that whatever we tossed at her, she would be able to catch and turn back at us with ten times the force.

"A hundred times the force," Natasha said in my mind.

"Oh, DOS!" I was such a blabber mind.

Grabbing Ona by an arm, I tried pulling her toward me. She wouldn't budge. "Damn it, Ona! Turn around!" I shouted.

"Zach, I don't want to miss the fun!" she said.

"Ona, it's not going to be fun!" I told her. "Natasha sees this coming!"

"Oh, Zach, you always see the negative side of things. You'll never make it in politics!"

"I don't want to make it in politics!" I said. "Just call off your dogs, Ona."

"They aren't my dogs, they are Threa's."

"There aren't any dogs," Threa added. "Though a wolf pack has just strolled in to join the party."

"Besides, it's too late," Ona added.

"Way too late," Threa concluded. "When my pets smell blood, there is just no turning back."

DOS! Things were sure to get dicey now. I didn't see any way this was going to end well for anybody.

Natasha was now surrounded by the biggest menagerie of cute and cuddly animals I had ever seen. Even the wolves were dancing a jig with a group of fiddle-playing pigs in blankets who had also joined the soon to be fray.

"Maybe they are trying to overdose her on cuteness?" HARV offered.

"Why are the pigs wearing pants and hats?" GUS asked.

"Doesn't really matter, GUS," I said.

"Shush," Ona ordered. "You're going to miss the good part!"

I could only assume the two super sisters who had been trying to lull Natasha into a false sense of security were about to strike. They knew that she knew that they knew that she knew they couldn't be trusted. But maybe, just maybe, they thought that if they kept her distracted long enough, Natasha would start to actually lose herself in the place and let her guard down.

"All these animals are sure cute," Natasha said, calling over to us. "But I'm guessing you had something else in mind when you brought me here."

Threa had the slyest, most evil grin I had ever seen on her. "You asked for it, honey!" she said.

The birds that had been braiding Natasha's hair started the attack. Mutating before our eyes from cute sweet tiny bluebirds into giant blue-winged monsters with long sharp talons as big as Natasha's head, their small rounded beaks turning into sharp jagged fangs. They looked like a sick cross between zombie vultures and vampire bats.

Truthfully, my first instinct was to zap the beasts out of the air, but then I remembered they were on my side. DOS! I wasn't sure I was on the right side, but I had to be.

Two of the bird creatures swiped at Natasha with their claws. The blows seemed to hit but do no damage.

"I phased myself out of this plane of existence," Natasha told the birds.

"Wow, I didn't know she could do that!" Threa said with a hint of awe in her voice.

The birds started swiping at Natasha again. They swiped. They swiped again. Then they were gone. Apparently this time Natasha chose to phase the bird things out of existence. Yikes!

Two more of the bird creatures came diving down toward Natasha, aiming to slice her with their beaks. They came to an abrupt halt, crashing into some sort of invisible force field, then crumpled to the ground.

"All creatures attack!" Threa shouted.

I've seen a lot of wacked-out crazy brawls in my day. DOS, I used to go to the mutant roller derby with my grandmother. But this was the strange brawl to pummel all strange brawls.

The wolves had sprouted fangs, claws, and scales on their backs and were rushing at Natasha. The cute bunnies were now in ninja outfits and leaping at Natasha with spin kicks and flying kicks. The mice grew to at least two meters tall, becoming hybrids of mice and men. They were lumbering at Natasha from another angle. The pigs in pants started using their suspenders as ninja choke cords and were hitting Natasha from another side. The dolphins were still dolphins, only now they were spraying Natasha with water, drilling her with more force than a high-powered fire hose. The squirrels were nipping at her heels and stomping on her feet. The chipmunks still looked the same, only now instead of singing to her, they were singing at her, bombarding her with high pitched tones. The butterflies that had been circling Natasha's head started to pulsate, flooding her eyes with bright blinding light.

"Apparently, Ona and Threa have studied our data on Natasha," HARV said.

The attacks were fierce. The strange thing (well, not the only strange thing but the strangest thing) was that Natasha was standing there in the middle of the animals gone berserk maelstrom, taking everything they could hit or bite or spit at her with.

"Are you trying to kill her?" I asked, not sure I wanted to hear the answer.

"Silly, silly Zach," Threa said. "My realm may be a physical place where I can be alone, but it also a mental place."

"Oh, okay . . ."

"Think of it as being in a holographic room where my mind is the projector," Threa said.

"A very warped projector," Ona added.

"Whatever the case, the damage she is receiving now is only mental. Our goal is to simply turn her mind off."

"Oh," I said. I wasn't sure if that was meant to make me feel better or not. Worse yet, I wasn't sure if it did.

Stranger yet, for all the force of all the creatures it

didn't look I needed to worry about Natasha's well-being, as she was taking everything they dished out.

"You know," Natasha said, wolves nipping at her heels. "I'm really trying to stay calm here, but you creatures, the noise, and the light are making it very hard."

"We live only to serve Master Threa!" all the animals said in chorus.

"I've never been prouder," Threa said.

"In that case," Natasha said. She said nothing else. She did nothing else. At least, it appeared she did nothing else. She obviously did do something else, because all of Threa's creatures simply turned to dust.

Natasha sat back down and dipped her feet in the pond again.

"Wow," HARV said.

"Dang!" GUS said.

"Impressive," Ona said.

"That bitch!" Threa shouted, stomping her feet. "That's it, now I'm taking the kid gloves off and letting her have it!"

"General Chen is right, she is too powerful," Ona said. "We have to stop her here!"

Threa arched her back and spread out her arms, glowing and surging with pure white energy. "I call on all my minions to attack!" Threa screamed.

A bolt of energy from Threa crackled up to the sky above us, splitting the sky open. Through the newly created ripple poured every creature I could ever imagine. Dragons of every color, ranging in size from large to mammoth, led the charge. They were followed by winged ogres and trolls, each of them wielding heavy spiked clubs. Wand-wielding fairies and pixies came next, blasting balls of energy at Natasha. Bringing up the rear was a mass of humanoid-shaped blobs. They were constantly forming and reforming hands, legs, and heads. It was an ugly sight. I couldn't pull away.

"Let's see how she deals with this!" Threa said.

Once again Natasha stood there taking the barrage. I've seen ants at picnics create more havoc than Threa's fantasy army.

"These attacks aren't going to work," HARV said. "They are mostly mental and mentally Natasha is nearly invulnerable."

Threa and Ona just smiled. Oh, how those smiles worried me.

The dragons were breathing fire, acid, and ice at Natasha. The pixies and fairies zapped her with balls of energy. The trolls and ogres were pounding away with their clubs. Waving her hand at the trolls and ogres, Natasha sent them flying away totally out of sight.

This simply gave an opening for the mob of bloblike creatures to move in. They combined into a giant ball and rolled over on top of Natasha, seemingly squishing her. The dragons and fairies stopped their airborne attacks. Everything was quiet. Was it over? Had the other attacks weakened Natasha enough that the blobs or blob could take her out?

I looked at Ona and Threa looking at the battlefield. "Is it over?" I asked.

The blob started rumbling and shaking.

"It's not over," HARV said.

"Not by a long shot," GUS said.

"DOS!" Ona said.

"Oh, dragon poop," Threa said.

The blob exploded into a mass of small dead blobs. The force of the blast knocked us all down, covering us with blob goo. I lay there on the ground for a nano surprised I wasn't dead. Ona and Threa were moving, so they weren't dead either. I stood up, wiping blob from myself.

I surveyed the battlefield. The force of the explosion had knocked all the flying creatures out of the sky. I didn't know if they were dead, but they wouldn't be fighting anymore.

"Major Wall was right on one account," Ona said.

"She would make a great tool if we could harness her."

Threa shook her head. "She is too wild to fully tame or control."

Ona nodded. "I agree."

"She is weak now, though, Sister. Now is our chance."

Ona pointed at Natasha, "Get her, Sister."

Threa leaped from our position over a hundred meters, crashing on top of Natasha.

Ona licked her lips. "Major Wall thought we could control her. Silly major. She must be killed."

"Ona, what are you going to do?" I asked, watching Threa and Natasha rolling across the ground, Threa pounding away, blow after blow.

"I just told you. I'm going to kill her," Ona said.

I jumped in front of Ona, spreading my arms out. "No. You can't! Don't you remember the plan?"

"Zach, the only plan I've ever really had was to take Natasha out," Ona said. "The first attacks were just to weaken her mentally. Now Threa is hurting her physically. So now I can hit her with a mental death blow!"

"Zach, Ona is right!" Threa said in my mind. *"I used to agree that Natasha could be tamed and controlled, but after seeing her in action I now must side with Ona and General Chen. Natasha must be stopped at all costs!"*

I pointed GUS at Ona. "I can't let you kill her!"

"Zach, she is a danger to all of Earth! I wouldn't be surprised if the aliens originally created psis on Earth knowing it would come to this."

"What?"

"Zach, the Council is aware of previous alien experiments on Earth. I wouldn't be surprised at all if aliens created the initial psis knowing we would create one with the power to destroy us all! Then they could take over our resources without lifting a finger."

Ona had become a true politician: blaming her

problems on others and rationalizing her decisions no matter what.

Threa had now rolled herself on top of Natasha. "Hit her fast, Ona. Not sure how long I can hold her!" she shouted.

Ona moved forward, pushing me to the ground. "Zach, I'm not going to debate this! You are either with us or against us! You can fire away with GUS or I will deal with you later!"

Ona concentrated her full attention on Natasha.

I aimed GUS. I wanted to fire. But I couldn't, not at Natasha. Sure, she may have been as big a threat as they said, but she didn't want to be. She didn't have to be. I wasn't going to have any part in killing her.

"Zach, you know this is wrong! I don't want to lose control!" Natasha screamed in my head. "Stop them before I stop them!" The government and the military had built a weapon they did not know how to use or control. Now they were just going to make things spin totally out of control. This wasn't just any weapon. This was a living, thinking, feeling human.

"Zach, keep her distracted!" Ona ordered. "I'm hitting her with the killing blow now!"

I had to stop this. I couldn't let Ona and Threa try to kill Natasha. Not only was it wrong, but I somehow sensed it wouldn't work. It would only make her madder and that would make things worse. I don't know how I knew, but I knew. There was only one way out of this. I had to knock Threa out.

Firing GUS, I heard and felt four blood-curdling screams that ripped from my brain through my bones. I was pretty sure one of the screams was mine.

Everything went black.

Chapter 44

The next thing I knew I was lying on the ground in the park outside of the convention center. Threa was lying next to me. Ona was lying next to her. A medical team was working frantically on Ona.

I sat up. My head was spinning and the ringing in my ears was deafening. I had been knocked out more in the last couple of days than a poor prize fighter is in their entire career. If this kept up I was going to have to consider changing careers. I noticed Tony was there.

"How long have I been out?" I asked.

"About an hour," he said.

"How'd we get out here?" I asked.

Tony shook his head. "Don't know. A passerby just said you three appeared out of thin air."

"What about Threa and Ona?" I asked.

"Threa is like the others. She was dead, but we were able to revive her."

"And Ona?"

"She's totally brain dead, Zach. They don't think she'll ever recover."

I stood up and looked around. "And Natasha?"

Tony shook his head. "No sign of her. What the hell happened to you guys?"

"Tony, I wish I knew."

I truly didn't know if I'd made matters worse. In trying to save Natasha, had I caused Ona's death?

I hitched a ride with Tony and the medical shuttle back to New Frisco. As we flew back, Tony and I talked in one of the side rooms. I was trying to make some sense out of what had happened.

"Sorry, I couldn't have gotten there sooner, Zach. I tried coming as soon as HARV sent the word out. Problem is, we don't have money in budget for extraneous travel. We're not politicians. You wouldn't believe the masses of red e-tape I had to cut through to get here."

"Sure, I would," I said leaning against the table we were sitting at. I took a hit of coffee. "Doesn't matter, you wouldn't have made a difference."

"Gee, thanks, Zach."

Shaking my head, I followed up on my point, "You and all your men wouldn't have made a difference. Natasha is too powerful . . ."

"What happened to you three in Threa's realm?" Tony asked. "You don't seem yourself."

"I shot Threa," I said. Maybe it was the concussion talking but I figured it was best to lay it out straight on the table.

"What?" Tony asked loudly. "You shot Threa Thompson! A standing member of the World Council."

"Not to kill, of course, just to stun her. I was hoping that would send us all out of her realm."

"So Threa and Ona couldn't kill Natasha?"

"Correct," I said.

"Therefore you shot Threa? Zach, I think I'm going to have to arrest you."

HARV appeared next to me in a formal gray suit and carrying an old-fashioned attaché case. He was in lawyer mode. DOS, as if things weren't bad enough already. "I assure you, Captain Rickey, Zach had nothing but the best intentions."

DOS, things had to be bad if HARV felt the need to defend me.

"Let me get this straight," Tony said, clearing his throat and taking a long, deep breath. "Ona and Threa couldn't stop the superpowerful vastly deadly Natasha, so Zach shot Threa."

HARV nodded. "Yes, that sums up the situation very well."

"Not helping here, HARV," I said.

HARV patted me on the shoulder. "Shush," he said, "let me handle this. Like they say, any person who defends himself has a fool for a lawyer."

"I'm not on trial, at least, not yet," I said.

"Zach, you're not leaving me a lot of choice here. First you escape from our headquarters . . ."

"I was being wrongly held," I said.

"He was," HARV agreed. "Zach was only defending himself." Opening up his case, he pulled out some papers. "I have the proof right here," he said thrusting the papers in Tony's face.

Tony waved the papers away. "I don't need to see those. I realize now we were all under false impressions planted in our brains by Natasha."

HARV stood up straight, crossed his arms, and smiled proudly, then said, "Then my client should be free to go."

"The thing is," Tony continued. "Just when it looks like Ona and Threa are about to put a stop to this Natasha, you go and shoot Threa." Tony paused for a nano, pointed and me and said, "How do you defend that?"

It was strange. I had followed my gut. I did what I thought was right. Problem was, I had no way of defending my action. As HARV would always tell me, my gut isn't admissible in court. Or anywhere else, for that matter.

"He had to do what he did to save us all," HARV said, showing better insight to my actions than I had.

"Come again?" Tony said.

"Zach realized that Ona and Threa couldn't stop Natasha, they could only make her angry. And if she got angry and lashed out, the damage would have been terrifying."

"Not sure that will hold up in court," Tony said.

"It won't have to. There will be no trial." A very familiar voice, Threa's voice, said. She was standing at the door. She looked weak and her skin was much closer to pale than it was golden with a hint of purple, but she was alive. "May I come in and sit?" Threa asked, very much out of character. "Being dead is hard on one's constitution."

Shooting up from my chair, I went over to Threa. Taking her arm, I guided her to a chair next to Tony.

"Thanks," she said with a smile.

"Threa, your recovering is remarkable," HARV said. "The other super ladies killed by Natasha are still bed bound."

Threa nodded. "I would be too except for two things. One, her attack happened in my realm. My constitution is much higher there, as I feel so secure there. At least, I did."

"And two?" Captain Rickey asked.

"Zach shot me," Threa said. "That knocked my mind out before Natasha's scream could damage me too much."

"So, Zach shooting you helped the situation?" Tony said not even trying to mask the surprise in his voice.

Threa lifted her head up high. Looking Tony dead in the eyes, she said, "In more ways than a simple little mind like yours can ever imagine."

I tried not to snicker. It certainly wouldn't have been appropriate.

"My sister Ona and I had gone a bit mad with power," Threa admitted, being shockingly blunt. "All we cared about was stopping Natasha and not even for the good of the world. DOS, it wasn't even for the good of our careers. We're mega-rich superbabes, we don't need any more credits or fame. We wanted to stop her for our egos. We couldn't stand the fact that we may not have been the biggest most powerful bitches on the block," Threa said. She stopped to collect her breath. "And by block I mean planet," she added.

Out of all the unbelievable things I have witnessed in my career, this may have been the most mind-boggling of all. A politician was telling the truth.

"We made a grave mistake that we almost compounded," Threa said, forehead in hand.

"Wow, a politician admitting to a mistake," I said. "Now I have seen everything."

Threa looked at me and forced a weak smile. "I am resigning from the World Council. At least for now. I need to need to set my life back on its proper path and before I can do that I need to discover the trail that leads to the path . . ."

"So, by shooting you, Zach saved you?" Tony said, probably not even believing he was saying what he was saying.

"Zach followed his sense and he was right," Threa said. "He saved not only me, but everybody, as the psychic scream Natasha was putting out because of our mindless attack would have mentally crippled us all."

"Really?" Tony said.

"I knew he did the right thing!" HARV said.

"Me, too!" GUS said.

"As it turns out, only the psis of the world were damaged," Threa said. "They weren't hurt, but their abilities have been greatly reduced . . ."

"I'm getting confirmation of this now," HARV said.

"It may be these effects are self-correcting," Threa said. "But if Zach hadn't acted how he did when he did . . ."

"But your sister Ona is dead, dead, dead," Tony said, unable to hold back the cop inside of him.

"That's not Zach's fault either," Threa said. "Natasha simply deflected Ona's killing blow back at her. My sister killed herself."

HARV closed his briefcase and set his hands on top of it. "I rest my case," he said.

Chapter 45

When I stepped in my front door, Electra was there waiting for me. I have never in my life been so happy to see her. We hugged for a good two minutes. Then we kissed—hard, even harder than normal.

"I'm glad you're here," I said.

She took my hand and led me to the couch. We sat.

"HARV told me what happened. Of course it's all over the press. Is Ona really dead?"

I lowered my head. "Her body isn't, but her brain is beyond repair."

"That's terrible," Electra said. "Truthfully, I never liked her that much, but nobody deserves that fate."

The thing that was eating at me now was that this was the fate Ona had intended for Natasha. She only got what she was attempting to give. She got greedy and power-mad. She got what she had coming. Yet, for better or worse, she was a friend. I felt bad that I had let her down.

"How are Carol and the others?" I asked.

Electra cracked a weak grin. "They are improving . . ."

HARV appeared in the room. Of course he did. No way he was letting Electra and me share a tender mo-

ment alone for too long. In some ways he was like a
needy dog who has to be petted when its owners hug.

"I am blocked from the medical records," HARV
said. "Did they suffer any new repercussions from Natasha's latest attack?"

"It wasn't an attack, it was a defense mechanism,"
I said defensively without thinking.

"From what I understand, she defended herself
quite well," Electra said. "EEGs show that their powers have been reduced, but they suffered no other
ill effects."

"Yes," HARV nodded. "The data is coming in now
from all over. It appears all psis in the world have
been greatly reduced in power."

"Is Natasha really that powerful?" Electra asked.

"She is powerful and resourceful and fairly well designed," HARV answered. "I surmise that she actually
broadcast over the P-Pod network. Maybe even seep-
ing her power out over other communication networks."

I thought of something. I should have thought of
this sooner. DOS, was I slipping? "What about the
Moon?" I asked HARV.

"Funny you should ask," HARV said. "I have been
in contact with your blue-haired friend Elena, as she
now leads the psi school on the Moon. The psi energy
bolt did reach them but they were able to somewhat
defend themselves. Their powers have been reduced
but not by as much as Earth's psis. That further
strengthens my belief that Natasha used the P-Pod
network. That network is not as strong on the Moon."

"So, nobody else died?" I said.

"Nope," Electra said. "Not to my knowledge."

"Not to my data, either," HARV said.

Things could have turned out a lot worse than they
did. I guess I should have felt better than I did. But
I didn't. Maybe it was because my old mentor used
to say, "When you start feeling good about a job,
that's when you know your ass is in trouble." But that

wasn't it. There was more going on here than met the eye, at least, at first glance. In a way, Natasha had just reset the psis a bit. It probably wasn't a bad thing for humanity. I had the feeling psis had been growing in power too fast. They were starting to make the masses anxious. Who knew if the changes were permanent? Either way I could live with them. I just couldn't live with this strange feeling in my gut.

Electra started stroking my shoulders. It felt good. "Something else is bothering you, my love."

She was right. She was almost always right.

"I'm still not sure what the right side is here," I said. "I know Natasha is a danger to all that exists and she needs to brought in and trained or frozen. I'm just not sure if the people who hired me have the world's best interests at heart. For once in my life I'm not sure if I'm part of the solution. In fact, I may be contributing to the problem. DOS! I may be the problem."

I held for a moment to let Electra and HARV think about what I had said.

"I know there is no such thing as absolute right. I know there is no such thing as absolute wrong, though some things, like putting ketchup on ice cream or ice in beer, come close. I know we all see the world the way we want or need to see the world. But I was always reasonably certain I was one of the better guys. The guy who would do the right thing. The guy who was fighting the good fight. Sure, I cared about myself, but I also cared about others. I wanted to make the world a better, safer place."

Electra and HARV both laughed at me. Not exactly the reaction I was expecting.

"Silly Zach," HARV said.

"I so agree," Electra said.

"Me, too!" GUS said.

Electra gently touched my hand. "Zach, for all your complications and flaws, you are the purest guy I know."

"I agree," HARV said. "Though I'd like to add you have a LOT of flaws."

"No more than any other human," GUS said. "And some machines . . ."

"Do I go after Natasha or just let her be?" I asked.

I waited for an answer. None came. I waited a bit longer. Still nothing. Then finally, "Only you know the answer to that," Electra said.

"Yeah," HARV agreed.

"I'm sure you'll make the right choice," GUS said.

"I'm sure you will, too," Electra said.

"I'm not totally sure," HARV said. "But the data suggests that you will."

I took a deep breath. One option was pure and simple. Just let Natasha go. Let the government and Earth Force do their best to try to stop her. It wouldn't be up to me. It wouldn't be my duty. The other was the sticky one, the one that would require a lot of leg- and brainwork on my part. To keep going to track Natasha down. Not to kill her, but to bring her in. There really was no choice. I had started the job. I know I needed to finish the job. I was going to find Natasha. Not sure why, yet I knew it was right.

Chapter 46

For the next few hours I just rested at home, collecting my thoughts. Trying to figure out where Natasha might be now and what I could do to stop her. Most of my thinking was done sitting on my couch with Electra by my side. We were kicking around ideas. After all, you never know when inspiration will strike. Like my old mentor would say, "It's always great when inspiration strikes as long you don't let it blindside you or kick you in the balls." (Yeah, she was a tough old broad, but thinking back she really wasn't that bright.) The good thing was, with Electra and HARV and GUS by my side I was less likely to be blindsided.

Electra, HARV, and I kicked around ideas, but none of them resonated in my brain. None of them felt right. So finally, I didn't believe I was going to ask this, but I had to.

"HARV, contact Major Wall at Roswell and ask her if she has any leads as to where Natasha might be."

"Major Wall is no longer Major Wall," HARV said.

"Don't tell me she got busted again!" I said.

"On the contrary," HARV said. "Since Natasha has

proved her true power and shown what a danger she is, the World Council promoted Wall back to general."

"Amazing," I said.

"She's actually a two-star general now," HARV added.

"Twice as amazing. What wonder brain at the Council thought of giving her an extra promotion?

"The newest Council Member," Electra said. "The one replacing Threa."

"They replaced Threa already?"

"Very good, Zach," HARV said. "Nice to see you still have that keen PI instinct."

"Yes," Electra said. "Out of respect to Ona's still-living body, they haven't replaced her yet. But they have replaced Threa."

"That's morbid and strange and all too believable," I said. "At least when it comes to the World Council."

"Zach, the Council isn't that bad!" Electra told me.

Something wasn't quite right here. Electra was trying hard not to show it, but her back was straight and her eyes sharper and more focused than they had been. She was in a defensive position. It wasn't like Electra to defend the World Council.

"Why are you so defensive of them?" I asked. Part of me was guessing at the answer, the other part of me was hoping the guessing part was wrong. "DOS!" I said. "Your mother has been named to the Council. Hasn't she?"

Electra looked away from me and then directly at me. She couldn't help but be proud of her mom. I mean, I may make fun of the Council, but even I must concede the people on it wield a lot of power.

"Yes. The other Council members figured her views actually match up quite nicely with Threa's. In fact, Threa totally endorses my mom."

"Well, Threa is a loon," I said.

Electra glared at me. (It was with love, but a glare

is a glare.) "Zach, this is my mom we're talking about. She is one of the more qualified people on the planet."

I couldn't argue. Even if I could, I was too smart to argue. I guess there could have been many worse choices. The good thing was Helena wasn't superpowered. I guess the Council had learned their lesson as the fates of the last super powered members weren't so good.

"So your mom promoted Wall?" I said.

"She thought it was prudent," Electra said. "After all, Wall knows Natasha better than anybody."

"Hence the reason I want to talk to her," I said. Turning to HARV I asked, "How are you coming at getting through to Roswell?"

"I got through," HARV said.

"And?"

"General Wall deemed that facility not secure enough, so she and her staff have transferred," HARV said.

"To where?"

"To the most secure base possible."

"The orbital base," I said.

"Right."

"Okay, then contact the orbital base and let them know I want to talk to General Wall."

"Done," HARV said.

"And?"

"The base communications officer says Wall now likes to be referred to as Two Star General Wall."

"Okay, tell them I'd like to speak to Two Star General Wall," I groaned.

There was a pause. "They say the Two Star General is very busy right now. She will contact you at the appropriate time."

"That's it?" I said.

HARV nodded. "They say they are very busy and not to call them but they'll call us."

"Not too helpful," I said.

Looking at Electra, I said, "Now may be the time to play the mom card."

"Zach, my mother hasn't even been on the World Council for twenty-four hours and you already want me to use her clout."

"Welcome to the world of politics. She promoted Wall. Wall owes her."

"I'll see what I can do!" Electra said.

"Now that's my girl," I said then kissed her.

"You know sometimes I think you only kiss me when you want something," Electra said, touching her P-Pod.

I shrugged. "I'm a man. I always want something."

There was a knock at my door. Probably saved me from getting into too much trouble.

"Who's there?" I asked HARV.

HARV morphed into an image of JJ standing at the door, wearing his full armor.

"Should I let him in?" HARV asked.

I stood up from the couch, stretching a bit. "I'll let him in," I said.

"Do you think that is wise?" HARV cautioned as I walked to the door. "He seems quite aggravated. Perhaps I should call the police, or at least send a security bot to deal with him."

"Nonsense, we're partners now," I said, reaching for the door knob. (Yes, my house still has door knobs.) "I'm sure I can reason with him."

I opened the door.

JJ hit me with a right cross to the jaw, sending me reeling back into my living room.

"Ah, yes, your legendary people skills!" HARV said. "How could I forget?"

Chapter 47

JJ stormed into my house and lifted me back to my feet. His hands were curled into fists and he had a look of angry determination in his eyes. I quickly motioned to Electra and HARV not to take action. I wanted to handle this alone. I needed to handle this alone.

"JJ, calm down," I said, arms held out straight.

He hit me with a left hook to the jaw, knocking me down again.

"So, your plan is to let him tire himself out by punching you so much?" HARV said. "I'm sure even you can see the flaws in that logic. You're just lucky I deactivated his battle armor."

"Yes, my thoughts exactly," I told HARV, making it clear from my tone I didn't mean it.

JJ lifted me back up off the floor again.

He started to throw a roundhouse right. Enough was enough. Blocking his blow with a left, I hit him with a quick back fist dead on the nose. I drew blood. He pulled back, holding his nose.

"DOS! Why'd you do that?" he screamed at me, though it was muffled by his hands over his nose, losing some effect.

"Sorry kid, I can only take being pummeled for so long before I hit back."

Electra got up from the couch and walked over to JJ. "Let me look at the nose," she said.

"No!" JJ said defiantly, pushing her away.

Electra put him down on the ground with a leg sweep. (She took precautions, though, so his head never hit the floor.) Standing over him, she said, "Listen, kid, I'm a doctor. Don't make me hurt you!"

JJ looked up to me. "Wow, now I see what you see in her."

"The question that has baffled experts for years is what she sees in him," HARV said.

"I think you're swell," GUS said from up my arm.

"Did your underarm just talk and actually use the word swell?" JJ asked from the floor.

"Don't worry about it, kid," I said. "Why in Gates' name did you attack me?"

JJ tried pushing himself up. Electra wouldn't let him. "Stay down, chico," she ordered.

"I'd listen to the lady," I said.

"When Zach is right, he is right," HARV said.

"Ditto!" GUS shouted from up my arm.

JJ pointed at me. "There it is again!"

"Just answer the question, JJ," I said.

JJ locked his gaze on me. "You let Fera die!"

Shaking my head, "I didn't let anybody die."

"You used her for bait to distract that Natasha bitch so you could be the hero!" JJ said.

I looked at him. "Excuse me? How did you come up with this?"

"I wasn't born yesterday," he told me. "You used them all so you could be the hero."

"Not true, kid," I said.

"I assure you, JJ, Zach is not nearly clever or devious enough to use a bevy of superhuman females the way you assumed he was."

"That's true," Electra said, checking out his nose

with a pen light. "Zach is many things, some of them
not so good, but devious is not one of them."

"Thanks," I said, making a mental note not to use
HARV and probably not Electra if I ever needed
character witnesses.

"Besides, Zach was killed, too!" GUS shouted from
under my arm.

I popped GUS into my hand so he wouldn't have
to shout. I showed him to JJ.

"Ah, it's your weapon," JJ said knowingly. Getting
back to the conversation at hand, "So you died, too?"

"Yes, I just wasn't as dead as the others," I said.
"May be my constitution."

"Or more likely that Natasha took it easy on you,"
HARV said.

"I'm with HARV on that one," GUS said.

"Whatever the case, I wasn't dead long," I said.
"And neither were any of the ladies that fought
with me."

"Yes," Electra, said helping JJ back to his feet.
"They will all be fine. It will just take some recovery
time. Being dead is hard on most people's systems."

"So you weren't just using them?" JJ said.

"Smart kid. Glad to see I don't have to punch you
again," I said.

JJ sat down on the floor, legs crossed, head in hands.
I assumed this was his thinking position. "So you're
not a complete ass after all," he said.

"No, at least not a complete one," I said. "I really
did have everybody's best interests at heart."

JJ pushed himself to a standing position.

"Do you still want my help?" he asked.

"I'll take all the help I can get," I said.

"What's the plan then? JJ asked. "Where is
Natasha?"

"That would be the billion credit question," HARV
answered.

I shrugged. "Not sure where she is. I just know I
have to find her and bring her in."

"How you going to do that?"

HARV and Electra just looked at me.

"Kid, if you're going to keep asking questions I don't have the answers to, I'm going to have to slug you again."

"You don't know," JJ said.

Touching me nose, I said, "Vingo."

"You have to have a plan . . ." JJ persisted.

"Do you have a place to sleep tonight?" I asked.

"I was thinking of sleeping in the hospital by Fera's side. Though she snores a lot and the chairs are uncomfortable, making it hard to get any rest."

"So you'll stay here tonight. I'll have the maidbot make up the guest room."

"But . . ." JJ started to say.

"No buts, JJ, stay here." Electra insisted. "Fera is in good hands. I'm certain that Zach will very shortly form a plan of attack. When that happens we're all going to need to be as rested as we can."

"How can you be so certain?" JJ said.

Electra turned to me and smiled. "Because I know Zach. "

Chapter 48

Lying in bed that night, a lot of thoughts raced through my mind, most of them about where Natasha could be. Some of them about what JJ had said. Had I used the ladies? Had I let everybody down?

"Zach, go to sleep," HARV said in my head. *"Don't tell me you let the words of that kid get to you."*

"They didn't get to me, they just made me think."

"Zach, how many times do I have to tell you, you've got me to do the thinking now!"

"Did I let everybody down?" I asked.

"Zach, no, of course not," HARV answered.

"I did get everybody killed," I said. *"Including myself."*

"You didn't get everybody killed," HARV corrected. *"Everybody got killed."* A slight delay to process. *"Besides, everybody ended up living. Think of it as the ultimate growth experience."*

I knew HARV was trying to be helpful and sensitive, which was a pleasant change. It even helped, at least a little. I knew, though, I had to find Natasha. Still wasn't sure why. Still wasn't sure how. I just understood that if I didn't things would somehow get even worse, and quickly.

"Zach, squirming," Electra mumbled, three quarters asleep.

"Sorry," I said.

Turning toward me, she hugged me. "Don't worry, you'll find her," she whispered in my ear.

"Then what?" I said softly.

"You'll do what you always do. What you do best. Improvise until you find a solution," Electra said.

I smiled, a little. I closed my eyes, trying to will myself to sleep. Like my old mentor used to say, "A sleepy PI ends up sleeping with the fishes." I don't know why I was thinking of the old battle-ax so much now. I guess I was wondering what she would do. She wouldn't have quit. I knew that. She didn't have the tools I have, HARV and GUS, but she was a stubborn lady who would follow a trail until it ran cold. Then she'd pick right up on the next trail and follow that until she got her man, woman, or bot. (There weren't as many kinds of bad guys in her day.)

I had trailed Natasha to a lot of different places, all leading to vacation spots. It never ended well for either of us. Natasha would probably try to find a new type of place to hide and hang out. I thought about our latest confrontation. Natasha seemed quite happy in Threa's realm. Maybe she would try to create a realm of her own? Nah, that wasn't it. Natasha didn't have the resources Threa did. Even if she did, from what I understood (mainly from HARV's educated guesses), Threa has spent years and years building her realm. Even if Natasha had both the resources and time to build her own realm, she wouldn't go that route. She wasn't that egotistical or that much of a loon.

No, Natasha would try something else. I had mentioned to Ona the possibility of putting Natasha on her own island. I traced back through the 411 I had on Natasha. I knew the government had isolated her at least for a few days each month when Natasha was in a particularly touchy mood. HARV had found some government worker's notes on that. It seemed Natasha reluctantly cooperated with the isolation but always hated her time alone. Maybe she needed to find herself an island with just a small population and live there. DOS, with her abilities she could easily make herself queen of the island. Thing is, that would mean inflicting her will over innocent people. That didn't seem to exactly match Natasha's m.o. Sure she would control people for the moment like she did in Vegas but totally taking over the lives of innocent civilians— I didn't think she would go that far.

I fell asleep dreaming of hula dancers on an island, a floating island. It was a weird dream, even by my standards. The dancers, instead of wearing the traditional hula dresses, wore military khaki micromini skirts. It had been a long few days, I had been dead— literally. I was allowed a strange, slightly erotic dream or three.

Waking up the next morning, I felt refreshed. Not great, but better than I had in a while. Turning to the side, I noticed Electra was out of bed. The smell of bacon (real bacon, not the soy stuff—I can tell the difference) came waffling into the room. Interestingly enough so did the smell of waffles. If that didn't get a man out of bed nothing would.

I popped up. Stretching, I didn't feel nearly as bad as I thought I should. I had taken a bit of beating the last few days. I was surprised more things didn't ache more.

HARV appeared behind me. "I've augmented your neurotransmitters, so you can now ignore minor aches and pains."

"I'm not sure I like you playing with my neurotransmitters, HARV!"

He just shook his head. "Do you have anything against taking painkillers when you are in pain?"

"No."

"Then think of me as just eliminating the middle-man. With no nasty side effects."

"Except, of course, for the supercomputer playing with my brain."

HARV put his hand on his chest. "I don't consider that a nasty side effect at all. I consider that a definite plus."

I didn't push the issue. I felt good. That had to count for something.

"Electra says if you don't hurry, JJ will eat all the food."

"Tell her I'll be out in five, after I take a quick shower, and to save me some food and that I love her."

"I'll tell her two out of the three," HARV said then disappeared.

When I joined Electra and JJ at the breakfast table, I could see from his plate and the syrup on his face that JJ had already consumed a good deal of food. He didn't act like he was ready to stop eating anytime soon.

"This is great!" JJ said, with a smile wider than old-Texas. "I haven't had a home-cooked meal in long time."

As I was sitting down at the table, a bot poured me a cup of joe. "Oh, I thought Fera would be the home-cooking type," I said sarcastically.

"You thought wrong," JJ said, diving into his latest waffle.

Electra brought me over a plate filled with waffles, bacon, and served with a kiss. "Sleep well?" she asked.

"Not as good as when I was dead, but all in all not bad."

I took a piece of bacon and munched on it. "HARV, any word from General Wall?"

HARV appeared, sitting at the table next to me.

He was reading an old-fashioned paper newspaper. "Two Star General Wall, remember?"

I sighed. "Any word, HARV?"

Putting the paper down, he peered at me. "Ah, no. Not yet." Lifting the paper up to block my view of him, he started reading.

"Have you tried contacting her again?"

"Yes, of course. I got the same reply every time. I'm starting to think it's a recording."

Sitting back in my chair, I looked at HARV. "This didn't strike you as odd?"

"Zach, they are the military. They always strike me as odd. I figured they were just planning some top secret way to stop Natasha and they want to be left alone."

"Normally, I might agree. But the military is big on team play, working together as long as they can call the shots. They can't call anything if they don't return our calls."

"Your point being?" HARV asked.

I spun toward Electra. "Time to play the 'my mom's a World Council member' card. We need her to contact the general to see if she gets the same response."

"And if she does?" Electra said.

"That means Natasha is there, running the show."

"But . . ." HARV said.

"But nothing, it's actually the perfect spot for her. It's secluded, secure, and everybody there is military, no innocent civilians."

"HARV, put me through to my mom," Electra said.

HARV morphed into Helena's form. She was sitting at a desk, stamping electronic form after electronic form. She looked up and saw us.

"Hi, honey. Hello, Zachary. JJ. Zachary, I suppose we owe you thanks for at least attempting to stop Natasha. I'm sure you won't mind, though, if we have the military take it from here."

I minded. I minded a lot. I wasn't going to tell her

that, though. "I see where you are coming from," I told Helena.

She tilted her head back away from the screen. "I was expecting more of a fight from you."

"I pick my battles carefully," I told her. "I realize Natasha is way out of my league."

Helena forced a smile, not a very big one, but I could detect faint traces. "Very good. What matters is that girl is out of any one person's league. I'm sure, though, General Wall and her team can handle her." Her smile widened briefly. "Excuse me, Two Star General Wall."

"Along those lines, Helena, I just thought of something that Natasha mentioned that I think the general might find a good clue to her whereabouts. Can you put me through to the general?"

Helena thought about my request. "The general is a very busy lady."

"This can help free up some of her schedule," I insisted.

"I've heard it, Mother," Electra said. "I believe this could really help the general nail Natasha once and for all."

"Yes," HARV added. "What a tremendous way to start off your World Council career. Putting the general in contact with the man who holds the key clue."

"Yes, I agree," Helena said.

Turning away from us, she pressed some buttons on a computer screen. She looked at the screen. Her image was covered in a dark black veil.

"She turned on the privacy mode," HARV said.

After a couple of minutes, the veil slid off, allowing us to see Helena again.

"Well?" I asked.

Helena looked a little puzzled, a little more perturbed. "Their communications officer wouldn't let me speak to her. He just repeated over and over, the general is unavailable at the moment. She will get back to you at her earliest opportunity."

"Did you point out that you were the World Council member responsible for making the general a general again?" I asked.

Helena nodded. "Of course I did. I may be new to the role but not the game."

"And?" I asked.

"Same response," Helena said. "If I didn't have so much to do I'd be offended."

"Thanks for your time, Helena," I said.

"Love you, Mom," Electra shouted.

"Your daughter makes great waffles," JJ shouted.

Helena's image morphed back to HARV.

I stood up from the table. "Natasha is on the orbiting base. I know it!"

"How can you be so certain?" JJ asked.

"I just am," I said.

JJ looked at Electra, then HARV. They each stood there, arms crossed.

"He's pretty good at things like this," Electra said.

HARV started scratching his head. "I can't explain it yet; but it's true. Zach is a really good, for lack of a better word, guesser. All humans have talents, Zach's happens to be he can examine an absurd situation and come up with the most likely outrageous outcome."

"Speaking of which, I dreamed of military micro-mini skirts," I said.

Electra raised an eyebrow. "Excuse me?"

"HARV, how do we get to the Earth Force Orbiting Space Station?" I asked.

"There's only one way in and one way out—the same way—of EFOSS. A space elevator, called the EFOSS SE."

"Yes, of course that's what they call it," I said.

"There was some talk of calling it Tsiolkovsky's Space Elevator, but people figured nobody would get that reference. Kind of like the New Brooklyn Bridge and the Bush Library."

"Where's the elevator located?" I asked. I looked at JJ. "I'm not a fan of teleporters, but thanks to them we can be anywhere in the world in a matter of hours, and that's a good thing."

"The base is here, located in the New Frisco Bay," HARV said.

"Well, that's even better."

Chapter 49

"I've got good news and bad news," HARV told Electra, JJ, and me.

"What's the good news?" I asked. I needed some good news.

"I have tapped into the Earth Force secure database and located the platform of the sky elevator. It sits ten kilometers away, pretty well isolated in the bay," HARV said.

"The bad news?" JJ asked.

"There is no way to get to it," HARV said. "The place is very secure. It can be reached only by a specially equipped hover and that hover is currently docked at the station."

"What about teleporting?" Electra asked.

HARV shook his head. "No Earth-based teleporters can go there. They are actually designed specifically so they cannot be tampered with to teleport there."

"Wow, very thorough," I said. "Especially for the military."

I knew I had to get to that elevator. I also knew

the faster I got there, the better. Not sure how I knew any of this, I just did.

"HARV, contact the Gladians orbiting above us. Tell them I need their help again."

HARV smiled. "Very good, Zach."

A few moments of silence. HARV frowned. "They are not responding to my pages."

"Tell them we're about to leak the story of them spying on Earth to the media. If they think they've had PR problems before . . ."

Before I could say another word, Electra, JJ, and I were standing on port pads in the alien ship. For me, this is old hat, but this was certainly a new experience for Electra and JJ.

"Are we where I think we are?" Electra asked.

"If you are thinking we are on a Gladian ship orbiting Earth, then yes," I said.

"Way cool!" JJ said, eyes and mouth both wide open.

"Why did you threaten us?" the lead alien asked.

Hopping down off the pad, I said, "To get your attention. How did you find me so fast?"

"The computer in your brain gives you a unique human signature, making it easy for us to locate you," the leader said.

"Why'd you bring my girlfriend and the kid?"

Silence. In fact, the aliens dropped back a step or two. "Okay, we can't that accurately locate you," one of the aliens admitted.

"No problem. Well, no big problem," I told them. "The key issue is I am here and you can put me where I need to go."

"Where do you wish to go?" one of the aliens asked.

"I need to get to the Earth Force Orbiting Space Station," I said. (I kind of thought they would know that. I guess the aliens weren't as advanced as I had thought.)

More silence. Silence may be golden, but it's not all that helpful.

"Well?"

"How do you know that we know about the existence of that base and its location?" one of the aliens asked.

"You're nosy aliens," I said bluntly.

They all shrugged at once.

"Fair enough," one said.

"Well put," another said.

"We like to keep up," the third said.

"So, can you teleport me to the base?" I asked.

"We cannot transfer you directly to the base. There is a magnetic field over it, preventing all teleporting in or out."

"I figured that," I said. "That would be too easy. Can you just get me to the elevator?"

They turned to each other and started chatting quickly in their own language. Interestingly enough, they decided to talk out loud instead of telepathically.

Electra walked over to me. "You know these aliens and work with them?"

"We're associates," I said.

"Sub absolute zero with three o's!" JJ exclaimed.

I patted him on the head. "Calm down, boy, we don't want to have an accident on the alien ship."

The aliens stopped their chatter. Turning to me, the lead one asked, "And what is in this for us?"

"You get to know you helped me take Natasha out of circulation while keeping her alive. Remember, that's what you wanted."

They conversed again, this time more briefly. "That's what we wanted, but that was before we knew you would want our help. It costs us energy to teleport you up and down. We're on a tight budget here. Energy just doesn't grow from stardust, you know."

The Gladians may very well be the cheapest beings in the entire universe. If they're aren't, I pity us all.

"I'm working for free now," I told them.

"Surely they paid you something for your troubles," one of the back aliens said.

"Not a lot," I said.

"Not a lot is more than nothing . . ."

"Why do you want Earth credits, anyhow?" Electra asked.

Silence.

"They like to shop," HARV answered for them.

"Understandable," Electra said with a nod.

Time was wasting and time was one of the many resources we didn't have a lot to waste. Sadly, so were credits.

"I'll give you three thousand credits," I said.

"That's not much," the leader said.

"More than it costs to teleport anywhere on Earth," Electra said.

The leader shook her bald head no. "This isn't Earth."

"Zach will also give you a percentage of sales of his memoirs when he, well, more likely, I write them. He'll give you one percent. A very generous offer," HARV said.

All three of the aliens looked at each other. They started buzzing away, chatting at high speed in their alien language.

"Excuse me, aliens!" JJ said armed raised.

The aliens stopped their buzzing. "Yes?" One of them said to JJ.

"Do you have a bathroom on board?" JJ asked.

"No. Being highly advanced beings we have no need to relieve ourselves," another alien said.

"Really?" JJ said.

"No, of course not," the lead alien said. "We have a public relievement facility in the main area of the craft that resides below the bubble section you are currently located in."

"How do I get there?" JJ asked.

"The ship is totally built from nanotechnology, meaning it has one hundred percent elasticity and can be molded to meet our ever changing requirements. And it has complete area to area teleport capacity."

"I repeat, how do I get there?" JJ said.

One of the aliens pointed to the ceiling. "Look upward and state your destination."

JJ looked up and said, "Bathroom fast!"

JJ was engulfed in a ball of energy and then disappeared. I assumed he was teleported to the can.

I turned to the aliens. "Now if we can please get back to the matter at hand. Getting me to the base."

"We need to discuss it among ourselves and our planet-based accountant consultants," one of the aliens said.

The three aliens looked at each other and started chirping away at high speeds. I could only assume they were debating. The debating went on and on. I started tapping my foot to show my displeasure, hopefully speeding up the process.

Electra leaned forwarded and whispered to me, "Are Gladians always like this?"

"Fraid so," I sighed.

"Um, guys, I have a superpowered lady to track down," I said to the Gladians.

Ignoring me they continued to chirp away either with or at each other. Just then a red light started flashing and siren started blaring. The aliens stopped their clattering.

"What's going on?" I asked. "Some sort of meteor heading our way? Has Earth Force launched missiles at you?"

"Worse," one of the aliens said. She touched a button on her sleeve and pointed to the middle of the room.

JJ materialized. One of his hands was outstretched and holding a couple of socks. He had a weak grin on his face.

"Somebody is trying to steal from us!" the alien finished.

The three aliens started to move toward JJ. Holding out an arm to stop them I said, "Let me deal with the idiot!"

I walked up to JJ. He was slumping over like maybe if he slumped over enough we wouldn't notice him. I gave him a slap on the back of the head.

"What the DOS were you thinking?" I shouted.

JJ put his arms behind him and slumped backward. "Uh, I figured nobody would miss three socks . . ."

"What were you doing with socks?" I demanded.

"Are you kidding?" JJ said. "Actually worn alien socks. I can make a small fortune selling these on e-square-Bay!"

I grabbed him by his collar. "You risked the safety of the Earth and interplanetary relationships over socks?" I said.

The three aliens moved forward. They were more curious than angry. "How much of a small fortune?" One of the aliens said to JJ.

"Probably ten thousand credits each," JJ told them. "I can act as your middleman selling the socks and keeping ten percent for myself."

"Two percent," an alien said.

"Eight," JJ countered.

"Three," the alien said.

"Five," JJ said.

The aliens looked at each other and smiled. "Release the boy," they said.

I let JJ go.

"This is a business opportunity our highly advanced aliens minds could have never before considered." The three of them bowed to JJ. "For that we are grateful."

"So now do we have a deal?" I said.

"Besides our deal with the young one, our pre-sock-stealing offer still stands?" one of the aliens said.

"It does," HARV said

All three of the aliens smiled. "We have a deal."

The leader pointed to the teleport pads. "Please stand on the pads."

No time now for thanks, complaints, or good-byes. Electra, JJ, and I moved to the teleport pads.

"This was cooool even if I didn't get to keep the socks," JJ said just as we disappeared.

Chapter 50

We appeared in a long plain corridor.

"Is this the right place?" JJ asked.

Three heavily-armed military men dressed in blue battle armor were coming at us from one side of the corridor. Two more were coming at us from the other side.

"I'd say yes," I said.

"Halt!" one of the military men, a sergeant, ordered.

We all put our hands up to show we meant no harm as the five men surrounded us. Something about them wasn't quite right. Their movements seemed forced and jerky, more like puppets than men.

"I'm Zachary Nixon Johnson!" I said.

"We know who you are," the sergeant said.

"I need to take the elevator to the base for official World Council business," I said.

The sergeant shook his head slowly. His eyes were glazed. "Sorry, the base is on lockdown."

"By whose orders?"

He thought a moment. "By the order of General Wall."

That was it. The final sign that I was dead right.

Sandy Wall had made it clear that whenever anyone referred to her, it would be as "Two Star General Wall." She'd have been especially firm about it with her own troops. Natasha, on the other hand, probably couldn't care less—and so neither did her puppets.

Natasha was on that base, in fact, she was running the base. It was up to me to get up there and talk her down. Of course, there were at least five heavily-armed men who felt differently. I've never been one to let something like that stop me. Linux, five heavily-armed, well-trained soldiers against Electra, JJ, and me. I would triple down on those odds any day.

Raising both of my arms so the troops knew I would be no trouble, I said, "Listen, my fine soldiers. I know you are just doing your duty, but I have to get up there."

All five of them lowered their guns and aimed them at us. They flipped off the safeties. That was my cue.

Flicking my wrist, I popped GUS into my hand. I blasted the first guy with a heavy electrical stun bolt. He may have been wearing body armor, but it wasn't built to take a shock. He dropped to the ground convulsing.

Spinning toward the others, I became a spectator. Electra put one down with a sidekick to his knee followed by a snap kick to the chin. She put the second guy down with a vicious spinning scissor kick to the top of his head. That's why I love her, she so knows how to inflect maximum damage with minimal effort, yet make it look so poetic.

JJ wasn't nearly so elegant, moving forward quickly at the two guys closest to him. He extended his arms, clotheslining them. Once behind them, he turned and used his body weight to drive them both into the floor face-first.

JJ looked up at me and said, "That was fun. Are there more?"

HARV appeared. "Nope, only those five guards at the elevator."

"Oh," JJ said.

I pointed to the door at the far end of the corridor. "Let's go."

Walking toward the door, JJ could barely contain his excitement. Even Electra seemed extra pumped.

"I forgot how exhilarating a real fight can be," Electra told me, drawing closer to the door.

"I can't wait until we get up," JJ said, fists clenched. We reached the door.

"There is no 'we,' only me," I said.

"No fair!" JJ said.

Electra looked me in the eyes. "*Mi amor,* you won't have much of a chance up there without us."

"It's too dangerous," I said. "I won't have much chance with you, either."

"But . . ." JJ started to say.

"If I fail, it's going to be up to you two to rally the troops and stop Natasha," I said.

Looking at the door, I asked, "HARV, can you open it and get me up there?"

HARV nodded. "Helena gave me the access code. So, yes."

"That was very helpful of her," I said. I could maybe get used to having a mother-in-law on the World Council.

"I gave her a dynamite ceviche recipe," HARV said, proudly.

"How long will the trip take, HARV?"

"Thirty-five minutes, and they will know you're coming. I can cloak you, of course, but the cloak doesn't do much good in a small enclosed area."

I tapped the door. "Open it up and let's get rolling," I said.

Electra took my hand. "Are you sure about this, Zach?"

"No, of course not. I just don't see another way."

"If we could convince Earth Force that Natasha has taken over their top secret base, I am sure they would nuke the place," HARV said. "I am also sure they would think the hundred people on the base were acceptable losses."

"They might. I don't," I said.

"No, of course you don't," Electra said with a smile.

"Besides, the base has to be worth billions of credits," JJ said. "They're probably not that anxious to nuke something so costly."

I looked the kid in the eyes. "You're smarter than you look."

"So are you," he retorted.

"Damn straight," I said.

"Let's hope you're a lot tougher, too," JJ said.

"Believe me, kid, I am."

"He is," Electra said.

"He surprises me all the time," GUS said. "Though he did cry watching *Old Yeller* last week."

"I wasn't crying. I had been peeling onions for a salad," I said.

"Zach is as surprisingly tough and persistent as a real stubborn, not particularly intelligent, bulldog," HARV said. "If anybody can pull this off, it is him."

"Thanks, HARV," I said, walking into the elevator.

I blew Electra a kiss. The door shut. The elevator started up.

"You *were* crying during *Old Yeller,* though," HARV said.

Chapter 51

The ride up to the station would take thirty-five minutes. Since we had nothing else to do, HARV, GUS, and I talked.

"So, what's the plan, Mr. Zach?" GUS asked.

HARV gave him a look of disapproval. "GUS, how long have you been with us now?" he asked.

"One year and twelve days," GUS said, chipper and as pleased as ever.

"And how many plans have you seen Zach devise in that time?" HARV asked.

"It depends on how you define the word 'plan,'" GUS said.

"The way you or I or any rational machine or being would define plan," HARV said.

We had time to kill, so I just let those two talk it out. I really had nothing to say.

"Define rational," GUS said.

"Oh, now you're just stalling!" HARV shouted, hands on hips, leaning forward.

"Define stalling," GUS said.

HARV looked to the ceiling and clenched his fists. "You are almost as irritating as Zach!"

"Oh, I think he's got a long way to go before he reaches my level," I said.

"I so agree with you, Mr. Zach," GUS said. "Not that I find you annoying."

HARV thrust a finger at GUS. "Okay, now you just contradicted yourself! You silly gun! Now I've got you!"

"I'm just playing with your central processor," GUS said to HARV.

"Me, too," I said.

HARV tilted his head back and rolled his eyes. "I should just let Natasha fry both of your brains," he said. "It would serve you right to be her lap dogs!"

"Oh, HARV, sir, you won't let that happen," GUS said.

"No, of course not," HARV said, hands back on hips and leaning toward us again. "I'm a professional!"

"So Mr. Zach pays you?" GUS asked.

"I get paid by the pride I get from doing my job well," HARV said. He processed his last words. He processed them some more. He put his head in his hands. "Oh, DOS! I let you both get to me."

Time to bail HARV out. It was nice, though, to see him take a mental licking for once.

"I do have a plan," I said.

HARV looked up. "You do?"

"You do?" GUS said.

"Well, I'm pretty sure the element of surprise is *not* on our side," I said.

"You can bet on that," HARV said.

"I'm not a betting weapon, but I agree," GUS said.

"So we won't even bother cloaking," I said loudly, figuring they had to be listening. "We won't put up any fight. We'll fake surrender and when they let their guards down, we'll blast away." I said.

"Actually we will cloak and we will blast away the nano the door opens," I thought.

"See, he does have a plan," GUS said.

"Not a very good one," HARV said.

"Nobody said it had to be a good plan." GUS thought about what he said. *"Though I believe in it."*

"Zach, whoever is running the station is clearly listening to our words and must know that we know that they know we know they are listening," HARV said.

"So?"

"Yeah, so?" GUS added.

"So therefore they must realize we won't do what you said," HARV said.

"Actually, I am betting they are thinking that since we said that and we know that they know that we know they are listening, they are thinking we are thinking they are thinking that we will do the opposite of what we said, but we'll actually try to do what we said."

HARV shook his head. *"You can't tell me even you actually followed what you just said."*

"See, that's why I don't like to plan," I thought. *"Things get too confusing. The thing is, we're in a small box, they know we are here, they know we are coming."*

"Not exactly inspiring my confidence there, Zach!" HARV said.

"So this is one of the times when our best plan is drop, cloak, blast away, hope for the best, and build from there," I said.

"I'm glad machines can't really die," GUS said. *"Oops, did I think that out loud?"*

"For once, GUS, you and I agree," HARV said.

"Since we have time to kill, how about those New New York Mets?" I said.

No, it wasn't much of a plan. In fact, even I had to admit it was a lousy plan. Thing was, we didn't have a lot of options. I was hoping that by at least stating my false plan out loud they might think that really wasn't my plan, as nobody would be stupid enough to say their plan out loud unless the plan was a red herring. Problem was, any way this played out Natasha held the best hand. She had all the advantages. When drop, shoot, and pray was the best plan you had, you better hope you get a lucky break.

Like my old mentor used to say, "I'd rather be lucky than good, lucky folks live longer." She was a wise old battle-ax. Sure, things weren't looking bright, but all I needed was one break or one lucky shot to turn the tide. My hunch was if we took Natasha out, at least knocked her out, whatever hold she had over everyone would be broken. All I needed was one lucky shot. I figured if I repeated it enough it might help increase my chances.

"I think the Mets need more pitching," HARV said, realizing the futility of talking strategy or lack of any longer.

"I think they need another bat," GUS said. "I like bats," he added.

"You would," HARV told him.

"I would what, think they need another bat or like bats?" GUS asked.

"Both," HARV said.

I listened for the next twenty minutes or so while the elevator ascended, as HARV and GUS discussed the pros and con of pitching versus hitting. Not to mention the pros and cons of preferring hitting to pitching based on one's shape.

I smiled. If this was going to be the last conversation I ever heard at least it would be a fitting one for my life. Plus, if this debate between my gun and my computer went on much longer I might actually welcome Natasha erasing my brain.

The elevator came to a stop.

HARV stopped his discussion with GUS and looked at me. "It's showtime," he said out loud.

"Right!" HARV said. *"Cloaking now."*

The door opened. Natasha was there, with a few troops on each side of her. "Nighty night, Zach," Natasha said.

Chapter 52

The next thing I knew, I was waking up in bed. Turning to the left, I saw Natasha sitting there watching over me.

"Welcome to my new home," she said.

DOS!

"HARV, are you there?" I thought.

"HARV and GUS are still sleeping," Natasha said.

Spam!

"I thought it would be better if we talked alone," Natasha said.

She took me by the hand and helped me up to a sitting position. "Come, I'll give you a tour."

I quickly ran through the course of options I had. GUS and HARV may have been deactivated, but I still had my good old knife down in my ankle holster, plus I had stuffed a backup backup gun behind my back. Knife versus superpowerful babe who can kill people simply by being in a bad mood.

I stood up. Pointing to the door, I said, "Give me the tour."

Natasha anxiously took me by hand and led me out of the room. "The place is perfect for me!" she said with a huge smile. "There are currently only fifty-five people up here, well, fifty-seven, counting you and me. So it's just enough to keep me company. And they are all military or military consultants. Even if I slip and actually kill somebody I don't feel overly guilty."

"How special for you," I told her.

She just looked at me. "Zach, I am letting you keep your brain as it is, but if you continue to get all spammy and snotty with me that can be remedied."

We walked by a couple of soldiers in the hallway. They meekly smiled and waved politely to us as we passed them.

"I can make you just like them," Natasha said.

"Ah, the Stepford Soldiers," I said.

Natasha raised an eyebrow. "I understand the reference and agree."

Natasha was certainly a happy camper as she took me to all the station's hotspots. First, she showed the male bunk area, where all her male "friends" slept and hung out. Blue walls surrounding beds and few tables surrounded by chairs. A couple of guys were lying in their beds, a few were playing cards. They all seemed happy and waved when they saw us.

Next we saw the female bunk area. Pretty much the same thing, only with pink walls and less card playing.

"I picked out the color scheme myself," Natasha said proudly.

For the next stage, we passed the lab areas. The labs looked very well equipped but we didn't stop there.

"The labs are so boring," Natasha insisted. "No need to go there."

We reached a big open area. One end of the area was filled with Ping-Pong tables, a pool table, a few virtual HV games. The other end had a stage, a popcorn popper and lots of seats. Semi-zombielike soldiers were going to and fro, smiles locked on their faces.

"This used to be the weapons range," Natasha said. "I converted it to a rec room. More fun this way."

"Yes, I can see that," I told her.

She led me to the gym, filled with treadmills, anti-grav weights, free weights, mats, medicine balls—pretty much any piece of equipment that workout enthusiasts would want. A few people were using the machines.

"Here's where General Wall and I share the same vision. We both agree that a first-class gym is important for both mind and body."

"I won't argue," I said.

Next stop was the mess hall. Not much different than any other cafeteria I had seen.

"Nice mess hall," I told Natasha. Like I said, it really wasn't anything special but I knew it was important to keep Natasha happy.

"It's not a mess hall!" she corrected.

"Oh?"

"We now call it the fine dining room," she said proudly. "Mess hall just sounded so messy."

I nodded. "True. Only the military can take something as basic and useful as food and make it seem unappealing."

"You are a wise man, Zach," Natasha said.

"I wish you'd tell that to HARV. He never believes me."

Natasha laughed.

"As a wise man I'd like to point out that taking control of other people's minds is wrong."

Natasha looked me in eyes considering what I had said. "Yes, I know," she agreed. "Sometimes though, Zach, survival of the fittest trumps doing the right thing. If I could figure out some way to live up here without controlling their minds I would. Just like if I could live on Earth without being hunted I would. I can't, so I make the best of it. One option I suppose would be to broadcast over the P-Pod network and make everybody on Earth love me; but I thought that would be even worse."

"I agree with you there," I said.

"I could very well rule Earth if I wanted to but I don't want to," she told me.

"Good," I said.

Natasha touched me gently on my shoulder. "I just want to live my life in peace. If that means turning a few troops into my very obedient friends so be it. It's not really that much different. Instead of taking orders from generals now they take requests from me."

It was then that I noticed General Wall sitting alone at the head of one of the tables. She was eating soup.

"Speaking of generals, I see you have the General Wall as one of your friends now."

"Yes," Natasha said. "I like her much better this way. Take away her meaness and most of her personality and she's okay."

Looking at the general, something else wasn't quite right. I moved closer to her.

"Where are you going, Zach? The tour is not over. I have to show you my favorite spots: the library and observation rooms!" I kept heading toward the general. "Are you hungry?" Natasha said.

I didn't know what set off my alarm about the general, but something was wrong. The general didn't have the right vibe. Getting closer, I noticed that she only had one star on her uniform. I knew Wall was not the kind of woman who would wear one star when she should be wearing two. Nope, not at all. Even in her reduced state, she'd still be proudly flaunting that new star.

Natasha studied me studying the general. "Something is wrong."

Natasha looked at me, then looked back at the general. "She only has one star. According to your mind, she should have two."

I shrugged. "My mind is probably wrong. I'm wrong a lot. Just ask HARV."

Natasha stared at the general. "Why don't you have two stars?" she asked.

The general looked up slowly from her soup. "I do not know," she said slowly. "Ah, lost in the mail . . ."

Natasha concentrated on the general. "You are not General Wall!" she said. "You have an organic brain with the general's memories and thoughts, but your body is artificial!" Natasha shouted.

"Are you sure?" I asked Natasha, though I was somehow sure she was right. I wanted to keep her off balance.

Natasha locked her eyes on the faux general. The body fell to the ground shaking. It started smoking. A brief flare and then it was a burn spot.

"How could I have let my guard down?" Natasha said.

"It can't be easy taking over an entire base," I told her.

An alarm went off. "Elevator arrival in three minutes," a computer voice said.

"What? I didn't okay any elevator activity!" Natasha said.

"This was an elevator override," the computer said. "By Two Star General Wall."

"How could I have let my guard down?" Natasha said again. "I was so happy. I wasn't thinking straight. I'll have to fix this."

I popped GUS into my hand. He may have been deactivated but he was still a fine club. Moving forward before Natasha even had a chance to think, I whacked her on the back of the head.

Natasha crumpled to the floor.

HARV activated. "What did I miss? What did I miss?" He noticed Natasha lying on the ground. He smiled. "Well, blow me down and call me a PlayStation. You can function without me!"

Chapter 53

Natasha hadn't been on the floor for a minute when General Wall and her team of heavily armed storm troopers burst into the fine dining room. The general, who was wearing her two stars proudly on her shoulders, smiled when she saw Natasha lying there motionless.

"Good work, Johnson," General Wall said, approaching me. "You've surprised the hell out of me."

"You're not the first."

"Is she dead?" the general asked, pointing at Natasha's body.

"No, of course not," I said. "She just underestimated me, too."

The general and her team reached us. Two of the troopers bent over Natasha. One put a helmet on her head, the other put bracers on her feet. General Wall's grin widened.

"My plan worked perfectly," the general said.

"Your plan was to confuse Natasha with a fake you so I could knock her out?"

General Wall pointed to her head. "I am a master strategist. Patton had nothing on me."

HARV appeared between us. All the troopers in the place who had been under Natasha's control were shaking their heads, trying to make sense of what had just happened.

"So you knew I was here?" I asked.

The general nodded. "Of course. I knew once your mother-in-law told you to give up, you'd have to push. I also knew you'd figure out Natasha was here." The general shook her head. "Not sure what it is, but you two do have some sort of funky connection. Perhaps it's from the computer in your brain?"

"How did YOU know Natasha would come?" HARV asked.

"We have profilers. They are very good at what they do. We knew she would consider this the perfect environment," the general said proudly.

I thought about what was going on here. "Plus you were subliminally conditioning her to come here in her dreams."

General Wall didn't answer at first. "Why do you think this?"

"Twoa mentioned it," I said.

"Damn civilians talk too much," the general spat.

"Yeah, well, it would be ugly if you cut all our tongues out."

"That's why you and she were connecting so well," HARV said, lightbulb blinking on top of his head. "They must have been broadcasting the messages on a frequency I, too, can pick up."

"It was just our emergency backup plan in case she escaped," the general admitted. "This way we would eventually know where to find her. A nice secure place where she can be controlled."

I looked for some point to argue about. I didn't find anything. Couldn't really find fault with the logic, especially since it had worked. Natasha was back where she should be, with the people that knew how to deal with her. They would treat her right. Wouldn't they? Yes, of course they would, I told myself.

The general put her hand on my shoulder. Funny, I hadn't pegged her as a touchy-feely kind of gal. She swayed me toward the door. "The job you've done here has been exemplary, Mr. Johnson. Rest assured your account has been credited at the agreed-upon rate."

"It has been," HARV confirmed.

"My best men will now walk you to the door," the general said. It was an order, even though it didn't sound like one.

Two beefy troopers in full armor positioned themselves behind me. One directed me toward the door. "Please move forward, sir," he said. Once again it was an order even though it didn't sound like one.

I took a step, then stopped. Turning to General Wall, I asked, "And what happens to Natasha now?"

The general was surprisingly forthright. "We'll keep her here for now. Heavily sedated, so we can run some tests. We'll keep her here. She'll be safe, just not in control."

"Are you sure?" I asked.

"Don't worry, Zach," the general said with a smile. "I promise you on my honor as a warrior, no harm will come to her."

I eyed her over. Being a PI I'm good at reading people. I got mixed feelings about the general. No eye twitches, no subtle tells. She was telling me the truth. It just didn't make me feel as good as the truth should make me feel.

"This way, sir," one of the troopers behind me said. "The elevator is waiting."

The troopers and I left the room and headed through the hallway toward the elevator. My job had been completed. Once again I had taken out a dangerous dame and made the world safer I told myself, trying convince me all was well.

Problem was, I still didn't feel better. I wasn't happy. I wasn't sad. I was just kind of indifferent. I'm not suppose to be indifferent after wrapping up a case this big. Something was rotten on the space station. Then it hit me like two metric tons of steel-reinforced bricks dropped from a rocket. They had been playing with my brain all along, too.

Chapter 54

"HARV, I've been used. Haven't I?" I thought.

"Zach, you're a PI. Of course you've been used. It comes with the job."

"But I've been used without my knowledge."

"True," HARV said. *"Though if it's any consolation I don't think they initially planned this. Somehow your link transmits over the same frequency as the messages they were sending to Natasha. You just picked up on them subconsciously."*

"But the general knew something was up," I said.

"Unless she is a moron. Which we really can't rule out," HARV said.

"So, she may not have planned for me being linked to Natasha through you, but she used it . . ." I thought.

It was abundantly clear that my work here may have been done but my mission wasn't. I needed to talk to General Wall. There was more to this story than met the eye at first glance or the brain at first thought. She was trying to muscle me out of the picture before I put the pieces together. I didn't like this at all. Not one little iota.

I stopped walking. The elevator door was within spitting distance.

"Please, Mr. Johnson, continue forward," one of the troops said.

I turned away from the door and faced them. I needed to see the looks on their faces. I couldn't because they had pulled down the dark visors attached to their helmets' rims. Ah, yes, they were here to make sure I got on that elevator whether I wanted to or not. Problem for them was I really didn't want to.

Each of the soldiers positioned one hand on his weapons and pointed to the elevator door with the other hand, just in case I had forgotten where it was. I hadn't. I just no longer gave a spam.

I led with playing it nice.

"Ah, there's something I forgot to tell the general," I said, taking a step forward.

They both drew their weapons.

"Send her a nice e-mail," one of them said. It really was kind of hard to tell who was talking from behind the visors.

So much for the nice guy approach. Thing was, I wasn't about to finish last. I lifted my arms and turned back toward the door. "Okay, you don't have to hit me with a cattle prod to let me know when I'm not welcome."

HARV transmitted himself from my wrist communicator and started walking by my side.

"Actually, Zach, most times you do have to be hit by a cattle prod to get the point."

"No, I don't," I insisted with a wink.

"Yes, yes, you do," HARV said.

"Name one time," I said.

HARV lifted a finger, "There was that time at police HQ in New Vegas." HARV lifted another finger. "Then the time at police HQ in Frisco." HARV started to violently vibrate like he was being electrocuted. He was mocking me but entertaining the guards.

"I said one time," I told HARV.

I heard a slight giggle from behind. That was my

cue to strike. Spinning around to my left, I popped
GUS into my left hand, striking the man on the left
in the neck where he wasn't protected by armor. The
blow sent him crashing to the floor. (It was thanks to
HARV's guidance that I was able to target my hit
so perfectly.)

The second trooper opened fire on me. His energy
bolt burned a hole in my shirt but glanced harmlessly
off my underarmor. I couldn't see his face under the
visor, but I was betting he had a look of shock.

"Just because I don't wear my armor on the outside
doesn't mean I don't wear armor," I said. Pulling the
trigger, I hit him with a concussion blast to the chest.
The force of the blast sent him rocketing hard into
the wall and then to the floor. He'd be out for a while.

"You're just lucky the World Council doesn't buy
their storm troopers the best energy and concussion-
proof armor," HARV said.

"Yeah, lucky me. I live in a world where politicians
save money on everything that's not their salaries."

I started back up the hallway to track down General
Wall and Natasha.

"Thanks for the help distracting the guard there,
buddy," I said.

"No problem," GUS said. "Though I hardly call
clobbering and shooting distracting."

"He was talking to me," HARV said to GUS.

"Oh," GUS said. "I knew that . . ."

"Anyway, thanks for the help, HARV."

"Who said I was helping?" HARV said straight-
faced as ever.

I let it go. HARV may never admit it, but he needs
to be helpful. Another time I might rub that in a bit,
but now wasn't the time. I was outnumbered fifty to
one and going to rescue a superdeadly being who
might or might not need rescuing. I figured right now
I needed all the assets I could muster.

"Do you know where General Wall is?" I asked.

"Still on this base," GUS said.

"Talking to HARV again, GUS," I said.

"Oops. I should have known that. Perhaps Natasha turning me off against my will has hampered my logic systems. Running diagnostics now."

"Just be ready to fire if I need you," I said.

No answer.

"I was talking to you that time, GUS."

"Oh, right!" GUS said.

"Now, HARV, can you tell me where I can chat with General Wall?" I asked, moving up the hallway.

"I've put you into stealth mode," HARV said.

"Great, thanks, that's helpful. It still doesn't answer my question, though," I said.

"Yes, well, her team has mostly blocked me from accessing their systems or cameras."

"Mostly blocked?" I said.

"I'm good, Zach. Very good."

"He is," GUS added.

"So, I can't tell exactly where she is but I have a fairly good idea," HARV said.

"Can you give me a clue?" I asked.

"Yeah, me, too!" GUS said.

"There are extremely high amounts of energy coming from a room up ahead. One of the rooms Natasha didn't bring us into."

"One of the research labs," I said.

"Yep," HARV said.

I don't know why, but I started to shudder.

Chapter 55

Heading toward the door, HARV was picking up extreme energy readings about which I was anxious to get some answers. Problem was, I didn't know how forthcoming the general would be. I was guessing she wouldn't be very open at all. She held most of the cards. I was either going to have to be forceful, charming, or tricky. My biggest chance of success would probably be the last.

"I've got okay news and really bad news about that door we're coming up to," HARV broadcast to my brain.

"What's the okay news?" GUS asked.

"I've managed to download and review the station's specs."

"So, what's the bad news?" I thought.

"The door is super-carbon-plexisteel reinforced with a manual bolt. Once closed, it can't be picked, shot up, or forced open from the outside."

"What about the wall next to the door?" I thought. "Nobody ever thinks about the wall."

"It is also reinforced with super-carbon-plexisteel," HARV said.

"I guess some people do think of the walls!" GUS said.

"Yeah, just my luck it would be these people."

Drawing closer to the door in question, I saw it was guarded by three more heavily-armed troopers. There was one on each side of the door. Plus another one across from the door.

"Apparently the general really wants her privacy," I said.

"Wouldn't you?" GUS asked.

"No, GUS, I'd make it as easy for my potential foes to get to me as possible," I said.

Silence. *"You're being sarcastic. Aren't you?"* GUS said.

"Vingo," HARV answered.

It looked like the only way I was going to get into that room was if they let me into that room. The only way that was going to happen was if I surrendered. Of course, I couldn't make it too obvious.

Nearing the guards I thought, *"Okay, HARV, let's make this look like an accident."*

"Zach, with you that will be easy," HARV said.

"You are very smooth," GUS said.

"That's not what I meant," HARV said out loud.

From the shimmer in front of my eyes, I knew he had lifted the cloak. It was showtime.

"HARV!" I shouted, kicking the guard across from the door in the gut. "My cloak is down!"

"Sorry, Zach," HARV said as I ducked under a roundhouse punch thrown by one of the door side guards. "My battery is drained!"

Okay, making up excuses wasn't HARV's strong point. Even so, I had to roll with it and the punches. The second door guard hit me with a right to the chin. I staggered against the wall. I could have fallen, probably should have fallen. But I didn't want to make it too easy. (Yeah, I can be stubborn. It's one of my worst yet more endearing traits.)

The guards pulled their energy weapons.

"Uh, Zach, what makes you think the guards will just capture you and not kill you?" HARV asked.

"Hell of time to bring up that potential flaw in my plan, buddy!"

"Yeah!" GUS said.

I kept GUS sheathed. If I did get captured, I was going to want him to be available for me.

The troopers all drew their weapons.

"The general will probably want him alive," one of them said. "Just use clubs on him!"

"You are so lucky," HARV said.

The guards drew in on me. I feigned some resistance, but I didn't want to make it very hard on them. Last thing I needed was to piss them off and have them forget to keep me alive. The first club rammed me in the back. Even with my body armor, it hurt. The next one got me in the back of the head. No body armor there. Right before I blacked out, I started thinking, I'm lucky they are only clubbing me. DOS! No wonder there are no other freelance PIs around.

Chapter 56

"Come on, Zach, wake up!" I heard HARV calling from the deep recesses of my mind. I knew what he wanted. I just wasn't in the mood to open my eyes yet. Everything hurt. I figured shooting my eyes open and exposing them to light would increase the pain. *"Come on, Zach, a beautiful damsel in distress needs us."*

"That's right, Mr. Zach! It's time for the good guys to save the day."

Opening my eyes, I was glad to see I was in the same room with Natasha and General Wall. I wasn't so glad to see that I was tied to a big wooden chair, surrounded by guards in every corner. I was even less glad to see Natasha had been strapped down on a large gray metal gurney. Her legs were still bolted. They had also placed a funky looking electronic headpiece across her forehead. The headpiece had optic lines running from it to a strange-looking machine, like an old-fashioned computer. I could see Natasha's chest rising and falling, so she was alive.

One lady in a lab coat was monitoring Natasha. Another lady in a lab coat was manning the machine. A balding guy in a lab coat was positioned next to the general. For her part, General Wall was supervising like a good general should. There was another gurney next to the one Natasha was lying on, only this one was padded and had pillows. I think I saw what was coming here.

"Somebody has been watching too many sci-fi flicks," I called out.

The general looked over to me and smiled. "How nice of you to be awake," she said. "And this is hardly sci-fi."

"More like horror," I said.

General Wall laughed. "Oh, Zachary, one man's horror is another woman's pleasure."

"That is kind of the story of your love life," HARV said.

"Not the time, HARV!"

"I'm going to drain Natasha's mental powers and put them into me," General Wall said proudly, too proudly.

"It can't be that easy," I said.

She laughed. "It hasn't been easy. I've been planning this for last six years."

"See, it pays to plan," HARV scolded me.

"I even convinced your good buddy Dr. Pool to slip some of my DNA into Natasha. Not a lot mind you, mostly just that which determines brain structure." Wall laughed.

"Natasha was basically your human guinea pig. Let her test out the power for you then you take it," I said.

The general shook her head. "Not at first. At first, my DNA being injected into her was just to make her more like me. Hopefully easier to mold. Turns out that wasn't the case. Too much of your niece in her. Would you believe she doesn't enjoy being able to kill people with a thought?"

"Hard to believe," I said.

"When it became apparent she wouldn't do our bidding, I changed the plan. I decided I would take her powers. I know how to use power!"

"See, a good plan is flexible," HARV said.

"So how do I fit into all this?"

"You, Zachary, were just an errand boy. Somebody to help fetch Natasha when she went astray."

"I'm actually much more than that," I said.

"I'll bite," the general said. "How much more are you?"

"I'm the guy who's going to stop you," I said bluntly.

General Wall's head shot back. She was laughing a hard faux laugh. "Zachary, Zachary, stop, you're killing me with your humor," she said holding her stomach. The laughing stopped abruptly. She glared at me. "Believe me, Zachary, while I was fake laughing outside, I was really laughing on the inside. You are tied to a chair and surrounded by my most loyal troops. You have no chance."

I love it when opponents talk like that. It means they've underestimated me and let their guard down. I've made a career out of taking advantage of people who make that mistake.

"Are you sure about that, General?" Natasha said, showing she was very much alive. Just not putting up a fight. "Zach has saved the world on a number of occasions."

The general sneered. "Please. He's just a glorified gofer. It's *my* job to save the world. I plan to do that better now by keeping order. Make them think how they are supposed to think!"

"He does have a highly advanced computer in his brain," Natasha said, unwilling to leave bad enough alone.

"Yeah, right, a flawed computer," the general said. "Some people had such high hopes for it once. I told them a machine would never have the guts to do what we needed."

"I'm not sure if I should be offended or honored," HARV said in my brain.

"Just stay calm, buddy," I coached.

I didn't need HARV drawing any unwanted attention to me. Gates knows Natasha was doing a good enough job of that on her own.

"Using computer implants to control people's minds," the general scoffed. "That's almost as lame as using civilians," she finished looking over at Natasha.

"I never asked for these abilities," Natasha told her. "I might be happier without them."

"Well then, my dear, I'm going to make you a very happy person," General Wall told her. She turned her attention to the female scientist diligently tinkering with the machine. "How's it coming?"

"Almost ready," the female scientist replied. "The machine just needs to recalibrate for three minutes." The scientist pointed to a switch in a middle of the machine. "Then I flip the switch and you have Natasha's powers."

"Lovely," the general smiled. "Begin the countdown!"

Now that was my cue to swing into action. As dangerous as Natasha may have been with her powers, it didn't take a genius to know that General Wall with those powers would be a much bigger danger. Time to break out and stop this. With everybody concentrating on the general and the device, it shouldn't be hard.

I tried moving my wrist in just that right way that pops GUS into my hand. Problem was, with arms tied to the chair as they were, that "just the right way" wasn't quite the right way. GUS didn't activate.

"Uh, Zach, you should probably break loose now," HARV whispered in my brain.

"I can't get GUS out," I thought.

"That's because with your hands tied, you can't properly catch him," HARV explained.

"Can you increase the strength in my arms so I can break these chains?"

"Highly unlikely. Those chains are made from extra high density flexi-iron," HARV said. *"It's one of Dr. Pool's newest patterns."*

I thought for a nano. Each of my hands and legs were chained separately to the chair . . . if I could just get my weapon arm free from the chair. The chair, that was it!

"HARV, can you increase the strength of my hips and butt?" I asked.

"Uh, sure. Why? Do you want do some aerobics so you'll die fitter?"

"HARV, if I smash the chair my arms and legs will be free!"

"Hey, that is good thinking!" HARV said.

"Way to go, Mr. Zach!" GUS shouted.

"You're ready," HARV told me.

I didn't feel any different, but I had to trust HARV. I arched my butt up as far as I could, then smashed it down on the chair. The chair shattered as I dropped through the seat to the floor. Quickly rolling to the side, I popped GUS into my hand.

The guards in the room quickly went for their weapons. Using a wide angle stun ray, I was able to easily take out the ones on the right side. The ones on left side opened fire. Spinning around, I was able to avoid two of their shots. Two others hit me square in the gut but my underarmor took all the damage.

"He's got body armor on, you fools!" the general shouted. "Aim for his head."

Firing another wide angle stun blast, I took out the entire left side. Smiling, I turned my attention to the general and her scientists. Waving GUS at the scientist manning the machine, I said, "Time to back slowly away from that switch."

The scientist lifted her arms and backed off.

"Smart girl," I told her.

I pointed to the scientist sitting next to Natasha. She was a younger lady. "Now free Natasha," I ordered.

The scientist stood up and waved a wand like electronic key over the shackles that were holding Natasha's legs down. The shackles opened up. She pointed the electronic key at Natasha's arm shackles. They popped up. Natasha sat up and smiled.

"I'd like to thank you for your efforts, Zach," she said.

"You'll never get away with this!" General Wall shouted at me. "My men won't let you."

"Sure, I will," I said, pointing GUS at her. "I'm guessing your most loyal troops, the ones who truly know what's going on, are in here and out of it for a while. I'm also guessing the Council doesn't know of your actions."

"Of course they don't!" the general growled. "Those pansy civilians can't see the beauty of my plan."

"Therefore, I am guessing that once my computer contacts the Council they will order the rest of your troops to stand down and they will," I said.

I was pleased with myself. I had saved Natasha and stopped the general. All in all, things had turned out pretty well.

"Natasha, you can disconnect yourself from the machine now," I told her.

"I know," Natasha said, walking near the machine. "I truly appreciate you efforts, Zach." Flipping the switch, she said, "Problem is, I don't want these powers!"

The machine made a sizzling sound. Both Natasha and General Wall shivered for a few seconds. Natasha fell to a knee. General Wall sat up from the gurney she was on.

One of the scientists, the young woman, touched her on the shoulder. "Did it work, ma'am?"

Wall smiled at the scientist. She fell lifeless to the ground. Wall smiled at the other two scientists. They held their chests and dropped dead. Wall removed the head piece and sat up.

Rising from the gurney, Wall said, "I'll let you be the judge of that."

Chapter 57

General Wall was laughing so hard I was surprised she didn't burst open.

"GUS, we have to take her fast before she really figures out how to use Natasha's powers," I said, aiming the weapon.

GUS went flying out of my hand, into the general's open hand. "Too late," she told me. Stroking GUS gently, she added "This is a fine weapon. Too fine a weapon for a civilian cretin like you to appreciate."

A squad of the general's men burst into the room. "We're here, General Wall!" the squad leader shouted very dramatically. He looked over the situation. "Oh, I see you have the hostile under control."

"Yes, of course I do!" Wall told him. "What took you and your men so long to respond?" she demanded.

"Ah, ma'am, the door is heavily reinforced and locked with a manual lock from the inside. It took us a while to cut through," the squad leader said.

Grabbing his throat, the leader gasped and fell to the ground. His men behind him looked on in fear. Then they all fell lifeless to the ground.

"Bad answer!" the general spat. She surveyed the

damage she had wrought. "I truly am an army of one!"

Pointing at the general dramatically, I told her, "You may have great mental powers now, but remember, you're not invulnerable!"

Slowly approaching the general, I continued my lecturing. "You may think you have all the power and all the answers, but you don't!" I shouted.

"Why are you shouting at me?" the general asked.

Natasha clunked her on the back of the head, knocking her out.

"To distract you," I said to the unconscious general.

Chapter 58

"Natasha, you have to take your power back!" I told her.

She lowered her head. "No, I don't want it. You were right—I abused it."

"You can learn to control your powers," I told her gently touching her shoulder.

She looked up at me, eyes searching for answers, "How do you know?" she asked.

"I just have faith in you. Not totally sure why I just do. My instinct tells me it's right." Pointing at the general I added, "If you don't, General Wall will just kill us both when she comes around," I said.

"You may not have to wait that long to die," HARV said. "With all the human troops now either dead or incapacitated, the base's backup robo-troops have activated. They are rolling here now."

Taking Natasha by the hand, I looked in her eyes. "Natasha, please, you have to take your power back."

"But I'm dangerous."

"Not nearly as dangerous as the wacko general," I said. "You were designed and conditioned to hold this kind of power. The general wasn't."

"True," she agreed with a slight nod. "But as long

as I'm alive and with the power they will never let me
live free."

"I may have a way around that," I told her.

Looking up at me, she smiled meekly. "You do?"

"Take back your power and I promise I'll find a
way for you to live free," I said.

"Zach, are you sure about this?" HARV said.

"Yeah, Mr. Zach, are you sure?" GUS also said.

"Trust me," I said to all three of them.

"I do trust you, Zach," Natasha said. "Not sure
why, but I do."

"I trust you, too, Mr. Zach," GUS said.

"I guess I trust you also," HARV said reluctantly.

"Good," I said, rubbing my hands together. "Since
we're all in agreement, the first step is to get Natasha
and Wall hooked back up the machine."

"That's actually two steps," HARV said.

"When he's right, he's right," GUS agreed.

Ignoring them, I bent down and lifted up the general. "Does it matter what gurney I put her on?" I
asked HARV.

"Going over the machine's specs now," HARV
said. "Nope, it doesn't matter."

Carrying the general over to the non-padded gurney, I quickly bolted down her arms and her feet.
Moving to her head, I grabbed the headpiece and
placed it on her.

"Is that I all I need to do?" I asked HARV.

HARV gave the connection a once-over. "Yes. For
a power-transferring machine, it is very user-friendly."

Pointing to the other gurney, I told Natasha, "Now
your turn."

She hesitated only for the briefest nano, then went
and laid down on the other gurney. "This one is much
more comfortable," she said.

"Good. Now put on the headpiece," I said.

Natasha placed the flat metal band on her forehead.

"Okay, Zach, now all you have to do is flip the

switch and in three minutes Natasha will have her power back."

"That should be pretty easy," I said moving to the switch.

"Yes, it will be," HARV said, pointing to the door. "Once the system powers up, all will be well . . ." There was a pause. HARV pausing is never good. "As long as you can hold off the battlebots!"

Chapter 59

"Battlebots?" I said.

"Yes," HARV said, rolling his eyes. "I told you, when all the human troops were disabled or, well, killed, the station's backup defense kicked in."

"DOS, that was fast!"

"Wouldn't be a very good backup if it wasn't," HARV said.

"True," GUS said.

"I'm a pacifist and I even see the wisdom in that," Natasha said from her gurney.

"How many of them are there?" I asked.

"Ten," HARV said.

"Of course there are," I sighed.

"Face it, Zach, you'd be disappointed if there weren't killer bots coming," HARV said.

The truth of the matter was, HARV was right. I kind of did dig the added danger. Not sure what that says about me. I was sure I didn't want to or have time to think of the social and moral ramifications of it either. It was time to react, not think.

Taking a firm grasp on GUS, I said, "How much trouble can a few battlebots be when I have GUS here?"

"Ah, about that, Mr. Zach, sir?"

"Yes, GUS?"

"You'll be mad," GUS said.

"No, I won't," I insisted.

"Then you'll be disappointed," GUS said.

"GUS! Get to the point! I don't have a lot of time before the battlebots get here."

"You have fourteen seconds," HARV said, helpful and annoying as ever.

"When that yucky general grabbed me, I deactivated myself. I figured her mental powers mixed with my firepower was a *bad* combination," GUS said very quickly.

Knowing what was coming next, I moved immediately toward one of the fallen guards. "So what you are saying is you are nothing but a fancy stick until you power up," I said running toward the nearest guard's gun.

"I wouldn't have said it with such humor, but yes," GUS said.

"He's such a brownnoser," HARV said.

"How long until you power up, GUS?" I asked, grabbing the guard's weapon.

"Three minutes. Sorry, I am very efficient."

"Guess I'll have to just make do," I said, pulling the gun up. "HARV, can you cloak me?"

"I can, but it won't matter, these are advanced model T2000 battlebots. They have the new patent-pending anti-hologram technology built in. It's really quite impressive."

Turning toward, the door I saw the first two bots had rolled into the room.

"Looks like I'm going to go old school," I said aiming the weapon.

Firing at the lead battlebot, I hit it in the head area. It started to spark. I had wounded it, but not put it out by a long shot. It turned its gun turrets toward me.

Opening fire, it said, "You will be neutralized!"

The two bots coming in behind it also aimed and opened up fire.

Diving toward the bots, I managed to avoid most of their hail of energy weapons. A couple blasts hit me, burning holes in my shirt and pants, but my armor took the damage. I was lucky; years of fighting battlebots have made me quite aware of their limitations. Most people let their massive frames, their multiple weapon turrets, and their retractable razor-sharp claw-like arms deter them. They see a battlebot rolling toward them and they either freeze in fear, surrender, run, or take cover. I've learned to take the opposite approach. I come right at them. It takes battlebots a while to figure out how to deal with an attacker who is bold enough or stupid enough to be an attacker.

Rolling toward them, I returned their fire the best I could, firing mostly randomly in their direction hoping to hit them.

"He is crazy!" one of the bots shouted.

"Ahh, we hate crazy!" another bot said.

"We must recalculate our offensive plan of defense."

After a few nanos, I stopped rolling, took aim, and fired from the ground. Jumping to my feet while firing away, I drew closer to the baffled bots. Concentrating my fire on the lead bot, I took him out. He blew up in a glorious yet contained explosion. That made me feel good.

"Time to use the Zachary Nixon Johnson defense," one of the remaining bots said.

That made me feel not so good. Though, in a way, I guess I should have been honored they would think enough of me to program their bots with a special defense meant for just me. Of course, you don't think of those things when battlebots are trying to kill you.

"Concentrate fire in the same spot," the new lead bot said. "We can burn through his armor."

"Will that work?" I asked HARV.

One blast hit me in the leg, then another, then another, all in the exact same spot. I fell to the ground, grasping the area they had hit.

"Offhand I'd have to say, yes, that will work," HARV said.

The bots turned their concentration to my shoulder area, hitting me with shot after shot, forcing me to not only scream in pain but to drop my weapon.

The two remaining bots rolled up to me. I was lying on the floor, writhing in pain. They extended their energy weapons out until they each were touching a side of my forehead.

"I surrender," I told them.

"Surrender is not an option," one of the bots said. It didn't matter which one. "You have invaded an Earth Force secure area and killed many of its personnel. You will be terminated as an example."

"I didn't kill anybody," I said. "The general did!"

They shook their gun turrets a little, not enough so they weren't locked on my head, though. "That makes no sense. The general is our leader. Besides, we saw you destroy battlebot unit 2703."

"That was self-defense," I said.

"How could it be self-defense when it was defending its base and doing its assigned task?" the bot asked.

"HARV, is the process complete yet?" I thought.

"Almost," HARV said.

"How much time left?"

"Ten seconds," HARV said.

"You have ten seconds to answer before we kill you," the bot told me.

This was really timing it close.

The bot started its countdown, "Ten, nine, eight, seven, six, five, four, three, two, on—"

I closed my eyes waiting, for it to happen. Nothing happened. I opened my eyes. Where there had once been two large intimidating battlebots, there were now two piles of smoking putty.

Natasha was at my side. "I see you have your powers back," I told her.

"Smart man," she said, gently touching me on the

forehead. I felt better, much better. Looking down at where I should have had wounds, there was no damage.

I smiled at her.

"I can also heal, you know."

Chapter 60

I stood up. I felt better than I had in years. "Wow, can you fix receding hairlines?" I asked Natasha.

"I prefer not to use my abilities for such trivial matters," she said with a half smile.

"I am now fully activated and ready for action!" GUS said.

"I've already wilted all the battlebots," Natasha said. The ease she said it with sent a slight shiver up my spine. "So, I'm happy to say, GUS, there is no need for you."

"Oh, 44 4F 53!" GUS said. "Oops, pardon my ascii."

"I also have to say, GUS and HARV, I need to shut you down for a moment longer," Natasha said.

GUS fell silent. I could sense HARV wasn't around either. It was weird, but not in a bad way.

"Zach, as long as I am alive and Earth Force is around, I will never be able to live in peace, and that's all I want. So, I will either have to destroy all of Earth Force or myself," Natasha said, head lowered. "Neither option is appealing to me." She looked up at me. "But you have another plan?"

"How many people are still alive on the station?" I asked.

"You, me, the general, and thirteen others," Natasha said. "Though I have mentally reverted the general to childhood. I am hoping they may do a better job with her when they reeducate her."

"In that case, there is another way," I said.

Natasha looked at me. She smiled. "Yes, that may work," she said. She bent over and kissed me.

Chapter 61

The next thing I knew, I was on the elevator heading back down to Earth with General Wall, who was sucking her thumb; thirteen of her troops; and the lady scientist who had been monitoring Natasha. They all had looks of confusion on their faces. They clearly had no idea what had just happened. It was a blur to me, too.

"Whoa, what's going on?" HARV said, appearing in front of me.

"I am back online, too, Mr. Zach!" GUS said. "I, too, wonder what happened!"

"I guess Natasha just wants to be alone forever on the base," I told HARV. "She mentally sent us all away."

HARV analyzed my face. "Yes, I guess that is true."

"She felt really bad about what happened up there. Sure, she didn't kill all of the soldiers or scientists, but her power did," I said.

HARV's head turned to the stunned lady scientist. "I thought General Wall killed her, too."

"She did," I said. "Natasha tried to revive them all, but Nancy here is the only one she could. Natasha guessed that it was because Nancy was the first one the general killed, so she still didn't really know how to use her power."

"That makes sense," HARV said. He looked at General Wall sucking her thumb. "I see Natasha took her revenge."

"Natasha doesn't consider it revenge," I said. "More of a safety precaution. Contact General Chen and Captain Rickey and tell them we're on the way down."

"No need, Zach. They already know."

"Oh, okay," I said.

The elevator stopped.

"The trip down seemed much faster," I said.

"That's because Natasha made us all into temporary zombies," HARV told me.

"I kind of liked it," I said.

"You would," HARV said. "I did not."

"I agree with HARV," GUS chimed in. "Zombies are yucky."

"Finally, you are wising up," HARV said with a smile.

The door rolled open. We were greeted by a dozen heavily-armed men pointing their weapons at us.

"No need to panic," I said, "Natasha isn't with us."

"What?" the somewhat familiar voice of General Chen said from behind the armed men blockade.

"I said, Natasha isn't with us!" I shouted.

"Give them room, men," General Chen ordered.

The sea of troopers parted, allowing me clear access to General Chen. I was relieved to see Tony, Electra, Randy, and JJ standing beside him. Walking through the troops, my first order of business was to hug and kiss Electra.

"Did you miss me?" I asked, lifting her off the ground.

"I did have plenty of company here," she joked. "But, yes, a little."

"I missed you, too!" Randy told me.

Ignoring Randy, I turned to General Chen, who was clearing his throat. "You know Electra here is a doctor. She may be able to give you something for that cough."

"Where's Natasha?" the general demanded.

"She decided to stay up there and deactivate the elevator. This way she can't hurt anybody else and you can't hurt her," I said with a smile. "Sounds like the perfect compromise. I'm sure when you review the station's video, you will see General Wall is the true monster here. Natasha did nothing wrong."

General Chen shook his head. "Still, it is unacceptable that an asset like Natasha be allowed to roam free."

"She's not exactly roaming, general. If you leave her alone, I'm sure she won't hurt anybody."

The general looked at me. "What makes you so certain?"

"Just trusting my gut," I said. I now truly believed that if we left Natasha alone, she would not harm anybody.

"That's not nearly good enough for me." The general turned to one of his men. "You're sure we are safe here?"

I didn't like the sound of that at all.

The man nodded.

I didn't like the look of that at all.

General Chen rolled up his sleeve, revealing a wrist keypad communicator. Much like the one I wear. He pressed a couple of buttons.

"No!" I shouted, moving forward.

All of the general's men aimed their weapons at me. Tony and Electra each grabbed one of my arms, restraining me.

"Lucky for you Johnson, your friend and woman are smarter than you," Chen sneered.

"And your computer," HARV added.

The general pushed two more buttons on his pad. I struggled to free myself. JJ helped restrain me more.

I couldn't stop Chen without possibly hurting Tony, JJ, or Electra.

We all heard a loud explosion. The platform we were on shook back and forth but we remained standing.

General Chen smiled. "The base has been totally destroyed. Natasha is dead."

"You would blow up a billion credit base just to stop Natasha?" I said.

General Chen nodded. "Yes, of course. She was far too big a clear and present danger to remain free. No matter what your gut may think."

Chapter 62

The next days were difficult ones for me. I had managed to save the world from General Wall gaining Natasha's power and creating a new world order. For that I guess I should have been happy. I just felt so used on so many levels. All General Wall had wanted all along was Natasha's power so she could shape the world the way she wanted. Not sure what General Chen wanted exactly, but I guess he figured if he couldn't control that power then nobody would.

The really ridiculous thing was, most of the press thought the general and I were heroes for what we did. Chen was very open about his actions (he had no choice with all those well-armed witnesses there), but he was able to convince much of the world that what he did was acceptable, that if Natasha roamed free she would, like General Wall, turn and try to destroy or control everything. The World Council and most people thought a billion credits and one life were worth sacrificing for saving everything. Not sure I totally agreed, but nobody really asked me.

A bit of good news did come from all this. Randy leaked to the media that P-Pods could be used to subliminally plant ideas into people's heads. Turns out most people didn't mind this, either, their logic being the less thinking they had to do about trivial stuff the better. Kind of scary, but not that surprising.

It was a beautiful day, so I decided to go for a walk. I got up from my desk and walked into Carol's reception area. It was nice to see her back at her desk.

"How you feeling?" I asked, my hand on her shoulder.

Looking up at me, she smiled. "Fine," she said. "My power levels have been reset some. Maybe they'll come back. Maybe they won't. Either way, I'm still more powerful than 99.99 percent of the population."

"Probably for the best for everybody," I told her. "I'm starting to doubt humans should be wielding that kind of power anyhow."

Carol nodded in agreement. "After seeing firsthand what Natasha could do, I agree, too." There was a slight pause, "I am sad she had to die though."

"Me too, chica. Me too. Hopefully a walk along the pier will ease some of that sadness."

Carol looked up at me. "I don't see how, but good luck . . ."

I left the office and headed toward the old pier, which was now more of an oceanside tourist attraction. It was only a five minute walk and I did need the fresh air.

Sitting down on a bench overlooking the water, I just watched all the people and birds go by. That is, until they all froze in place.

I felt a hand on my shoulder.

"Took you long enough to get here," I said.

"Sorry, I had a client," Nancy the scientist said as she walked up and sat down next to me.

"You okay?" I asked.

"I resigned my commission from Earth Force. I told them after seeing what I saw up there, I couldn't take it any longer," Nancy said.

"And they were good with that?"

She smiled, her hair falling over her shoulders. I noticed it was a lighter shade of blond than before. "Of course."

"Now what?" I asked.

She touched me gently on the arm. "This poor Nancy woman was all alone in this world. No family. All she had was work."

"Looks like you picked the perfect person to replace," I said.

Her head lowered slightly. "I still feel bad I couldn't save any of them. It's just the general was so evil, she had so much hate in her mind. She killed them all very dead. I dared not try to revive them for fear of what it would do to their brains. Or worse."

Putting my finger under her chin, I lifted her head up gently. Even though she looked like Nancy the scientist, the eyes showed me she wasn't. "You did nothing wrong. You deserve a life. A nice normal life."

Nancy smiled. "I know. I've started a massage business. I'm renting an office just a few blocks away from yours."

"Put me on your client list," I said.

"I already have, Zach," she looked around. "I shouldn't keep things suspended like this long. It can't be good for the universe."

I nodded. "Good idea." So she was learning not to abuse her powers. "I'm sure when and if you do use your abilities it will be for good."

She got up. "I'll see you for a massage next Wednesday at eleven a.m. It's on the house, of course, since I wouldn't be here if it wasn't for you."

"Kind of ironic since at first you were warning me not to take the case," I told her.

"Silly Zach, I was just doing that because I knew it would make sure you'd take the case. You may not have trusted the military but you certainly weren't going to let me scare you away."

Didn't know if that was totally true. But I was giving

her the benefit of the doubt. I took her hand. I hoped
I had done the right thing here. Leaning over, she
kissed me on the cheek, smiled, and said, "A wise
man once said sometimes you have to trust your gut."

She walked away and the world turned back on.

HARV popped on, sitting next to me on the bench.
"What happened?"

"Nothing," I said. "The world is perfectly normal."

"I could swear my temporal sensors are out of
whack," HARV said.

"Don't you just hate it when that happens?" I said.

"I do!" GUS said.

HARV processed for a nano, slapped himself in the
forehead and moaned, "I can't believe I just said 'out
of whack!' " he moaned. He thrust a finger in my face.
"I've been connected to you for too long!"

I just smiled. I knew I had made the right choice.
Yep, sometimes you just have to trust your gut.

Jim Hines

The Jig the Goblin series

"Clever satire... Reminiscent of Terry Pratchett
and Robert Asprin at their best."
—*Romantic Times*

"If you've always kinda rooted for the little guy,
even maybe had a bit of a place in your heart for
Gollum, rather than the Boromirs and Gandalfs
of the world, pick up *Goblin Quest*."
—*The SF Site*

"This exciting adult fairy tale is filled with
adventure and action, but the keys to the fantasy
are Jig and the belief that the mythological creatures are real in the realm of Jim C. Hines."
—*Midwest Book Review*

"A rollicking ride, enjoyable from beginning to
end... Jim Hines has just become one of my
must-read authors." -—Julie E. Czerneda

GOBLIN QUEST   978-07564-0400-0
GOBLIN HERO   978-07564-0442-0
GOBLIN WAR   978-07564-0493-2

To Order Call: 1-800-788-6262
www.dawbooks.com

DAW 100

Tanya Huff

The Confederation Novels

A CONFEDERATION OF VALOR
Omnibus Edition
(Valor's Choice, The Better Part of Valor)
978-0-7564-0399-7

THE HEART OF VALOR
978-0-7564-0481-9

and now in hardcover:

VALOR'S TRIAL
978-0-7564-0479-6

To Order Call: 1-800-788-6262
www.dawbooks.com

DAW 73

John Zakour

The Novels of
Zachary Nixon Johnson
The Last Freelance P. I.

"If you like your humor slapstick and inventive,
you need look no further for a good fix."
—*Chronicle*

"No one who gets two paragraphs into this
dark, droll, downright irresistable hard-boiled-
dick novel could ever bear to put it down until
the last heart-pounding moment..." —*SFSite*

To Order Call: 1-800-788-6262
www.dawbooks.com